WRASSLE CASTLE

LEARNING THE ROPES

WONDERBOUND
PUBLISHER DAMIAN A. WASSEL
EDITOR-IN-CHIEF ADRIAN F. WASSEL
ART DIRECTOR NATHAN C. GOODEN
EVP BRANDING & DESIGN TIM DANIEL
MANAGING EDITOR REBECCA TAYLOR
SALES & MARKETING, DIRECT MARKET DAVID DISSANAYAKE
SALES & MARKETING, BOOK TRADE SYNDEE BARWICK
PRODUCTION MANAGER IAN BALDESSARI
PRINCIPAL DAMIAN A. WASSEL SR.

LIBRARY OF CONGRESS CONTROL NUMBER: 2021938892
ISBN: 978-1-638-490098
PRINTED IN THE USA BY AVENUE 4. FIRST EDITION 2021.

10 9 8 7 6 5 4 3 2 1

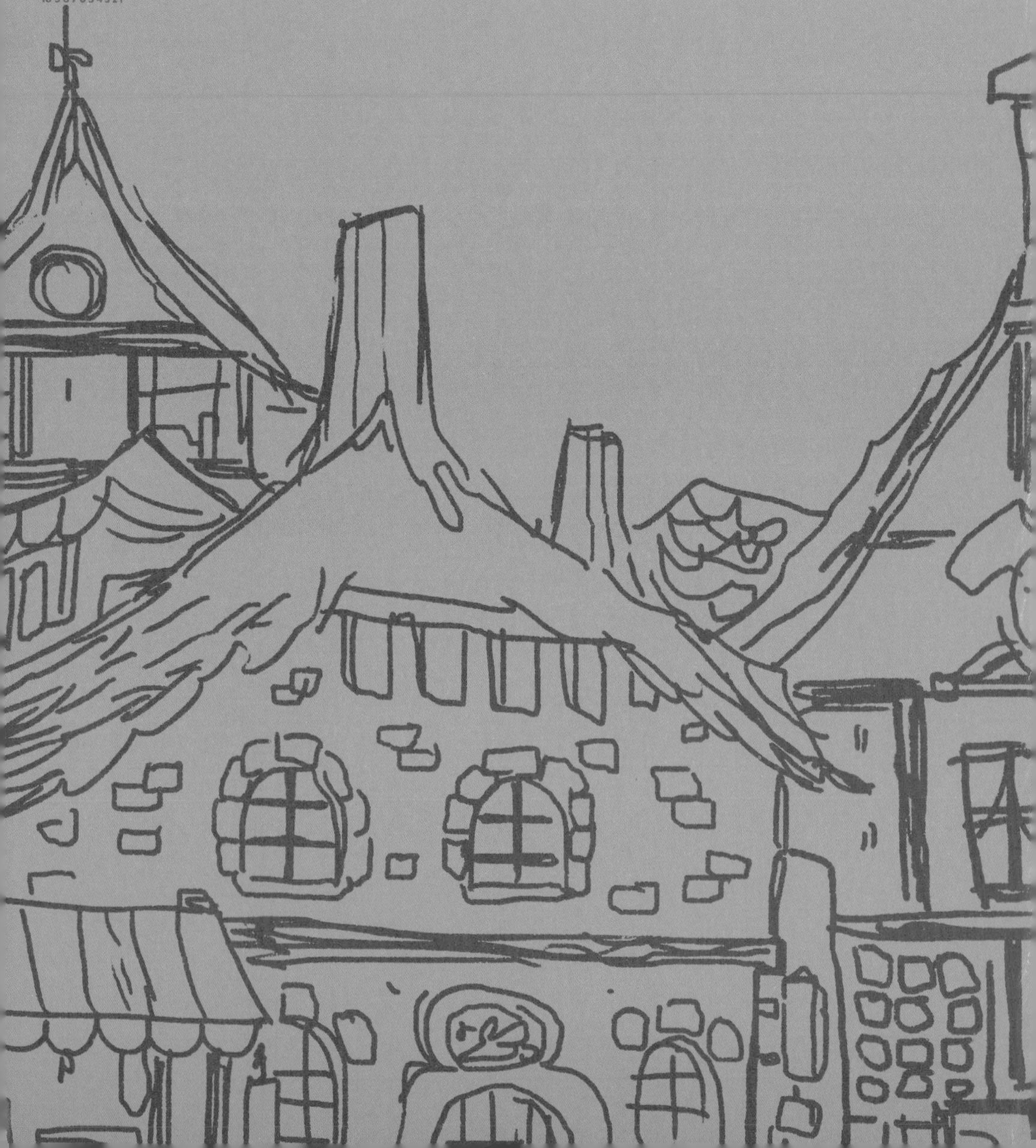

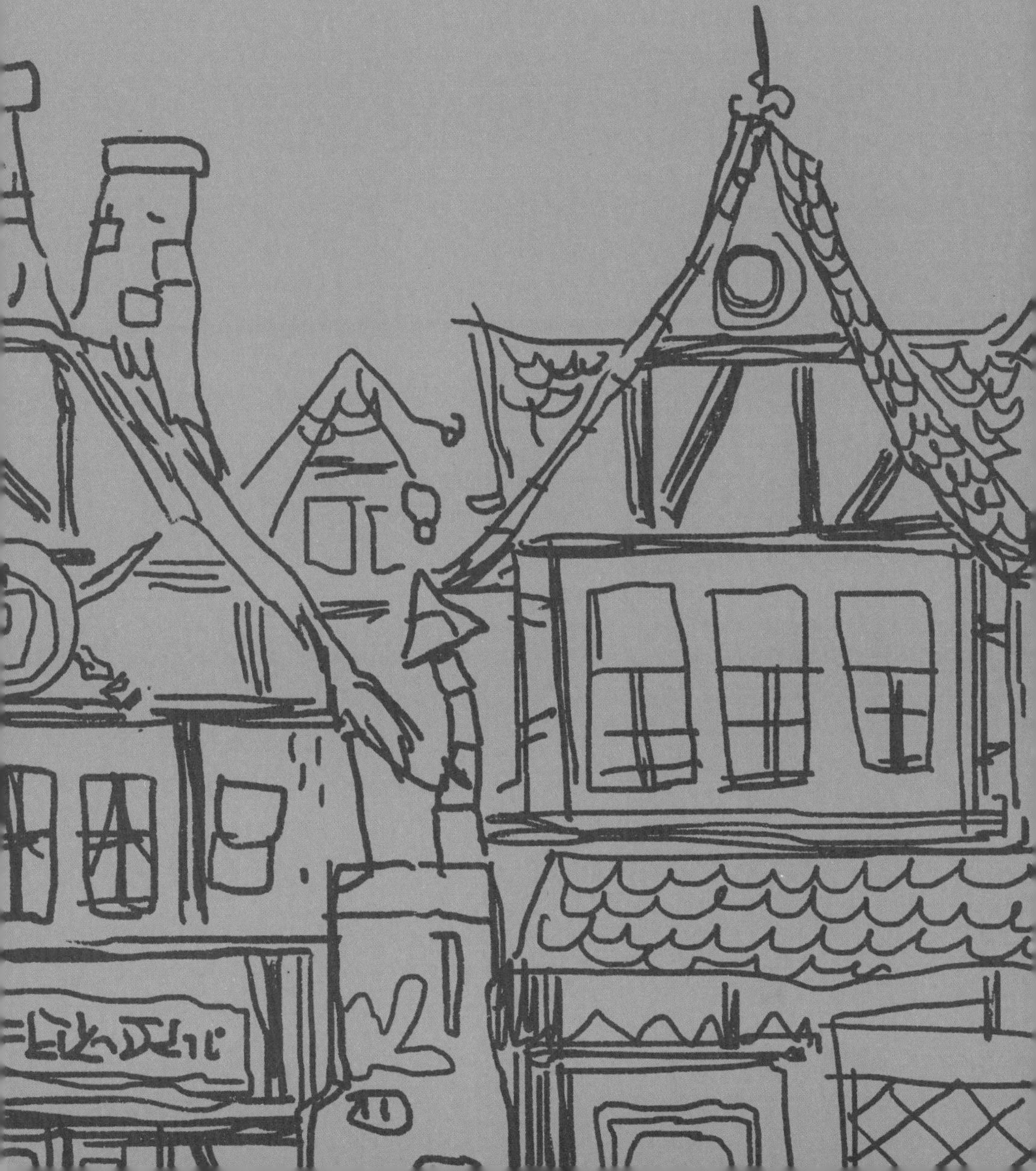

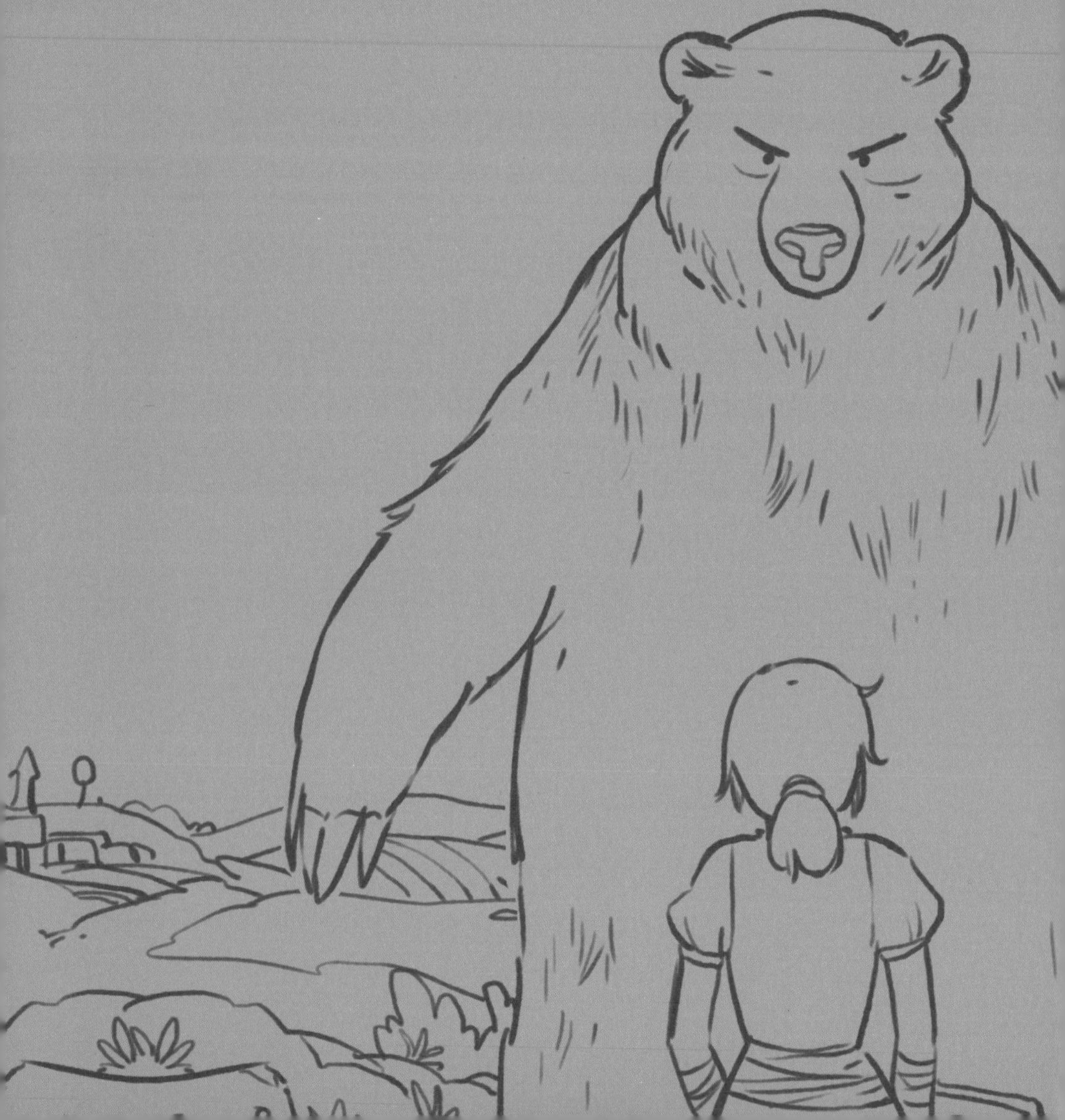

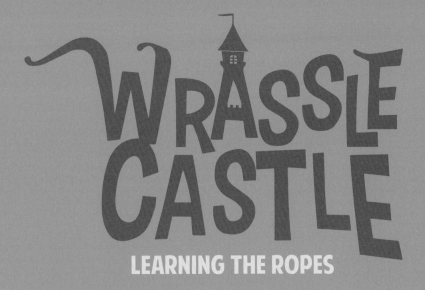

WRASSLE CASTLE

LEARNING THE ROPES

WRITTEN BY
COLLEEN COOVER & **PAUL TOBIN**

ILLUSTRATED BY
GALAAD

LETTERED BY
JEFF POWELL

DESIGNED BY
BONES LEOPARD

EDITED BY
REBECCA TAYLOR

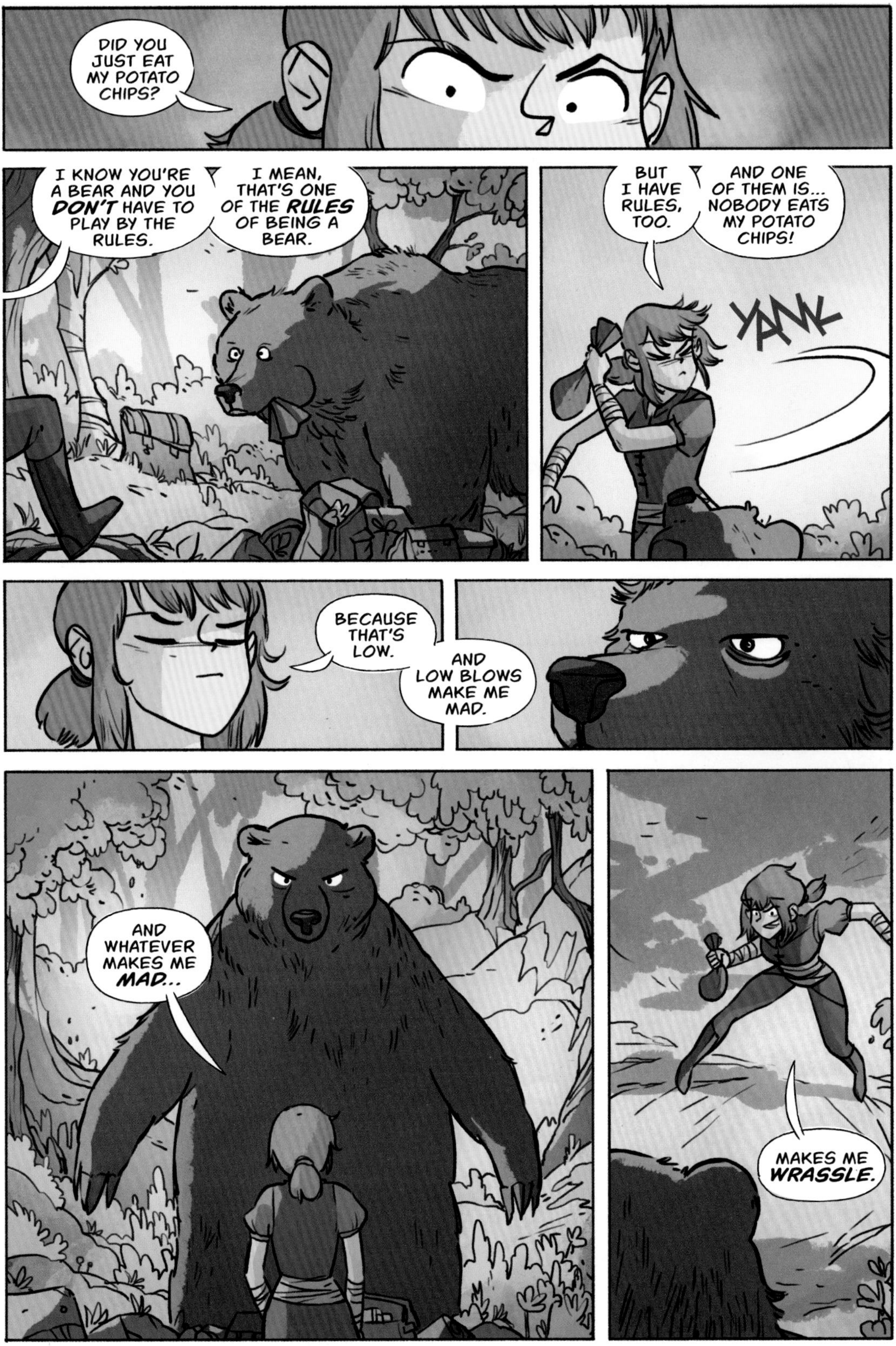

DID YOU JUST EAT MY POTATO CHIPS?
I KNOW YOU'RE A BEAR AND YOU DON'T HAVE TO PLAY BY THE RULES.
I MEAN, THAT'S ONE OF THE RULES OF BEING A BEAR.
BUT I HAVE RULES, TOO.
AND ONE OF THEM IS... NOBODY EATS MY POTATO CHIPS!
YANK
BECAUSE THAT'S LOW.
AND LOW BLOWS MAKE ME MAD.
AND WHATEVER MAKES ME MAD...
MAKES ME WRASSLE.

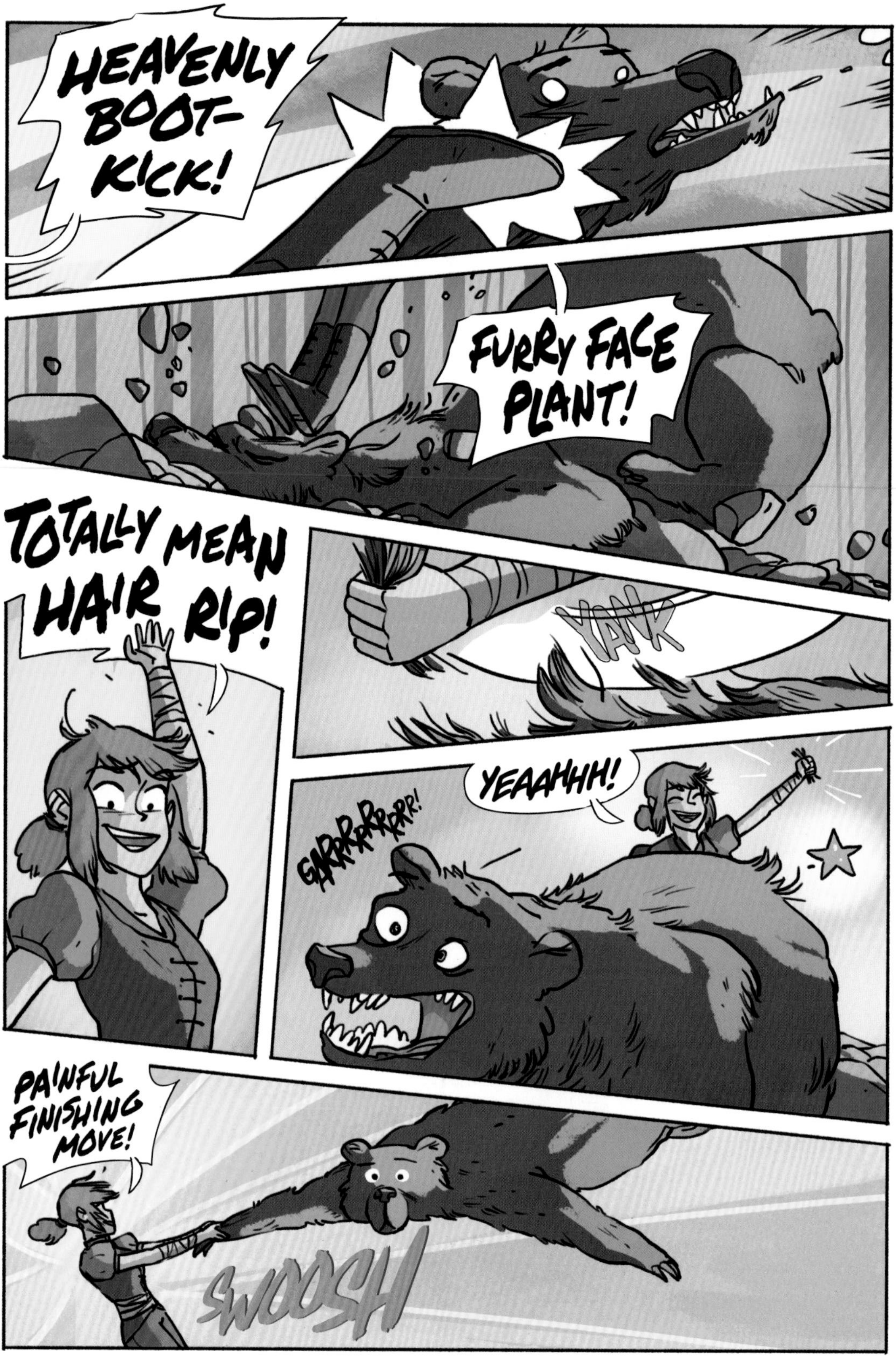
HEAVENLY BOOT-KICK!
FURRY FACE PLANT!
TOTALLY MEAN HAIR RIP!
YANK
YEAAHHH!
GARRRRRRRRR!
PAINFUL FINISHING MOVE!
SWOOSH

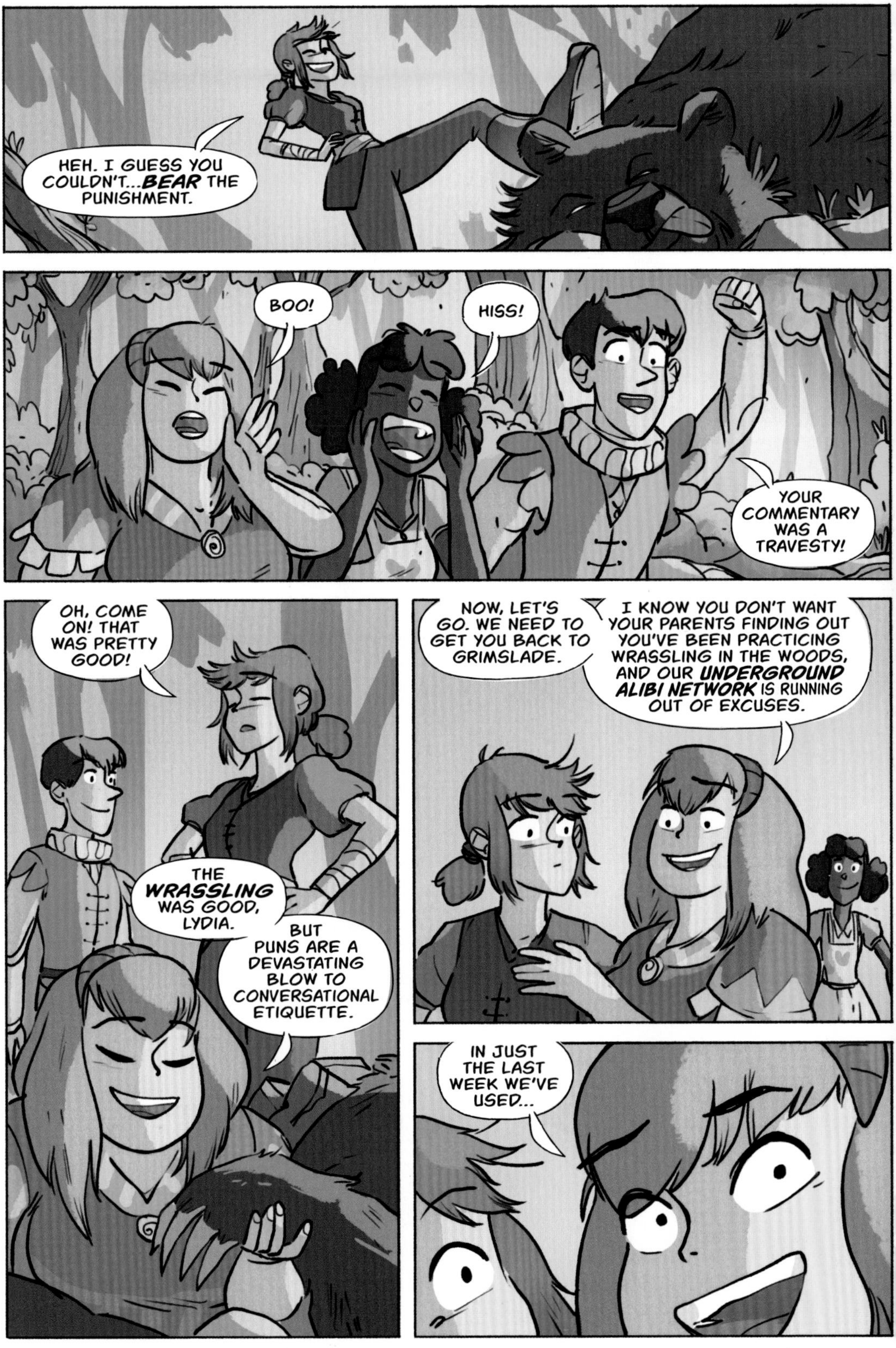
HEH. I GUESS YOU COULDN'T...BEAR THE PUNISHMENT.
BOO!
HISS!
YOUR COMMENTARY WAS A TRAVESTY!
OH, COME ON! THAT WAS PRETTY GOOD!
THE WRASSLING WAS GOOD, LYDIA.
BUT PUNS ARE A DEVASTATING BLOW TO CONVERSATIONAL ETIQUETTE.
NOW, LET'S GO. WE NEED TO GET YOU BACK TO GRIMSLADE.
I KNOW YOU DON'T WANT YOUR PARENTS FINDING OUT YOU'VE BEEN PRACTICING WRASSLING IN THE WOODS, AND OUR UNDERGROUND ALIBI NETWORK IS RUNNING OUT OF EXCUSES.
IN JUST THE LAST WEEK WE'VE USED...

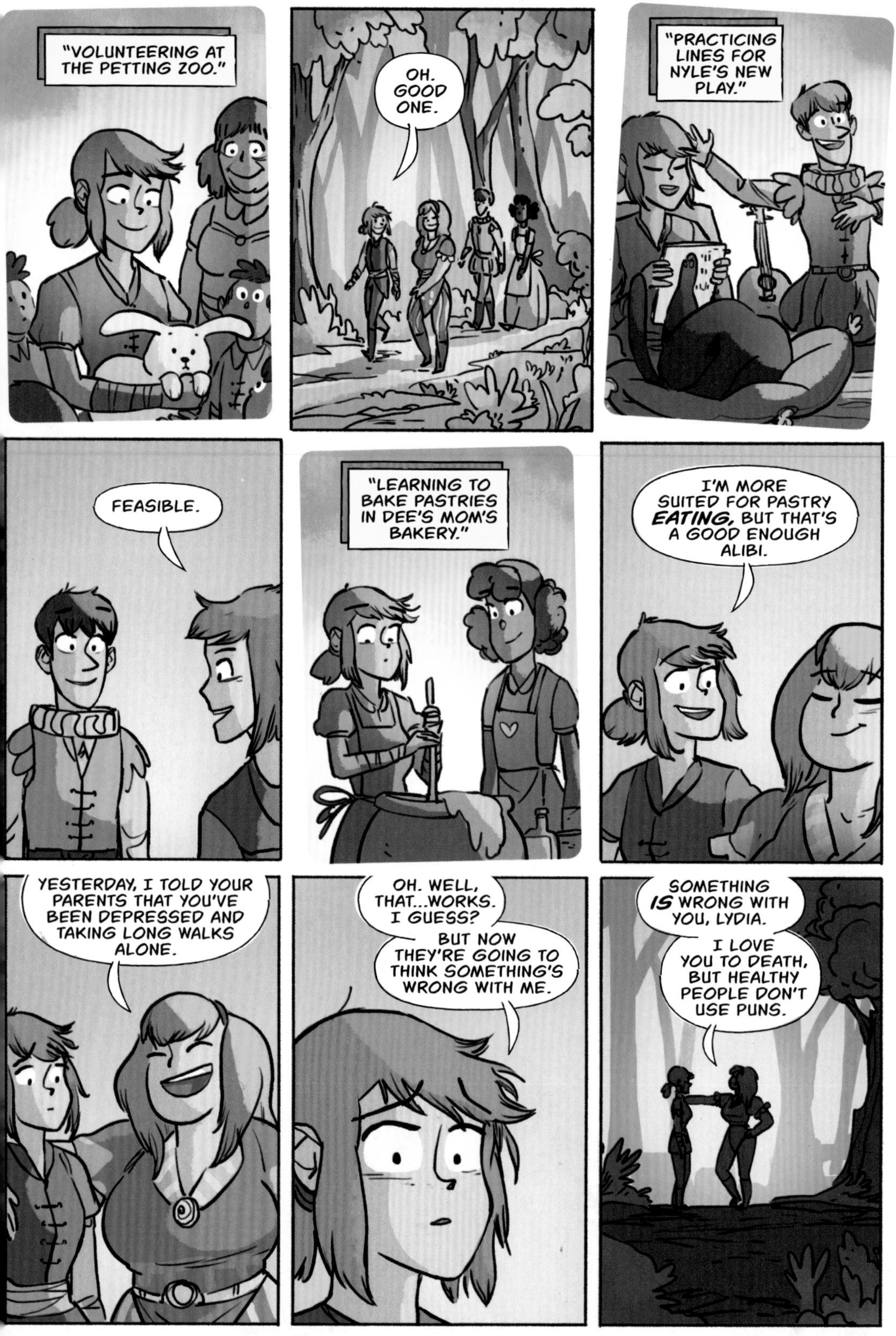
"VOLUNTEERING AT THE PETTING ZOO."
OH. GOOD ONE.
"PRACTICING LINES FOR NYLE'S NEW PLAY."
FEASIBLE.
"LEARNING TO BAKE PASTRIES IN DEE'S MOM'S BAKERY."
I'M MORE SUITED FOR PASTRY EATING, BUT THAT'S A GOOD ENOUGH ALIBI.
YESTERDAY, I TOLD YOUR PARENTS THAT YOU'VE BEEN DEPRESSED AND TAKING LONG WALKS ALONE.
OH. WELL, THAT...WORKS. I GUESS?
BUT NOW THEY'RE GOING TO THINK SOMETHING'S WRONG WITH ME.
SOMETHING IS WRONG WITH YOU, LYDIA.
I LOVE YOU TO DEATH, BUT HEALTHY PEOPLE DON'T USE PUNS.

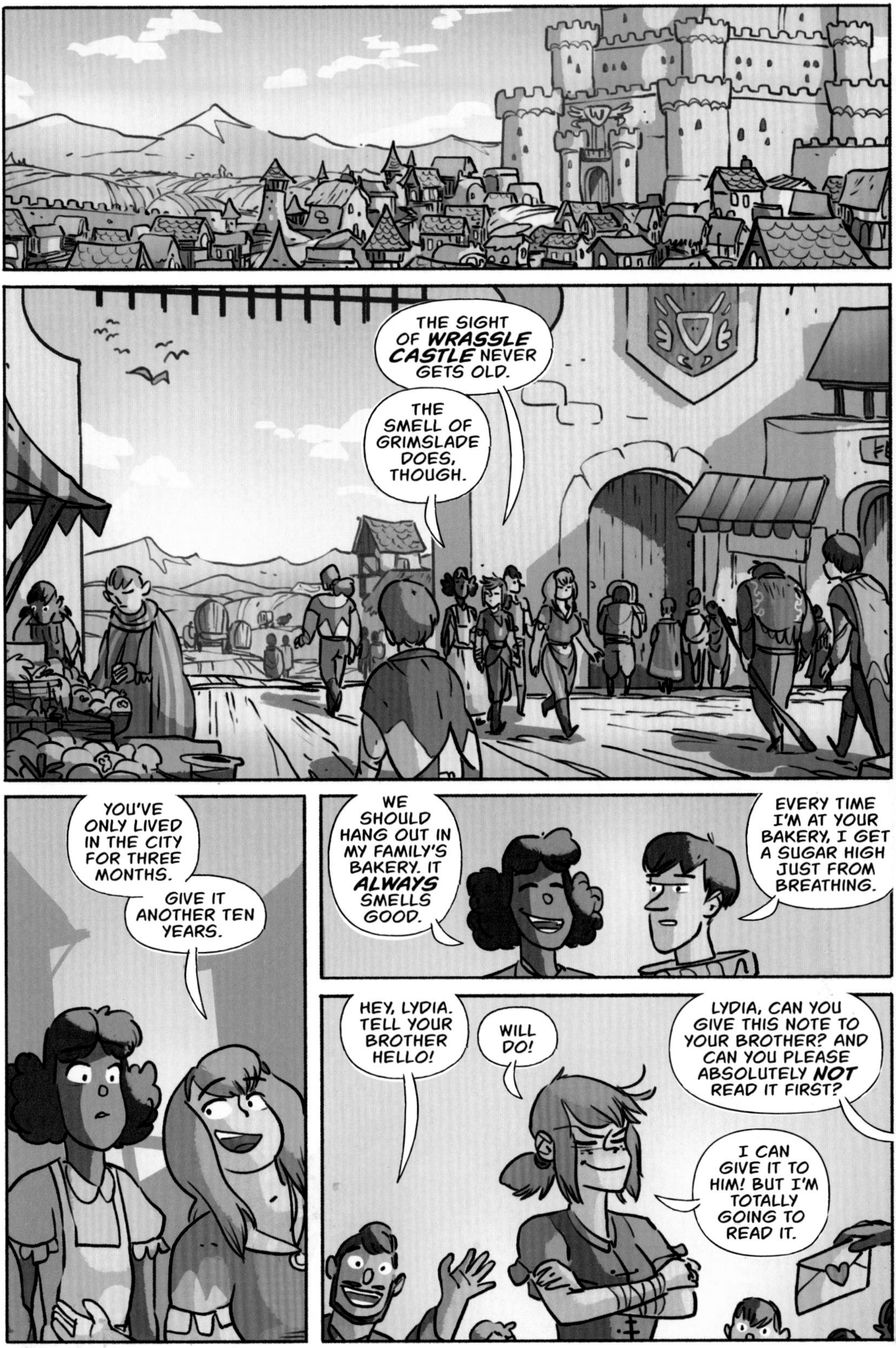
THE SIGHT OF WRASSLE CASTLE NEVER GETS OLD.
THE SMELL OF GRIMSLADE DOES, THOUGH.
YOU'VE ONLY LIVED IN THE CITY FOR THREE MONTHS.
GIVE IT ANOTHER TEN YEARS.
WE SHOULD HANG OUT IN MY FAMILY'S BAKERY. IT ALWAYS SMELLS GOOD.
EVERY TIME I'M AT YOUR BAKERY, I GET A SUGAR HIGH JUST FROM BREATHING.
HEY, LYDIA. TELL YOUR BROTHER HELLO!
WILL DO!
LYDIA, CAN YOU GIVE THIS NOTE TO YOUR BROTHER? AND CAN YOU PLEASE ABSOLUTELY NOT READ IT FIRST?
I CAN GIVE IT TO HIM! BUT I'M TOTALLY GOING TO READ IT.

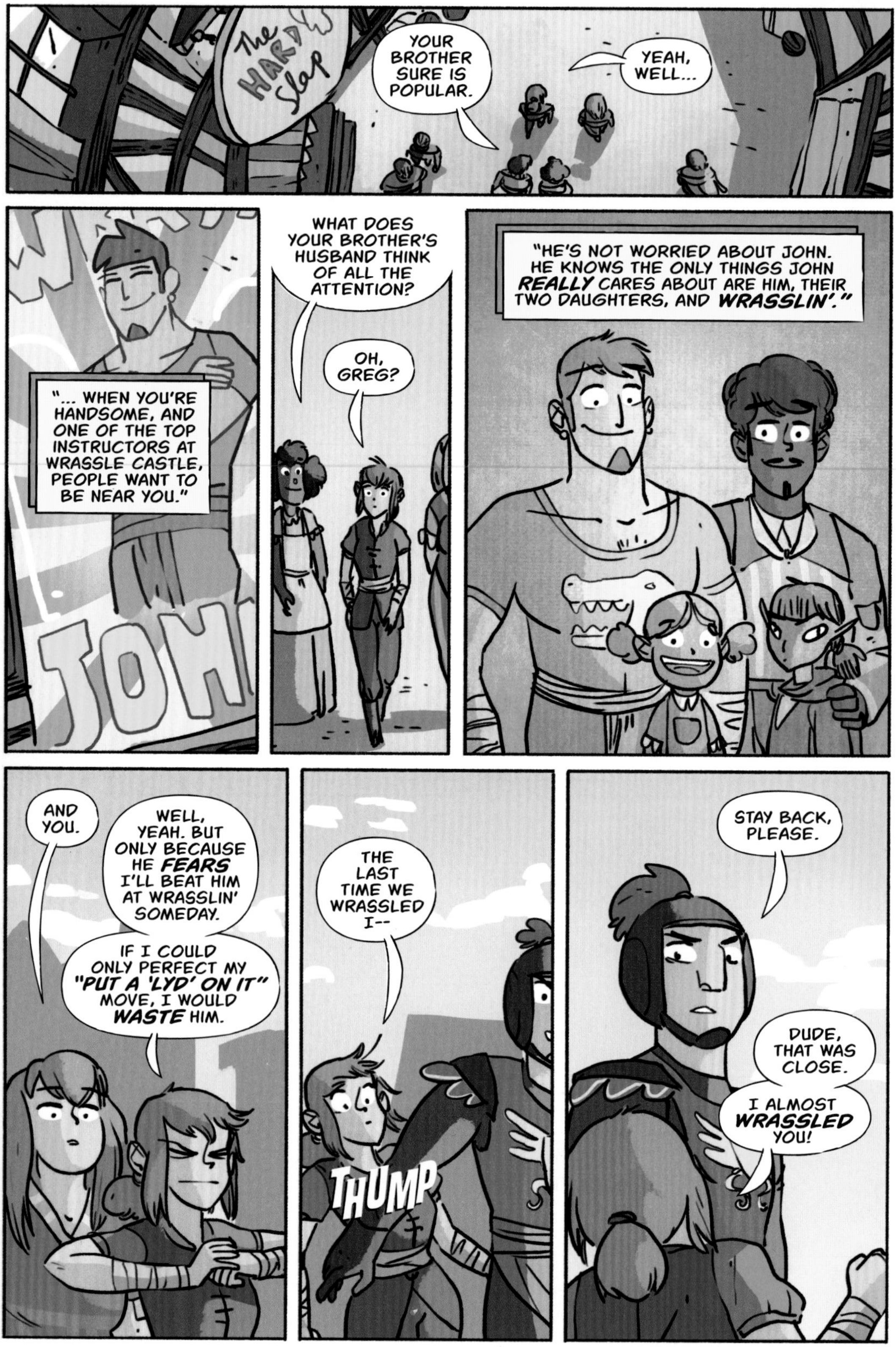
The HARD Slap
YOUR BROTHER SURE IS POPULAR.
YEAH, WELL...
"... WHEN YOU'RE HANDSOME, AND ONE OF THE TOP INSTRUCTORS AT WRASSLE CASTLE, PEOPLE WANT TO BE NEAR YOU."
JOH
WHAT DOES YOUR BROTHER'S HUSBAND THINK OF ALL THE ATTENTION?
OH, GREG?
"HE'S NOT WORRIED ABOUT JOHN. HE KNOWS THE ONLY THINGS JOHN REALLY CARES ABOUT ARE HIM, THEIR TWO DAUGHTERS, AND WRASSLIN'."
AND YOU.
WELL, YEAH. BUT ONLY BECAUSE HE FEARS I'LL BEAT HIM AT WRASSLIN' SOMEDAY.
IF I COULD ONLY PERFECT MY "PUT A 'LYD' ON IT" MOVE, I WOULD WASTE HIM.
THE LAST TIME WE WRASSLED I--
THUMP
STAY BACK, PLEASE.
DUDE, THAT WAS CLOSE.
I ALMOST WRASSLED YOU!

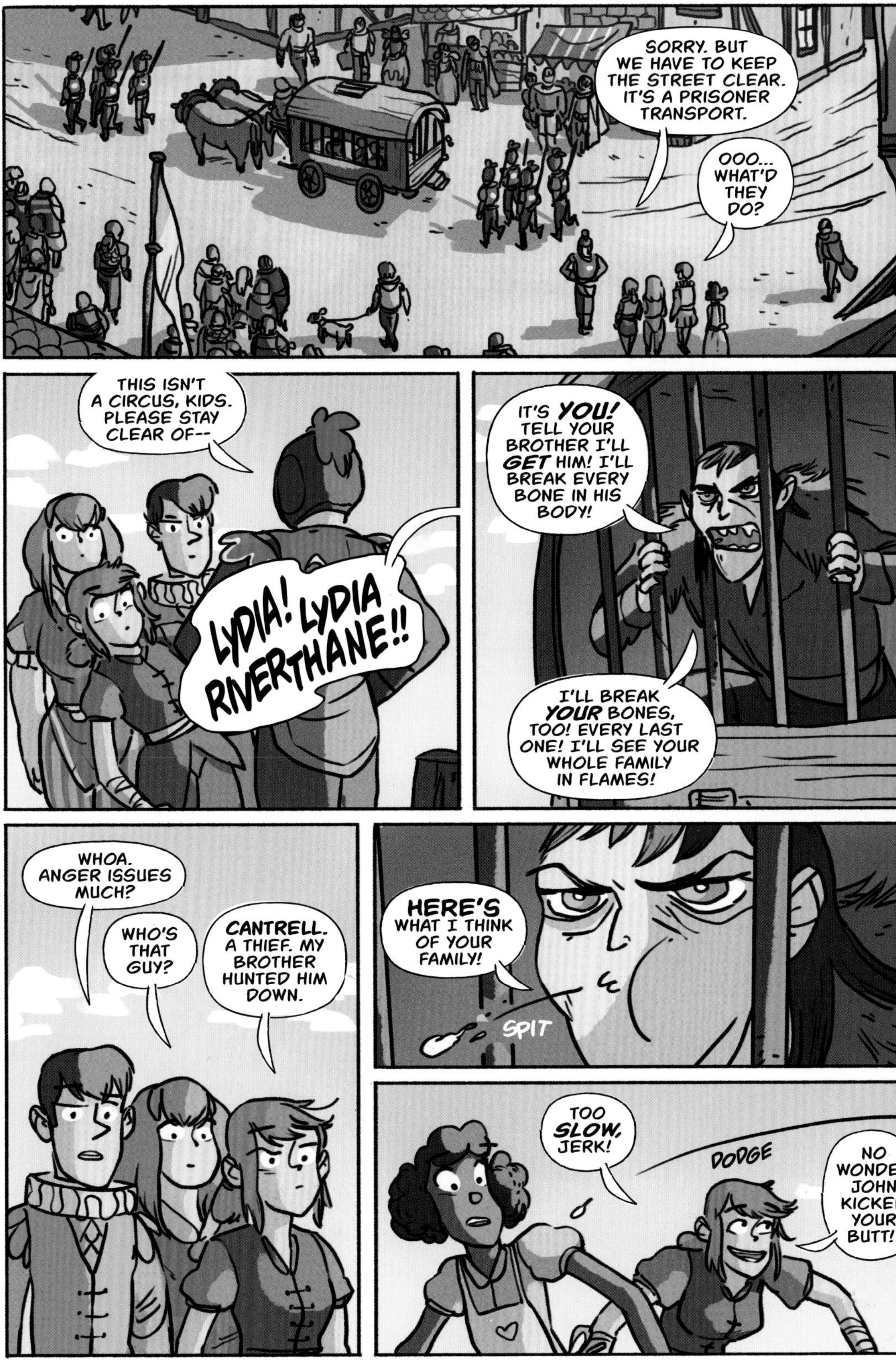
SORRY. BUT WE HAVE TO KEEP THE STREET CLEAR. IT'S A PRISONER TRANSPORT.
OOO... WHAT'D THEY DO?
THIS ISN'T A CIRCUS, KIDS. PLEASE STAY CLEAR OF--
LYDIA! LYDIA RIVERTHANE!!
IT'S **YOU!** TELL YOUR BROTHER I'LL **GET** HIM! I'LL BREAK EVERY BONE IN HIS BODY!
I'LL BREAK **YOUR** BONES, TOO! EVERY LAST ONE! I'LL SEE YOUR WHOLE FAMILY IN FLAMES!
WHOA. ANGER ISSUES MUCH?
WHO'S THAT GUY?
CANTRELL. A THIEF. MY BROTHER HUNTED HIM DOWN.
HERE'S WHAT I THINK OF YOUR FAMILY!
SPIT
TOO **SLOW,** JERK!
DODGE
NO WONDER JOHN KICKED YOUR BUTT!

Lydia Riverthane

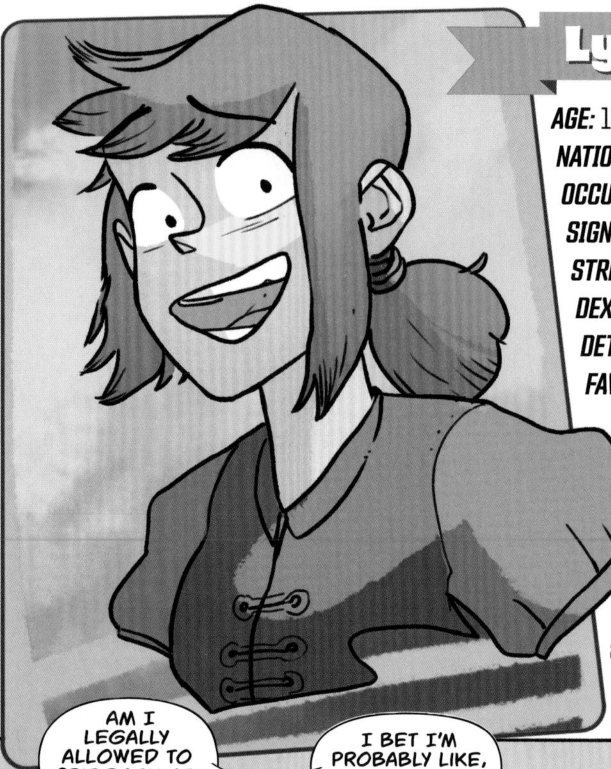

AGE: 15
NATIONAL RANKING: n/a (amateur)
OCCUPATION: Student.
SIGNATURE MOVE: Put A "Lyd" On It (pending)
STRENGTH: 12
DEXTERITY: 16
DETERMINATION: 20
FAVORITE FOOD: Chocolate Potato Chips.
HOBBIES: Community theater. Rock climbing. Defeating things.
NOTES: Lydia's awkward, self-taught wrasslin' style is surprisingly effective, but precludes accruing ranking points in any of the 112 classically recognized wrasslin' techniques.

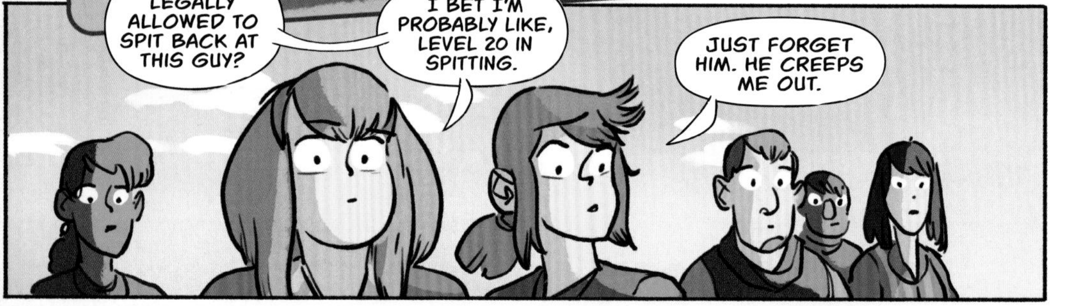
AM I LEGALLY ALLOWED TO SPIT BACK AT THIS GUY?
I BET I'M PROBABLY LIKE, LEVEL 20 IN SPITTING.
JUST FORGET HIM. HE CREEPS ME OUT.

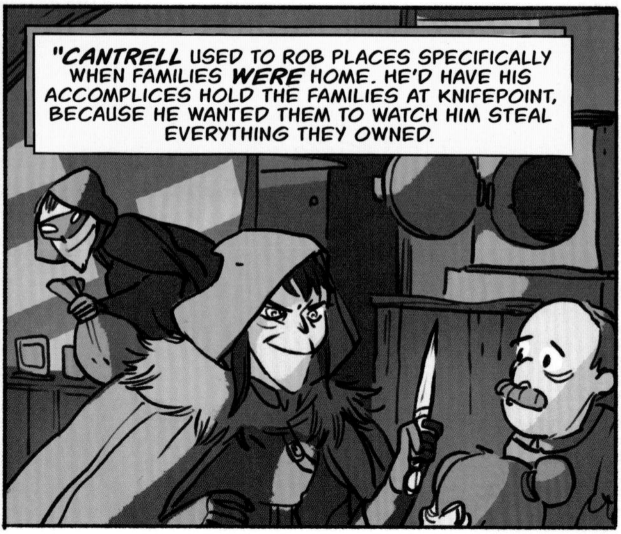
"CANTRELL USED TO ROB PLACES SPECIFICALLY WHEN FAMILIES WERE HOME. HE'D HAVE HIS ACCOMPLICES HOLD THE FAMILIES AT KNIFEPOINT, BECAUSE HE WANTED THEM TO WATCH HIM STEAL EVERYTHING THEY OWNED.

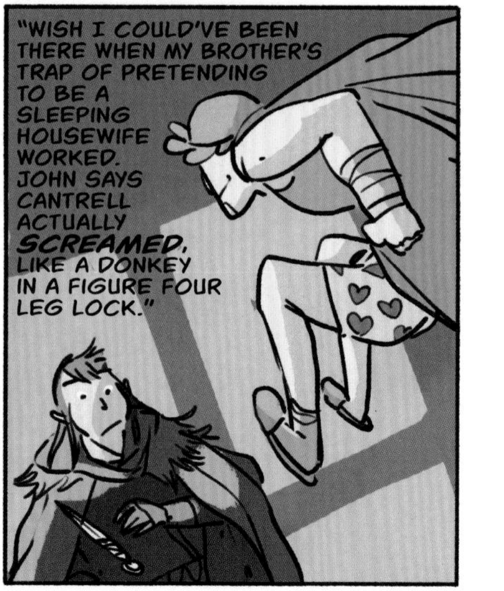
"WISH I COULD'VE BEEN THERE WHEN MY BROTHER'S TRAP OF PRETENDING TO BE A SLEEPING HOUSEWIFE WORKED. JOHN SAYS CANTRELL ACTUALLY SCREAMED, LIKE A DONKEY IN A FIGURE FOUR LEG LOCK."

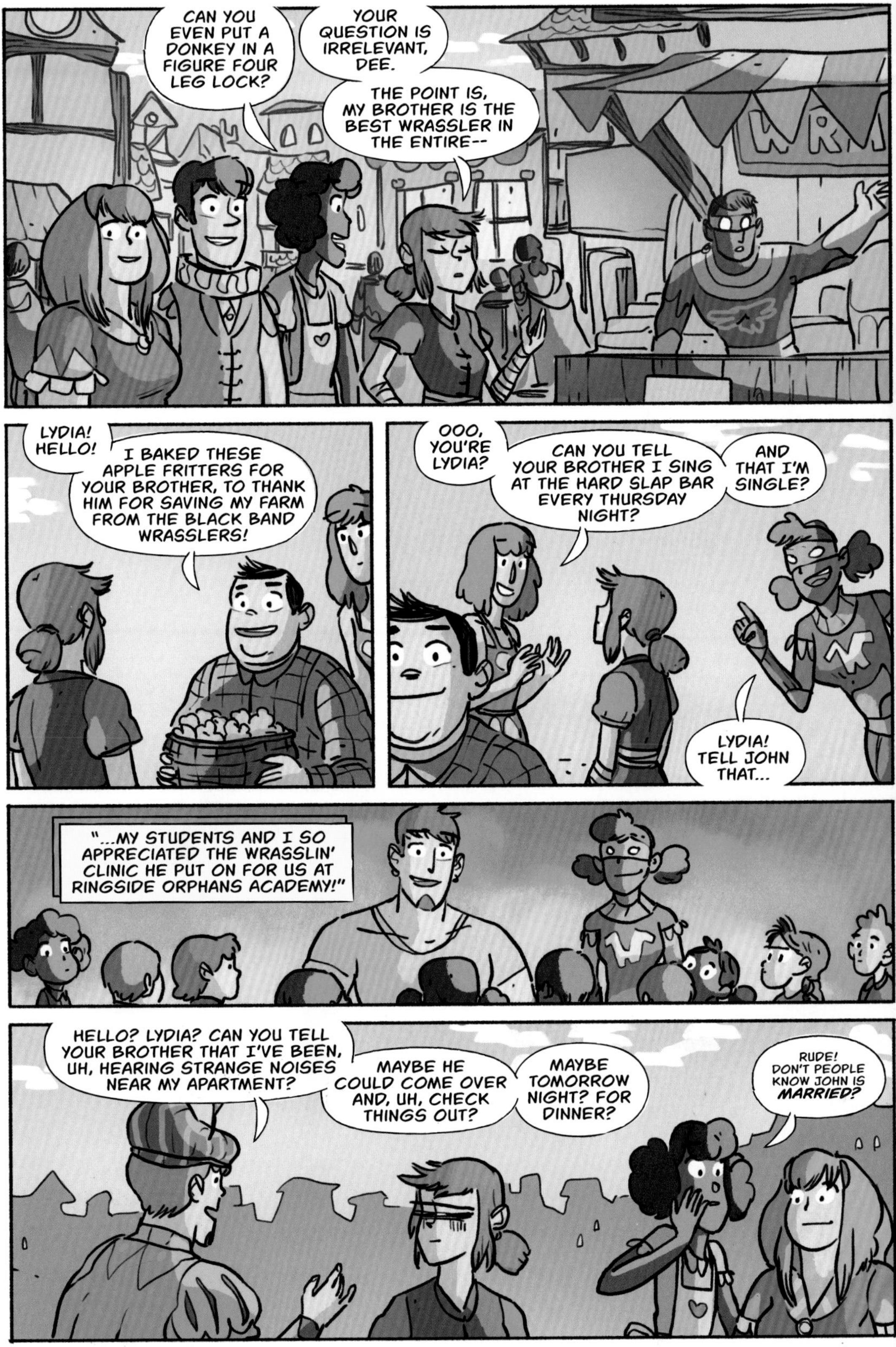
CAN YOU EVEN PUT A DONKEY IN A FIGURE FOUR LEG LOCK?
YOUR QUESTION IS IRRELEVANT, DEE.
THE POINT IS, MY BROTHER IS THE BEST WRASSLER IN THE ENTIRE--
LYDIA! HELLO!
I BAKED THESE APPLE FRITTERS FOR YOUR BROTHER, TO THANK HIM FOR SAVING MY FARM FROM THE BLACK BAND WRASSLERS!
OOO, YOU'RE LYDIA?
CAN YOU TELL YOUR BROTHER I SING AT THE HARD SLAP BAR EVERY THURSDAY NIGHT?
AND THAT I'M SINGLE?
LYDIA! TELL JOHN THAT...
"...MY STUDENTS AND I SO APPRECIATED THE WRASSLIN' CLINIC HE PUT ON FOR US AT RINGSIDE ORPHANS ACADEMY!"
HELLO? LYDIA? CAN YOU TELL YOUR BROTHER THAT I'VE BEEN, UH, HEARING STRANGE NOISES NEAR MY APARTMENT?
MAYBE HE COULD COME OVER AND, UH, CHECK THINGS OUT?
MAYBE TOMORROW NIGHT? FOR DINNER?
RUDE! DON'T PEOPLE KNOW JOHN IS ***MARRIED?***

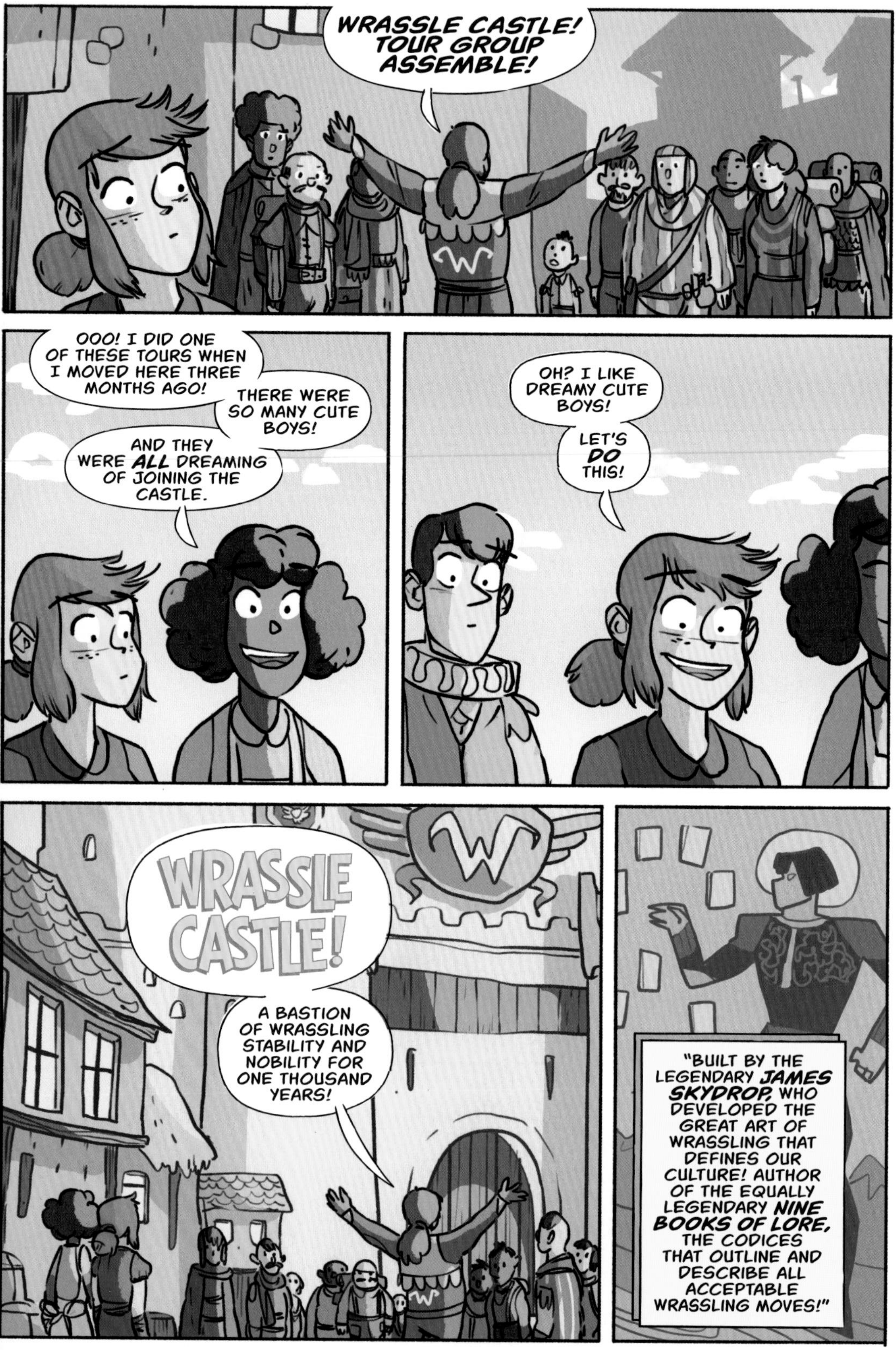
WRASSLE CASTLE! TOUR GROUP ASSEMBLE!
OOO! I DID ONE OF THESE TOURS WHEN I MOVED HERE THREE MONTHS AGO!
THERE WERE SO MANY CUTE BOYS!
AND THEY WERE ALL DREAMING OF JOINING THE CASTLE.
OH? I LIKE DREAMY CUTE BOYS!
LET'S DO THIS!
WRASSLE CASTLE!
A BASTION OF WRASSLING STABILITY AND NOBILITY FOR ONE THOUSAND YEARS!
"BUILT BY THE LEGENDARY JAMES SKYDROP, WHO DEVELOPED THE GREAT ART OF WRASSLING THAT DEFINES OUR CULTURE! AUTHOR OF THE EQUALLY LEGENDARY NINE BOOKS OF LORE, THE CODICES THAT OUTLINE AND DESCRIBE ALL ACCEPTABLE WRASSLING MOVES!"

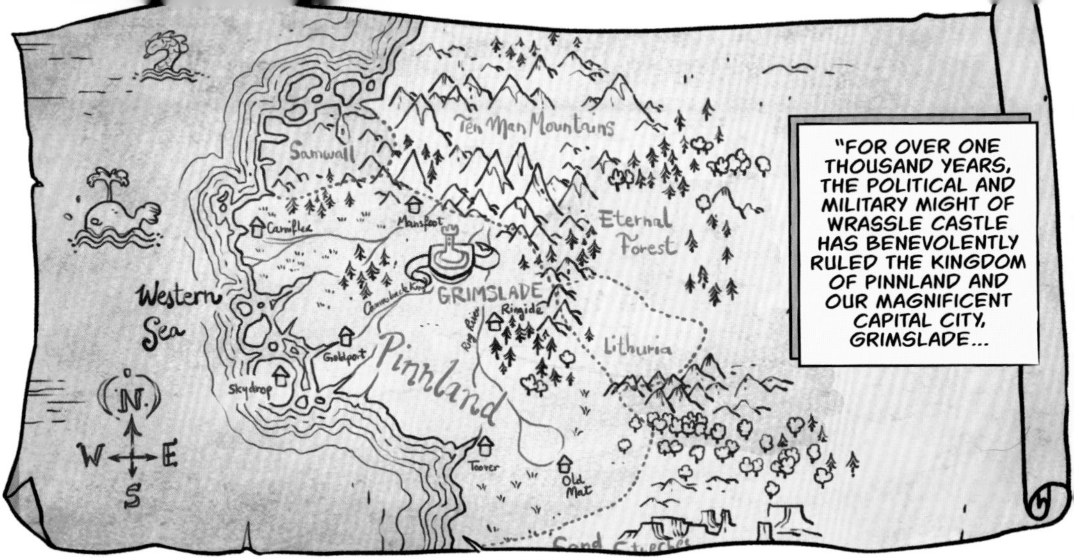
Ten Man Mountains
Samwall
Mansfoot
Eternal Forest
Western Sea
GRIMSLADE
Lithuria
Goldport
Skydrop
Pinnland
Toover
Old Mat
N.
W
E
S
"FOR OVER ONE THOUSAND YEARS, THE POLITICAL AND MILITARY MIGHT OF WRASSLE CASTLE HAS BENEVOLENTLY RULED THE KINGDOM OF PINNLAND AND OUR MAGNIFICENT CAPITAL CITY, GRIMSLADE...

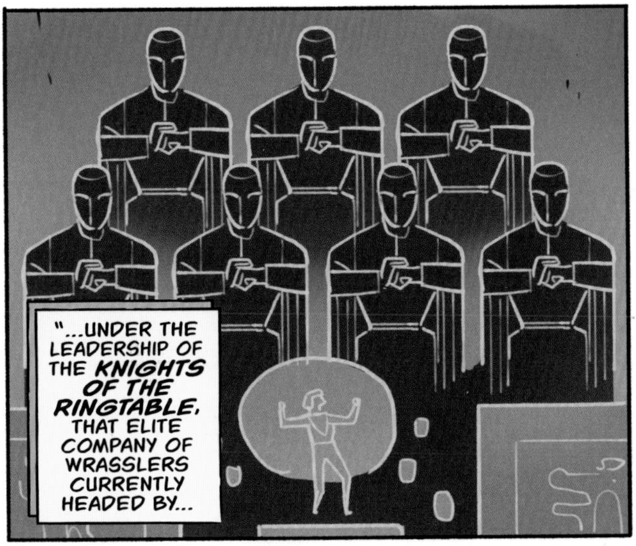
"...UNDER THE LEADERSHIP OF THE ***KNIGHTS OF THE RINGTABLE,*** THAT ELITE COMPANY OF WRASSLERS CURRENTLY HEADED BY...

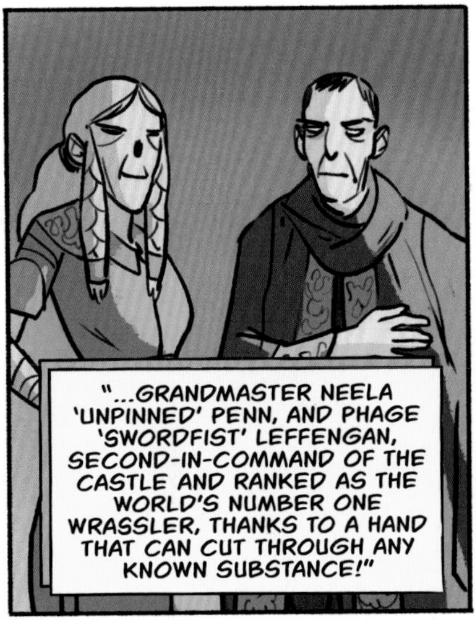
"...GRANDMASTER NEELA 'UNPINNED' PENN, AND PHAGE 'SWORDFIST' LEFFENGAN, SECOND-IN-COMMAND OF THE CASTLE AND RANKED AS THE WORLD'S NUMBER ONE WRASSLER, THANKS TO A HAND THAT CAN CUT THROUGH ANY KNOWN SUBSTANCE!"

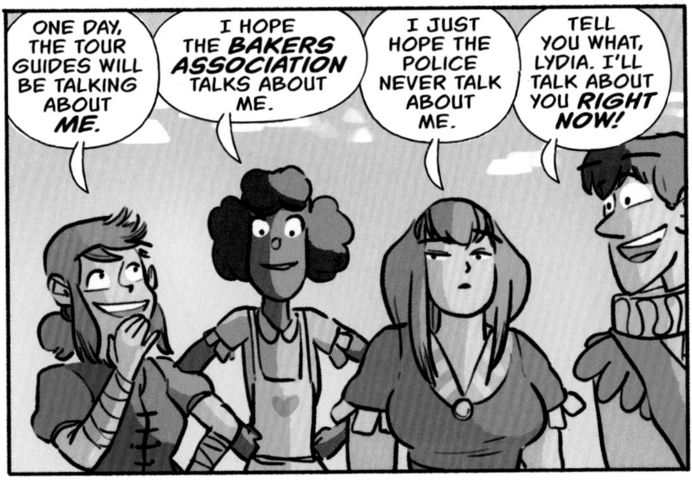
ONE DAY, THE TOUR GUIDES WILL BE TALKING ABOUT ***ME.***
I HOPE THE ***BAKERS ASSOCIATION*** TALKS ABOUT ME.
I JUST HOPE THE POLICE NEVER TALK ABOUT ME.
TELL YOU WHAT, LYDIA. I'LL TALK ABOUT YOU ***RIGHT NOW!***

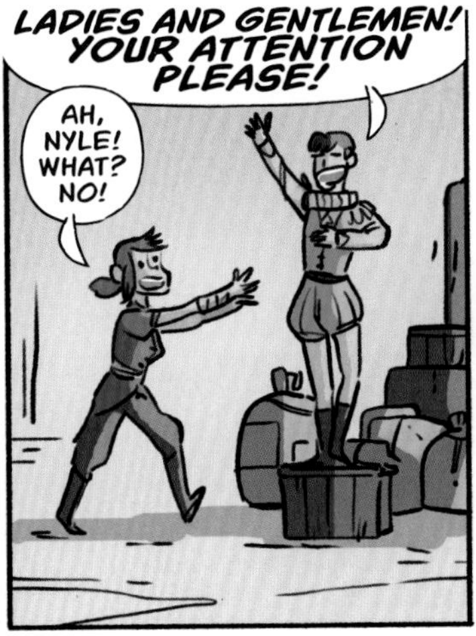
LADIES AND GENTLEMEN! YOUR ATTENTION PLEASE!
AH, NYLE! WHAT? NO!

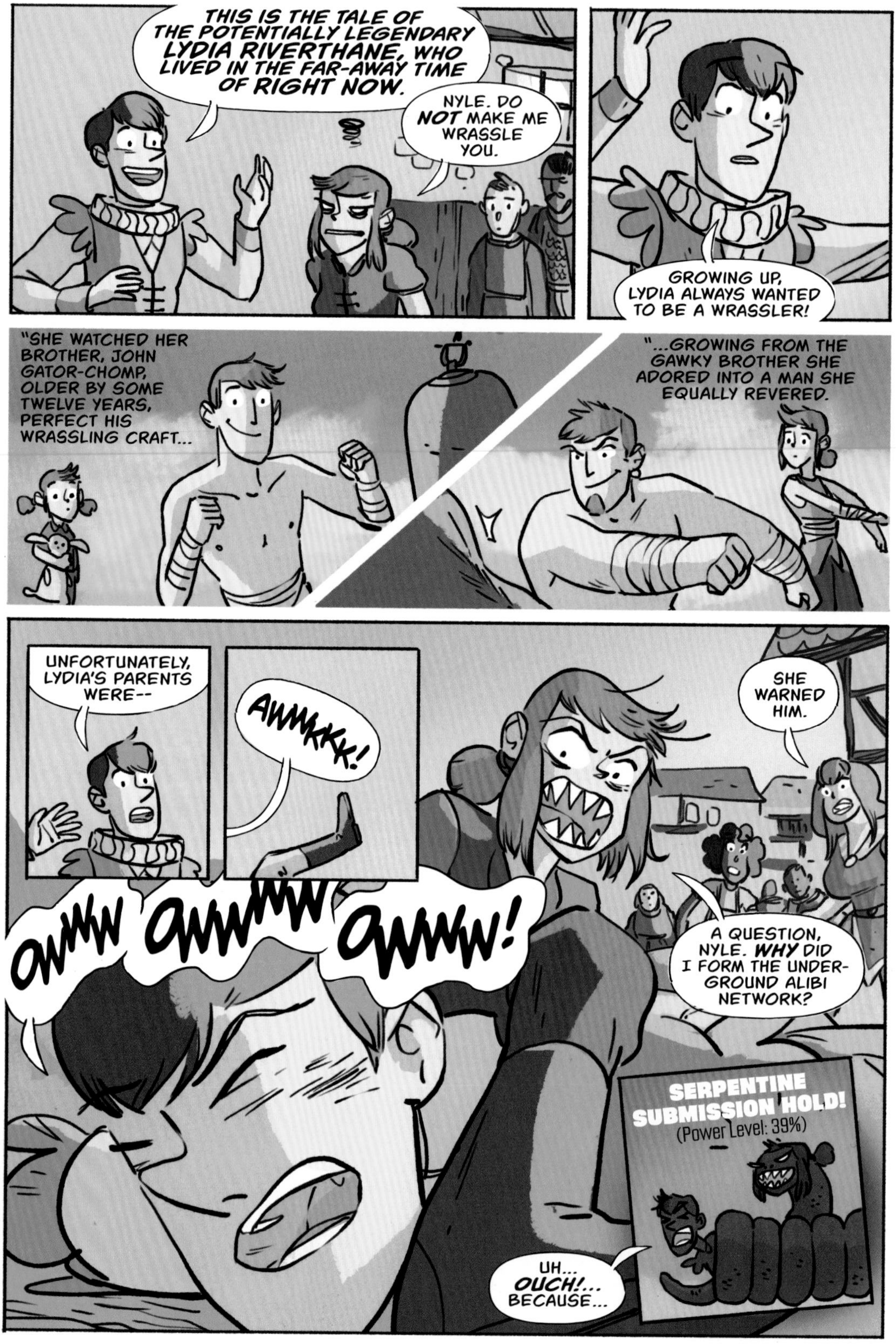
THIS IS THE TALE OF THE POTENTIALLY LEGENDARY LYDIA RIVERTHANE, WHO LIVED IN THE FAR-AWAY TIME OF RIGHT NOW.
NYLE. DO NOT MAKE ME WRASSLE YOU.
GROWING UP, LYDIA ALWAYS WANTED TO BE A WRASSLER!
"SHE WATCHED HER BROTHER, JOHN GATOR-CHOMP, OLDER BY SOME TWELVE YEARS, PERFECT HIS WRASSLING CRAFT...
"...GROWING FROM THE GAWKY BROTHER SHE ADORED INTO A MAN SHE EQUALLY REVERED.
UNFORTUNATELY, LYDIA'S PARENTS WERE--
AWNKKKK!
SHE WARNED HIM.
OWWW AWWWW AWWW!
A QUESTION, NYLE. WHY DID I FORM THE UNDER-GROUND ALIBI NETWORK?
SERPENTINE SUBMISSION HOLD!
(Power Level: 39%)
UH... OUCH!... BECAUSE...

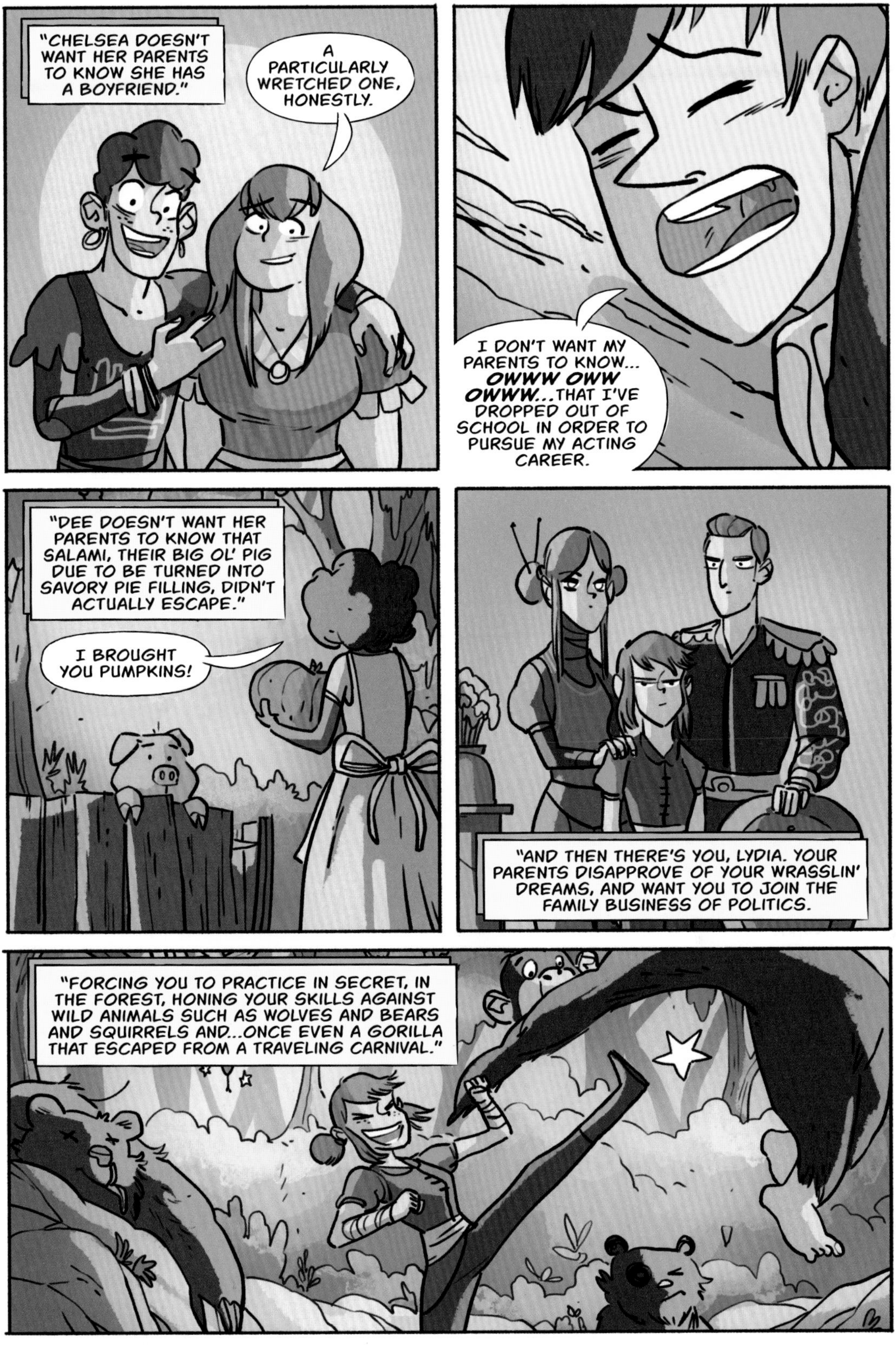
"CHELSEA DOESN'T WANT HER PARENTS TO KNOW SHE HAS A BOYFRIEND."
A PARTICULARLY WRETCHED ONE, HONESTLY.
I DON'T WANT MY PARENTS TO KNOW... ***OWWW OWW OWWW...*** THAT I'VE DROPPED OUT OF SCHOOL IN ORDER TO PURSUE MY ACTING CAREER.
"DEE DOESN'T WANT HER PARENTS TO KNOW THAT SALAMI, THEIR BIG OL' PIG DUE TO BE TURNED INTO SAVORY PIE FILLING, DIDN'T ACTUALLY ESCAPE."
I BROUGHT YOU PUMPKINS!
"AND THEN THERE'S YOU, LYDIA. YOUR PARENTS DISAPPROVE OF YOUR WRASSLIN' DREAMS, AND WANT YOU TO JOIN THE FAMILY BUSINESS OF POLITICS.
"FORCING YOU TO PRACTICE IN SECRET, IN THE FOREST, HONING YOUR SKILLS AGAINST WILD ANIMALS SUCH AS WOLVES AND BEARS AND SQUIRRELS AND...ONCE EVEN A GORILLA THAT ESCAPED FROM A TRAVELING CARNIVAL."

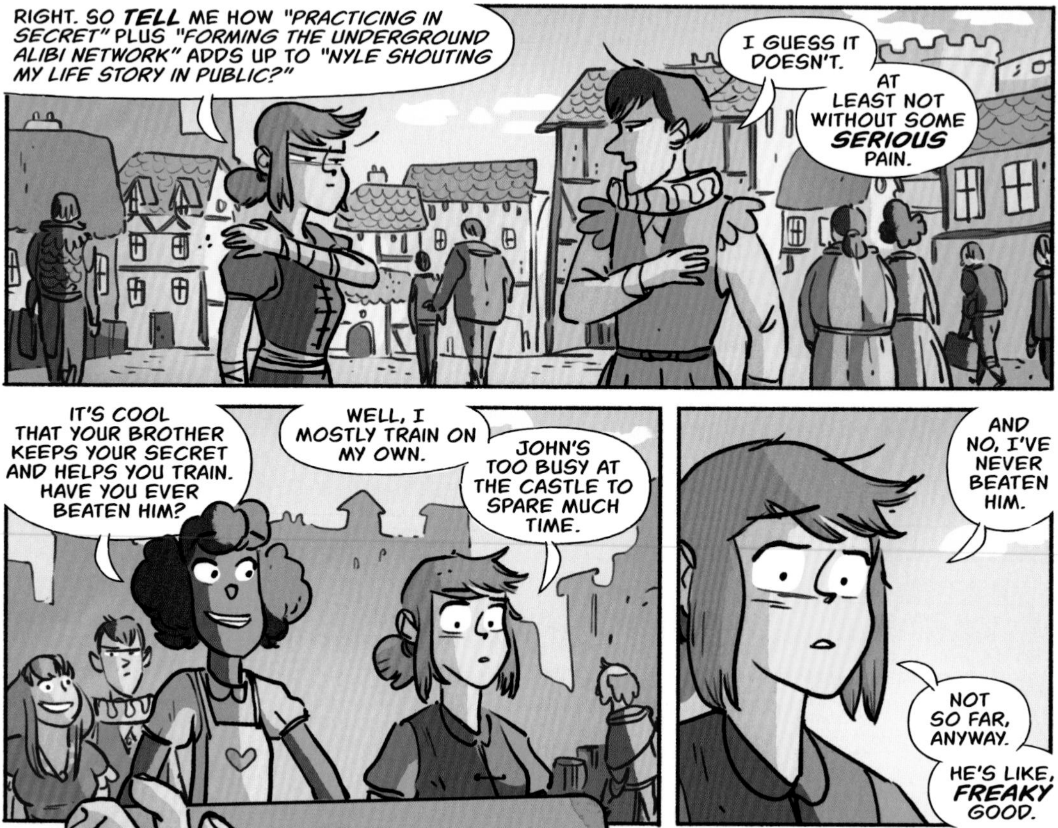
RIGHT. SO TELL ME HOW "PRACTICING IN SECRET" PLUS "FORMING THE UNDERGROUND ALIBI NETWORK" ADDS UP TO "NYLE SHOUTING MY LIFE STORY IN PUBLIC?"
I GUESS IT DOESN'T.
AT LEAST NOT WITHOUT SOME SERIOUS PAIN.
IT'S COOL THAT YOUR BROTHER KEEPS YOUR SECRET AND HELPS YOU TRAIN. HAVE YOU EVER BEATEN HIM?
WELL, I MOSTLY TRAIN ON MY OWN.
JOHN'S TOO BUSY AT THE CASTLE TO SPARE MUCH TIME.
AND NO, I'VE NEVER BEATEN HIM.
NOT SO FAR, ANYWAY.
HE'S LIKE, FREAKY GOOD.

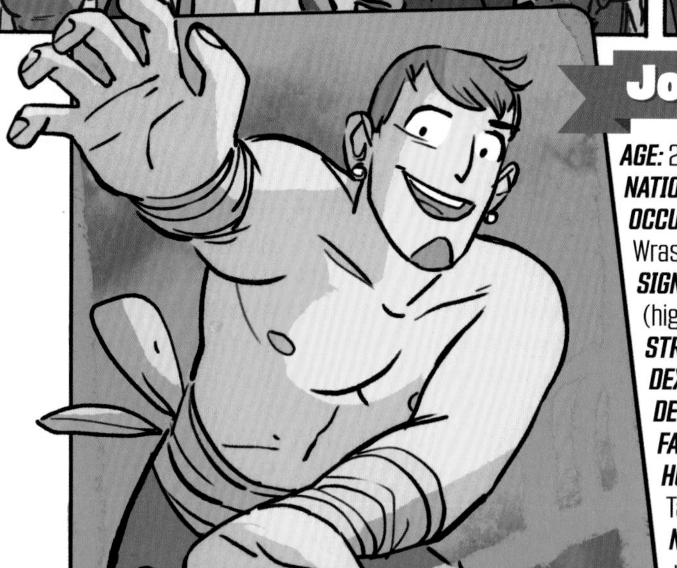

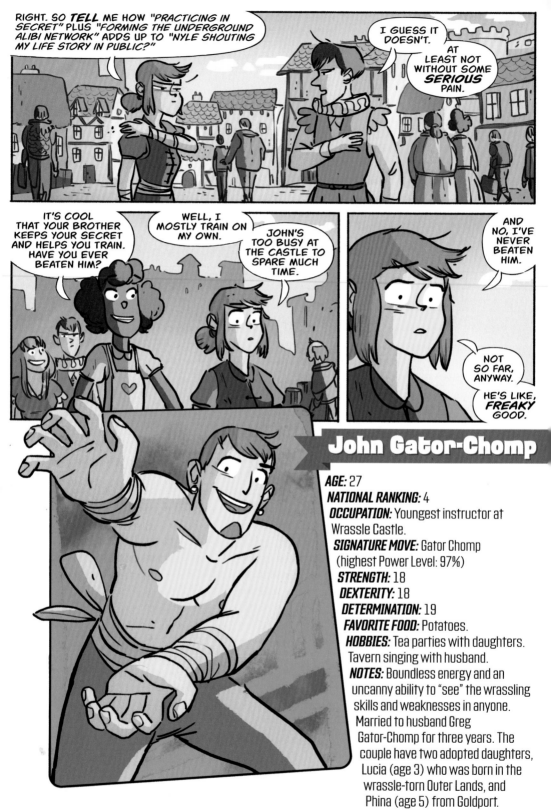

John Gator-Chomp

AGE: 27
NATIONAL RANKING: 4
OCCUPATION: Youngest instructor at Wrassle Castle.
SIGNATURE MOVE: Gator Chomp (highest Power Level: 97%)
STRENGTH: 18
DEXTERITY: 18
DETERMINATION: 19
FAVORITE FOOD: Potatoes.
HOBBIES: Tea parties with daughters. Tavern singing with husband.
NOTES: Boundless energy and an uncanny ability to "see" the wrassling skills and weaknesses in anyone. Married to husband Greg Gator-Chomp for three years. The couple have two adopted daughters, Lucia (age 3) who was born in the wrassle-torn Outer Lands, and Phina (age 5) from Goldport.

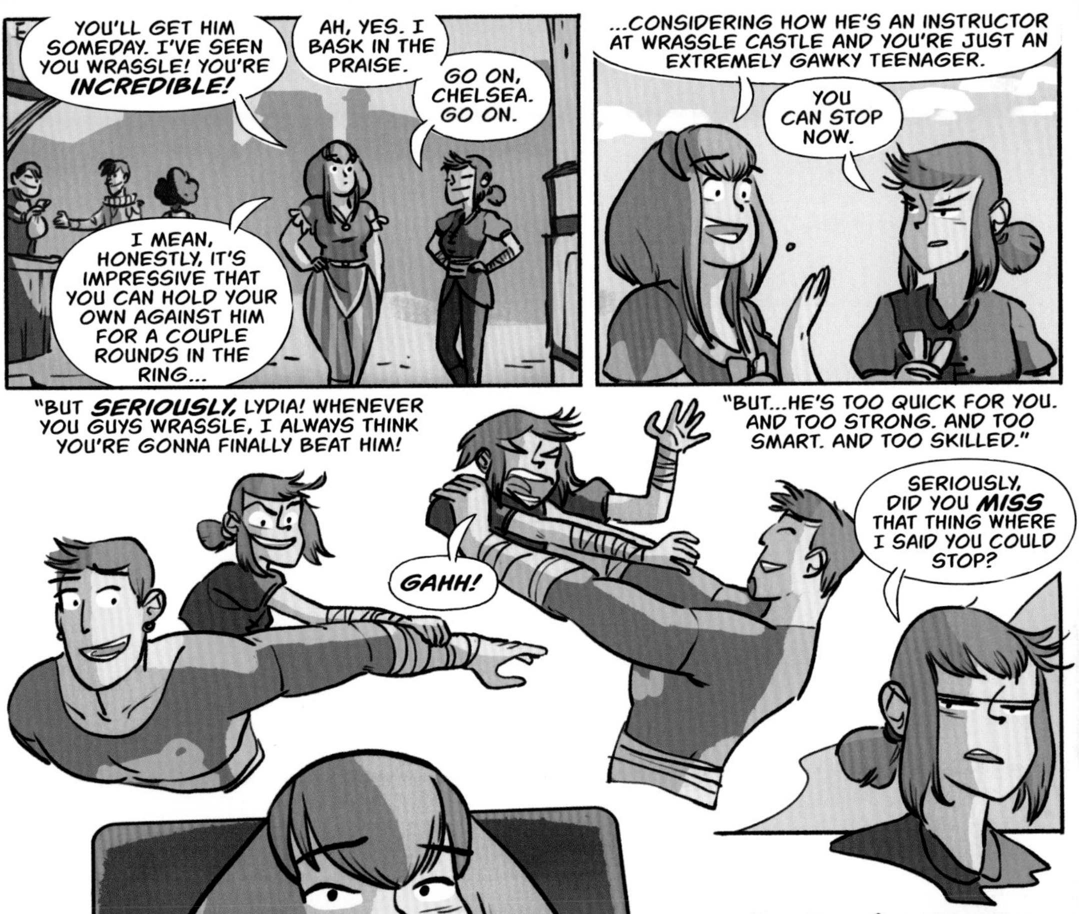
YOU'LL GET HIM SOMEDAY. I'VE SEEN YOU WRASSLE! YOU'RE *INCREDIBLE!*
AH, YES. I BASK IN THE PRAISE.
GO ON, CHELSEA. GO ON.
I MEAN, HONESTLY, IT'S IMPRESSIVE THAT YOU CAN HOLD YOUR OWN AGAINST HIM FOR A COUPLE ROUNDS IN THE RING...
...CONSIDERING HOW HE'S AN INSTRUCTOR AT WRASSLE CASTLE AND YOU'RE JUST AN EXTREMELY GAWKY TEENAGER.
YOU CAN STOP NOW.
"BUT *SERIOUSLY,* LYDIA! WHENEVER YOU GUYS WRASSLE, I ALWAYS THINK YOU'RE GONNA FINALLY BEAT HIM!
GAHH!
"BUT...HE'S TOO QUICK FOR YOU. AND TOO STRONG. AND TOO SMART. AND TOO SKILLED."
SERIOUSLY, DID YOU *MISS* THAT THING WHERE I SAID YOU COULD STOP?

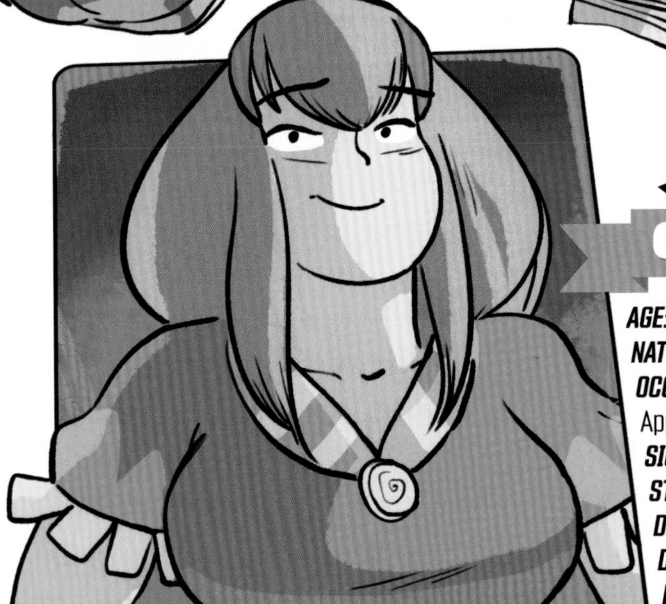

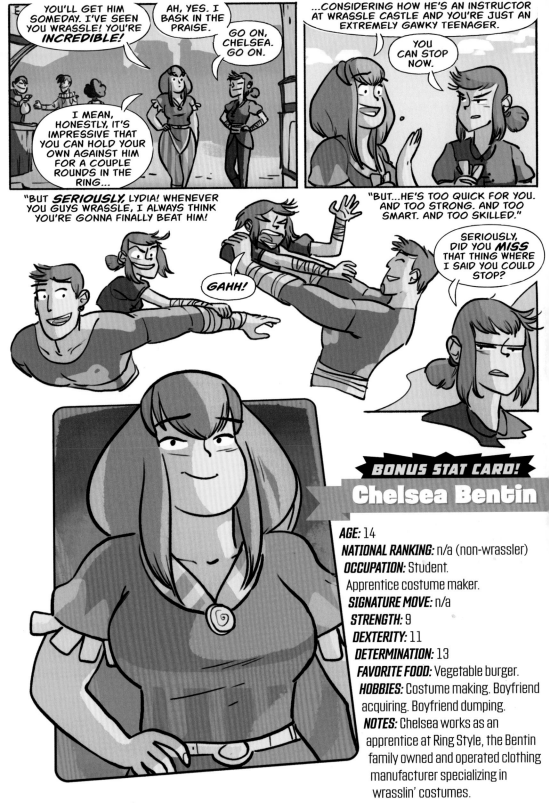

BONUS STAT CARD!

Chelsea Bentin

AGE: 14
NATIONAL RANKING: n/a (non-wrassler)
OCCUPATION: Student. Apprentice costume maker.
SIGNATURE MOVE: n/a
STRENGTH: 9
DEXTERITY: 11
DETERMINATION: 13
FAVORITE FOOD: Vegetable burger.
HOBBIES: Costume making. Boyfriend acquiring. Boyfriend dumping.
NOTES: Chelsea works as an apprentice at Ring Style, the Bentin family owned and operated clothing manufacturer specializing in wrasslin' costumes.

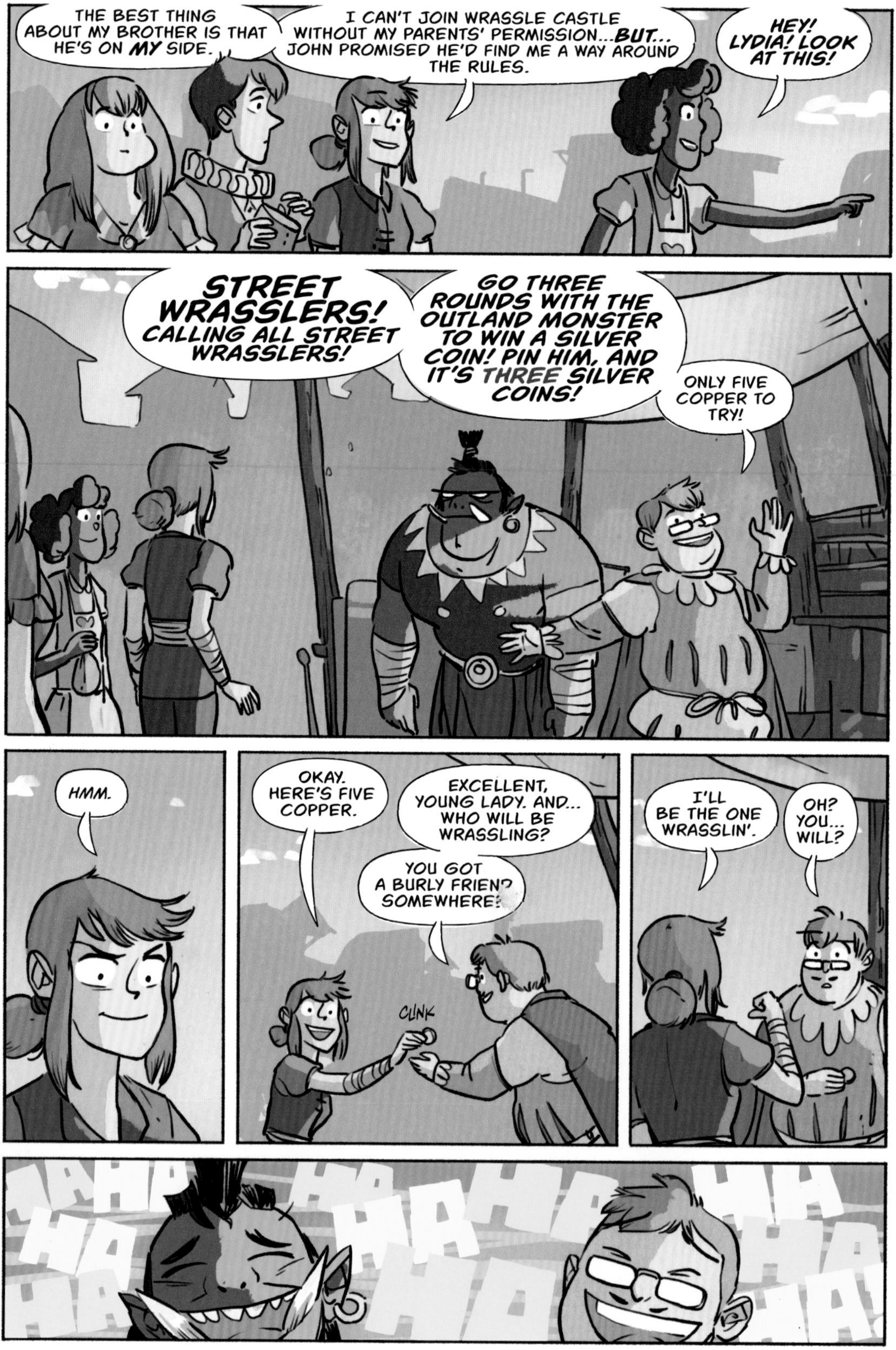
THE BEST THING ABOUT MY BROTHER IS THAT HE'S ON MY SIDE.
I CAN'T JOIN WRASSLE CASTLE WITHOUT MY PARENTS' PERMISSION...BUT... JOHN PROMISED HE'D FIND ME A WAY AROUND THE RULES.
HEY! LYDIA! LOOK AT THIS!
STREET WRASSLERS! CALLING ALL STREET WRASSLERS!
GO THREE ROUNDS WITH THE OUTLAND MONSTER TO WIN A SILVER COIN! PIN HIM, AND IT'S THREE SILVER COINS!
ONLY FIVE COPPER TO TRY!
HMM.
OKAY. HERE'S FIVE COPPER.
EXCELLENT, YOUNG LADY. AND... WHO WILL BE WRASSLING?
YOU GOT A BURLY FRIEND SOMEWHERE?
CLINK
I'LL BE THE ONE WRASSLIN'.
OH? YOU... WILL?
HA HA HA HA HA HA HA HA HA HA HA HA HA HA

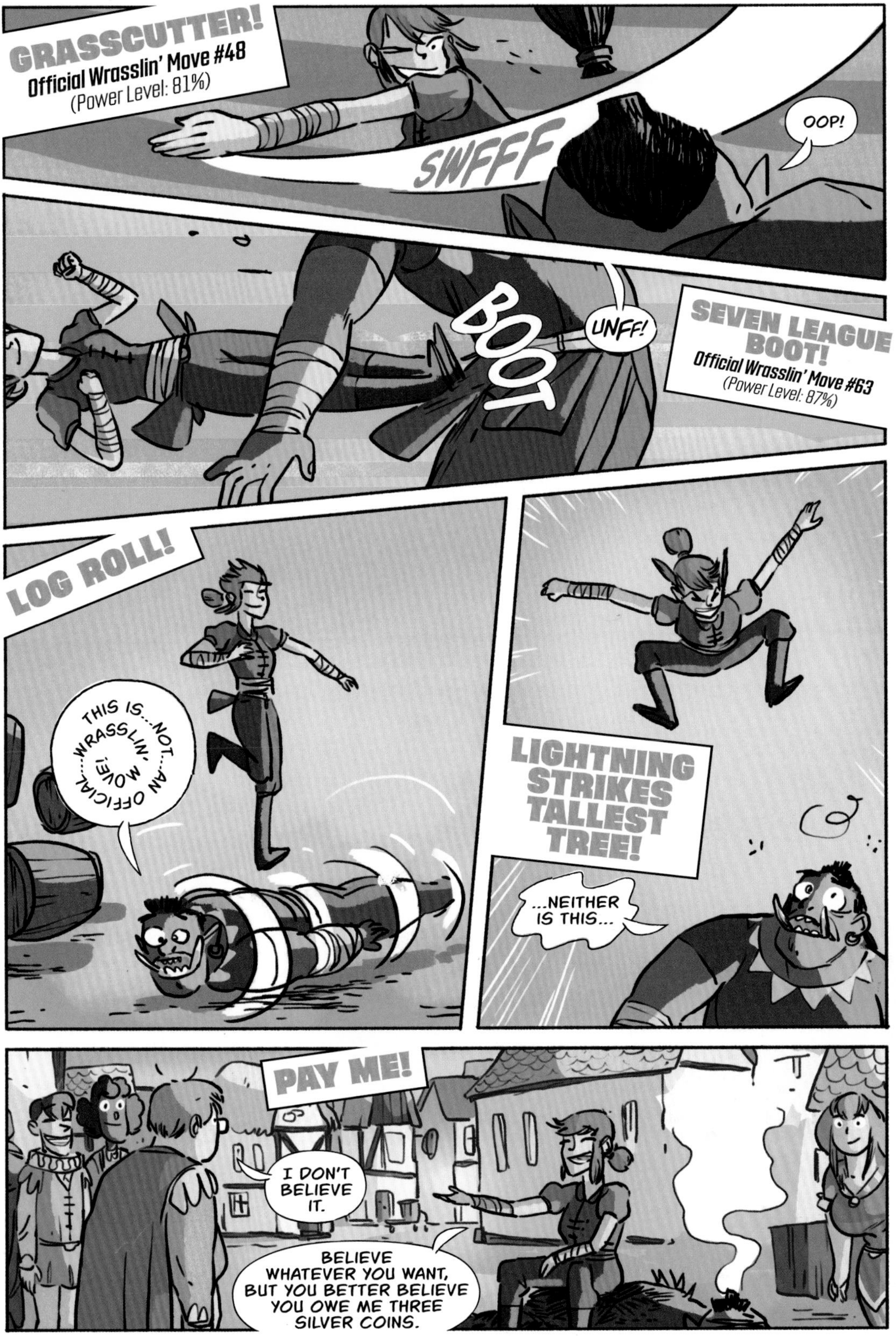
GRASSCUTTER!
Official Wrasslin' Move #48
(Power Level: 81%)
SWFFF
OOP!
BOOT
UNFF!
SEVEN LEAGUE BOOT!
Official Wrasslin' Move #63
(Power Level: 87%)
LOG ROLL!
THIS IS...NOT...AN OFFICIAL...WRASSLIN' MOVE!
LIGHTNING STRIKES TALLEST TREE!
...NEITHER IS THIS...
PAY ME!
I DON'T BELIEVE IT.
BELIEVE WHATEVER YOU WANT, BUT YOU BETTER BELIEVE YOU OWE ME THREE SILVER COINS.

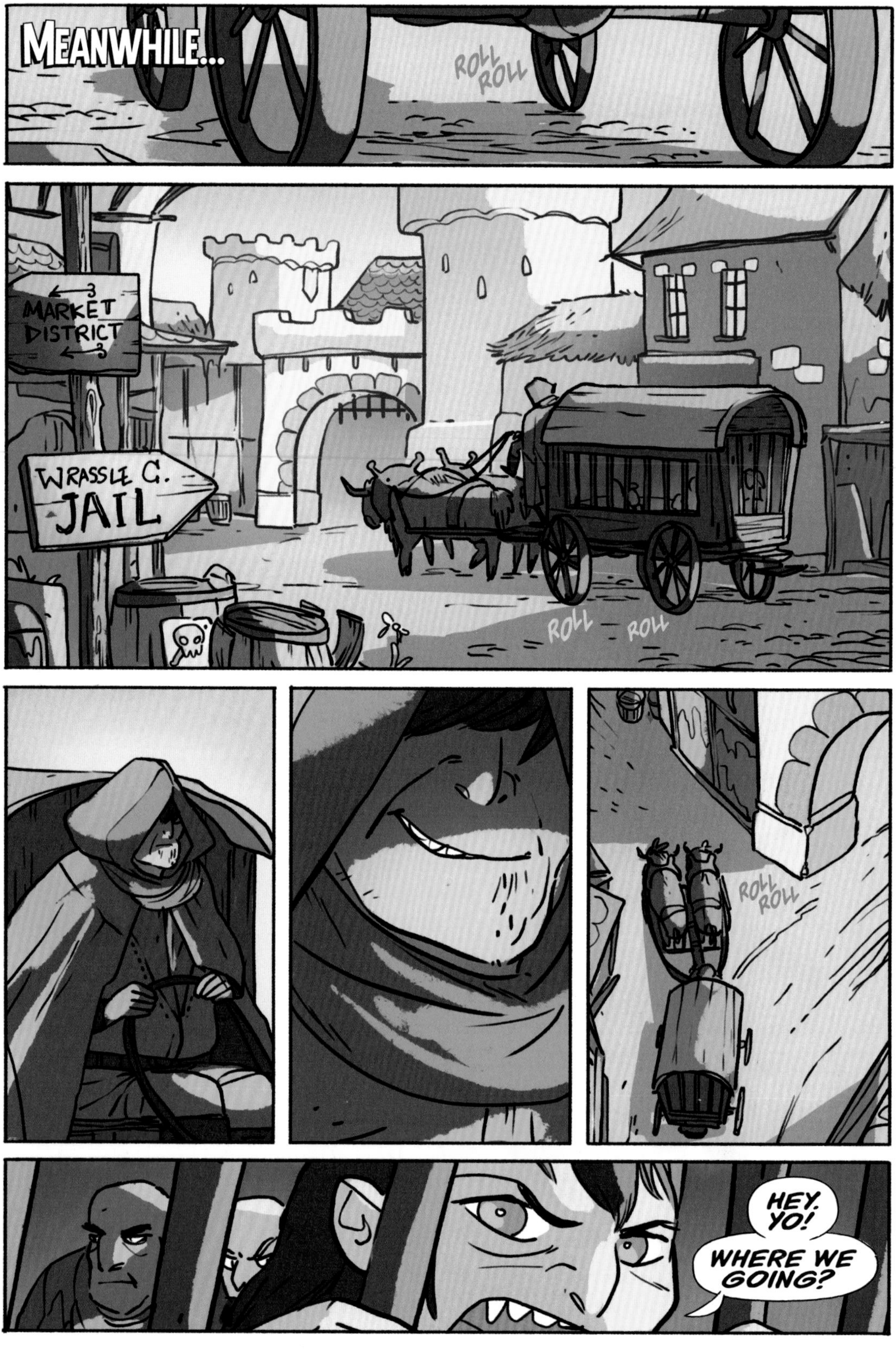
MEANWHILE...
ROLL ROLL
MARKET DISTRICT
WRASSLE C. JAIL
ROLL ROLL
ROLL ROLL
HEY. YO!
WHERE WE GOING?

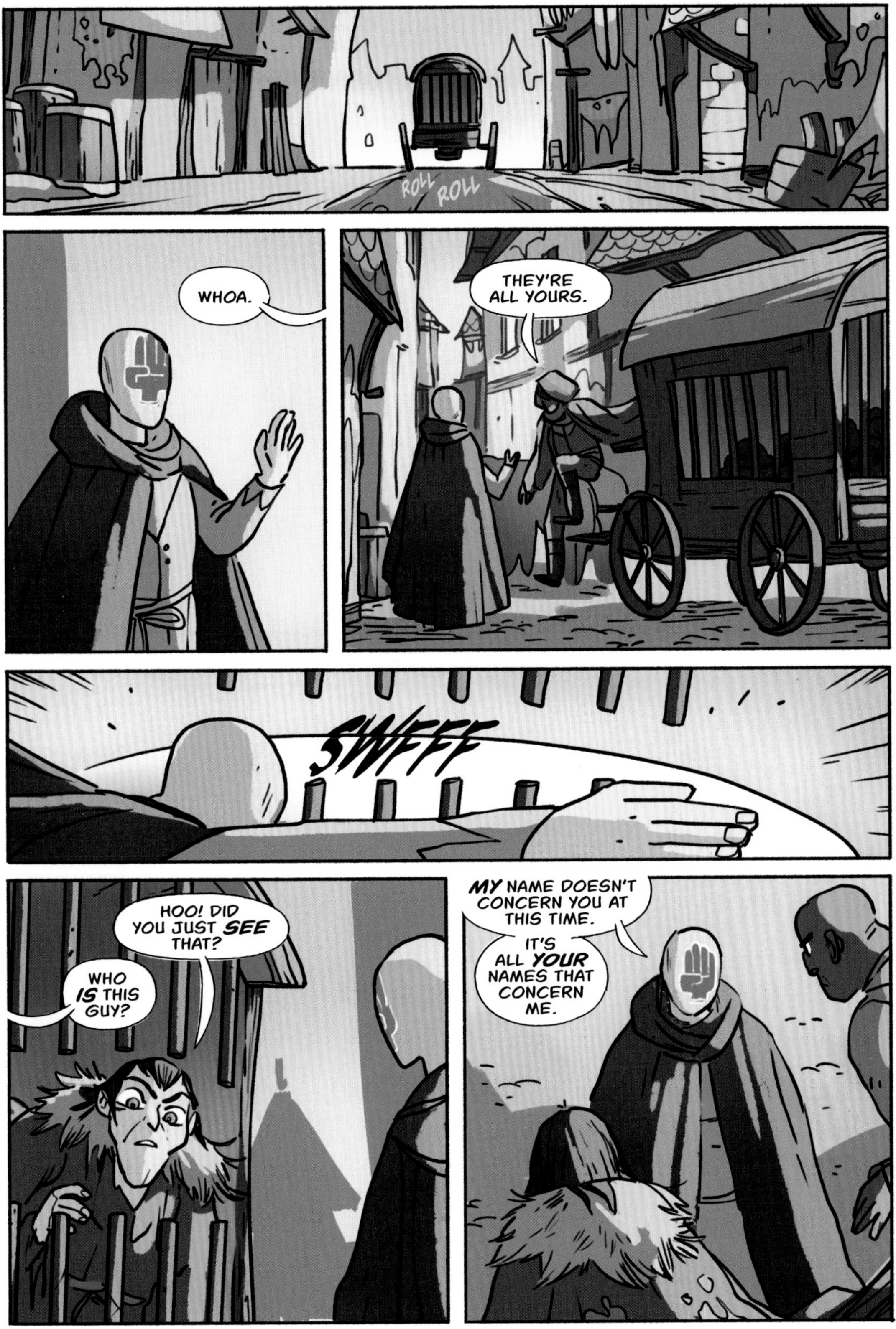
ROLL ROLL
WHOA.
THEY'RE ALL YOURS.
SWFFF
HOO! DID YOU JUST SEE THAT?
WHO IS THIS GUY?
MY NAME DOESN'T CONCERN YOU AT THIS TIME.
IT'S ALL YOUR NAMES THAT CONCERN ME.

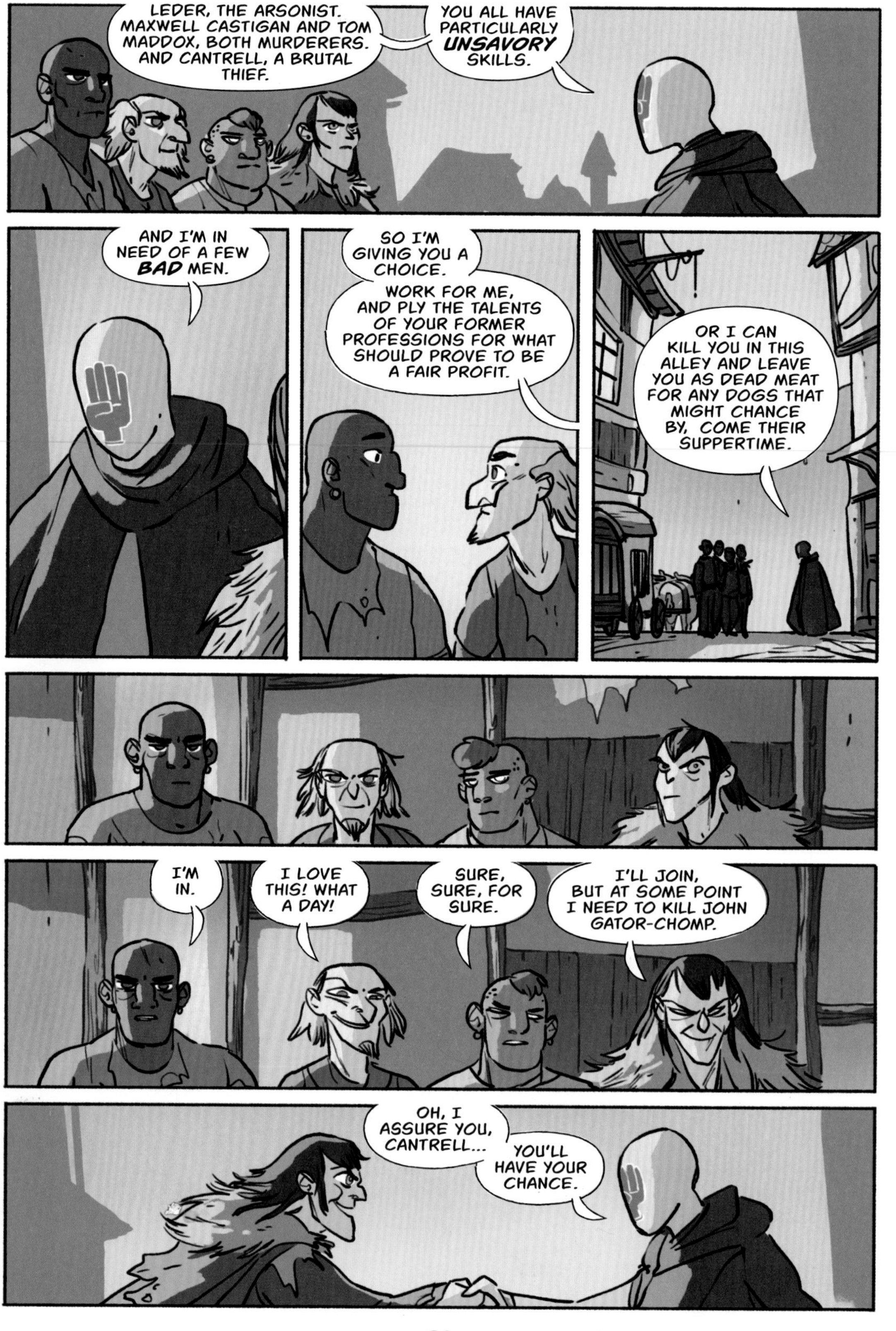
LEDER, THE ARSONIST. MAXWELL CASTIGAN AND TOM MADDOX, BOTH MURDERERS. AND CANTRELL, A BRUTAL THIEF.
YOU ALL HAVE PARTICULARLY **UNSAVORY** SKILLS.
AND I'M IN NEED OF A FEW **BAD** MEN.
SO I'M GIVING YOU A CHOICE.
WORK FOR ME, AND PLY THE TALENTS OF YOUR FORMER PROFESSIONS FOR WHAT SHOULD PROVE TO BE A FAIR PROFIT.
OR I CAN KILL YOU IN THIS ALLEY AND LEAVE YOU AS DEAD MEAT FOR ANY DOGS THAT MIGHT CHANCE BY, COME THEIR SUPPERTIME.
I'M IN.
I LOVE THIS! WHAT A DAY!
SURE, SURE, FOR SURE.
I'LL JOIN, BUT AT SOME POINT I NEED TO KILL JOHN GATOR-CHOMP.
OH, I ASSURE YOU, CANTRELL...
YOU'LL HAVE YOUR CHANCE.

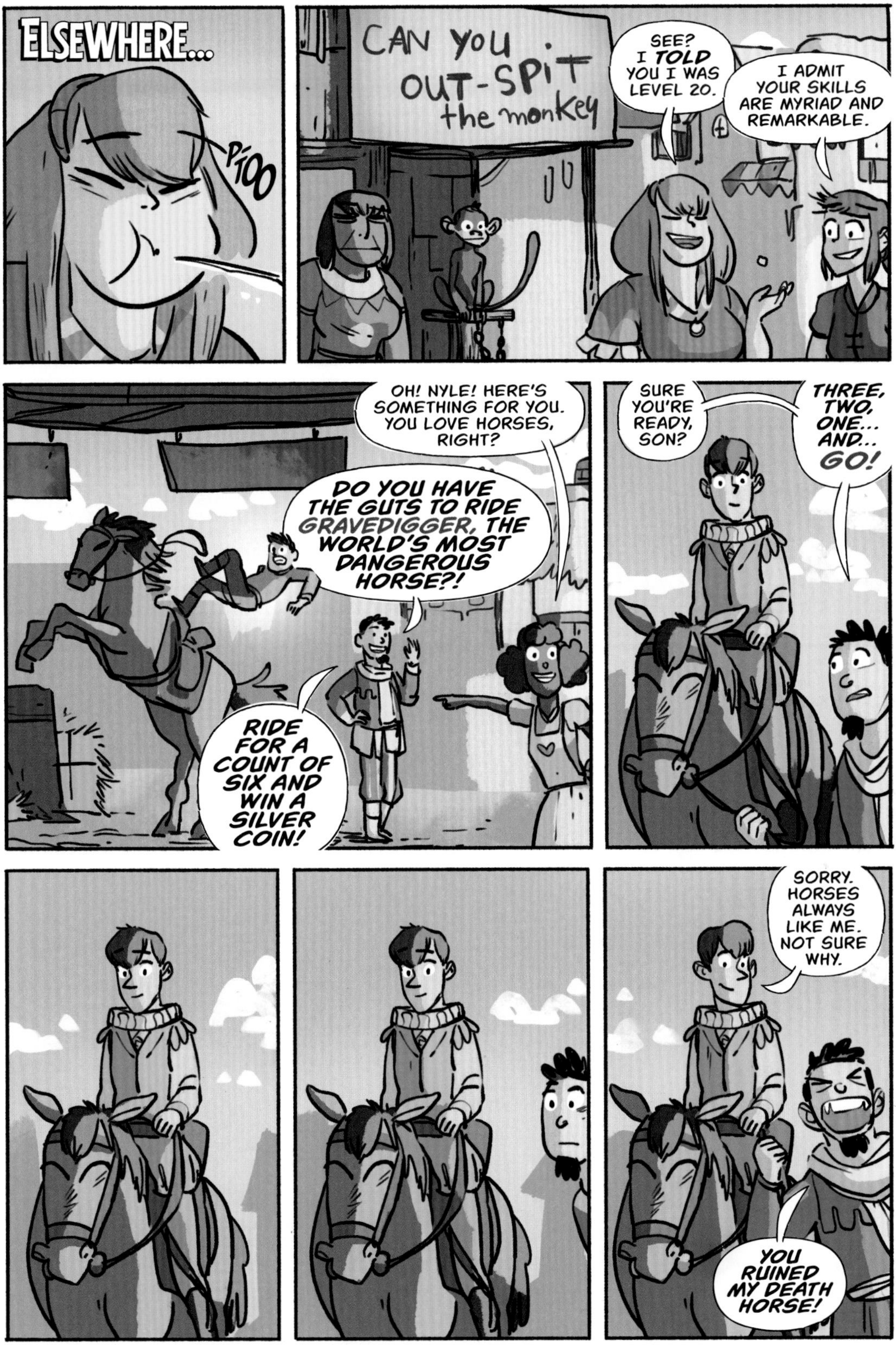
ELSEWHERE...
P'TOO
CAN YOU OUT-SPIT the monkey
SEE? I TOLD YOU I WAS LEVEL 20.
I ADMIT YOUR SKILLS ARE MYRIAD AND REMARKABLE.
OH! NYLE! HERE'S SOMETHING FOR YOU. YOU LOVE HORSES, RIGHT?
DO YOU HAVE THE GUTS TO RIDE GRAVEDIGGER, THE WORLD'S MOST DANGEROUS HORSE?!
RIDE FOR A COUNT OF SIX AND WIN A SILVER COIN!
SURE YOU'RE READY, SON?
THREE, TWO, ONE... AND... GO!
SORRY. HORSES ALWAYS LIKE ME. NOT SURE WHY.
YOU RUINED MY DEATH HORSE!

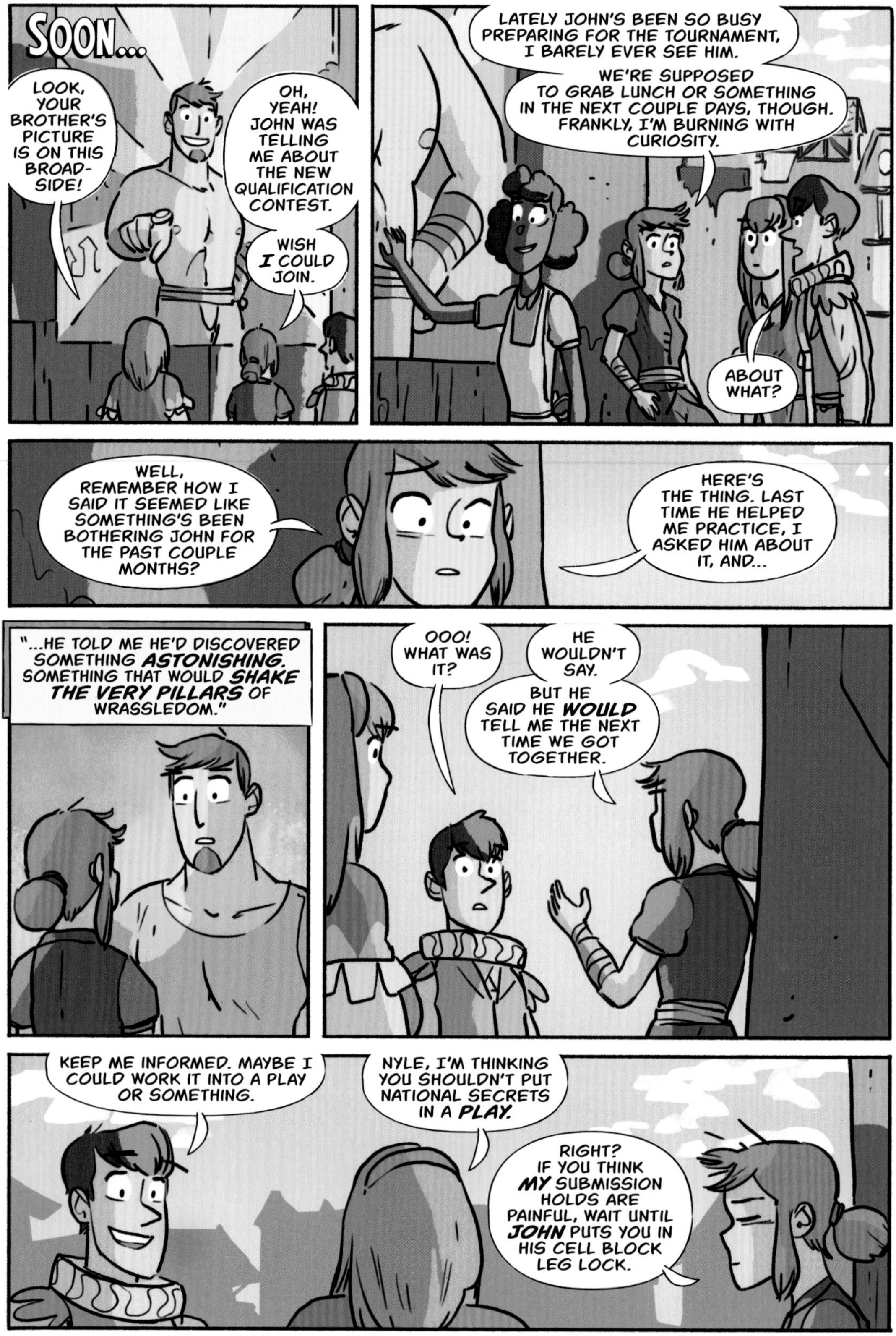
SOON...
LOOK, YOUR BROTHER'S PICTURE IS ON THIS BROAD-SIDE!
OH, YEAH! JOHN WAS TELLING ME ABOUT THE NEW QUALIFICATION CONTEST.
WISH *I* COULD JOIN.
LATELY JOHN'S BEEN SO BUSY PREPARING FOR THE TOURNAMENT, I BARELY EVER SEE HIM.
WE'RE SUPPOSED TO GRAB LUNCH OR SOMETHING IN THE NEXT COUPLE DAYS, THOUGH. FRANKLY, I'M BURNING WITH CURIOSITY.
ABOUT WHAT?
WELL, REMEMBER HOW I SAID IT SEEMED LIKE SOMETHING'S BEEN BOTHERING JOHN FOR THE PAST COUPLE MONTHS?
HERE'S THE THING. LAST TIME HE HELPED ME PRACTICE, I ASKED HIM ABOUT IT, AND...
"...HE TOLD ME HE'D DISCOVERED SOMETHING ***ASTONISHING.*** SOMETHING THAT WOULD ***SHAKE THE VERY PILLARS*** OF WRASSLEDOM."
OOO! WHAT WAS IT?
HE WOULDN'T SAY.
BUT HE SAID HE ***WOULD*** TELL ME THE NEXT TIME WE GOT TOGETHER.
KEEP ME INFORMED. MAYBE I COULD WORK IT INTO A PLAY OR SOMETHING.
NYLE, I'M THINKING YOU SHOULDN'T PUT NATIONAL SECRETS IN A ***PLAY.***
RIGHT? IF YOU THINK ***MY*** SUBMISSION HOLDS ARE PAINFUL, WAIT UNTIL ***JOHN*** PUTS YOU IN HIS CELL BLOCK LEG LOCK.

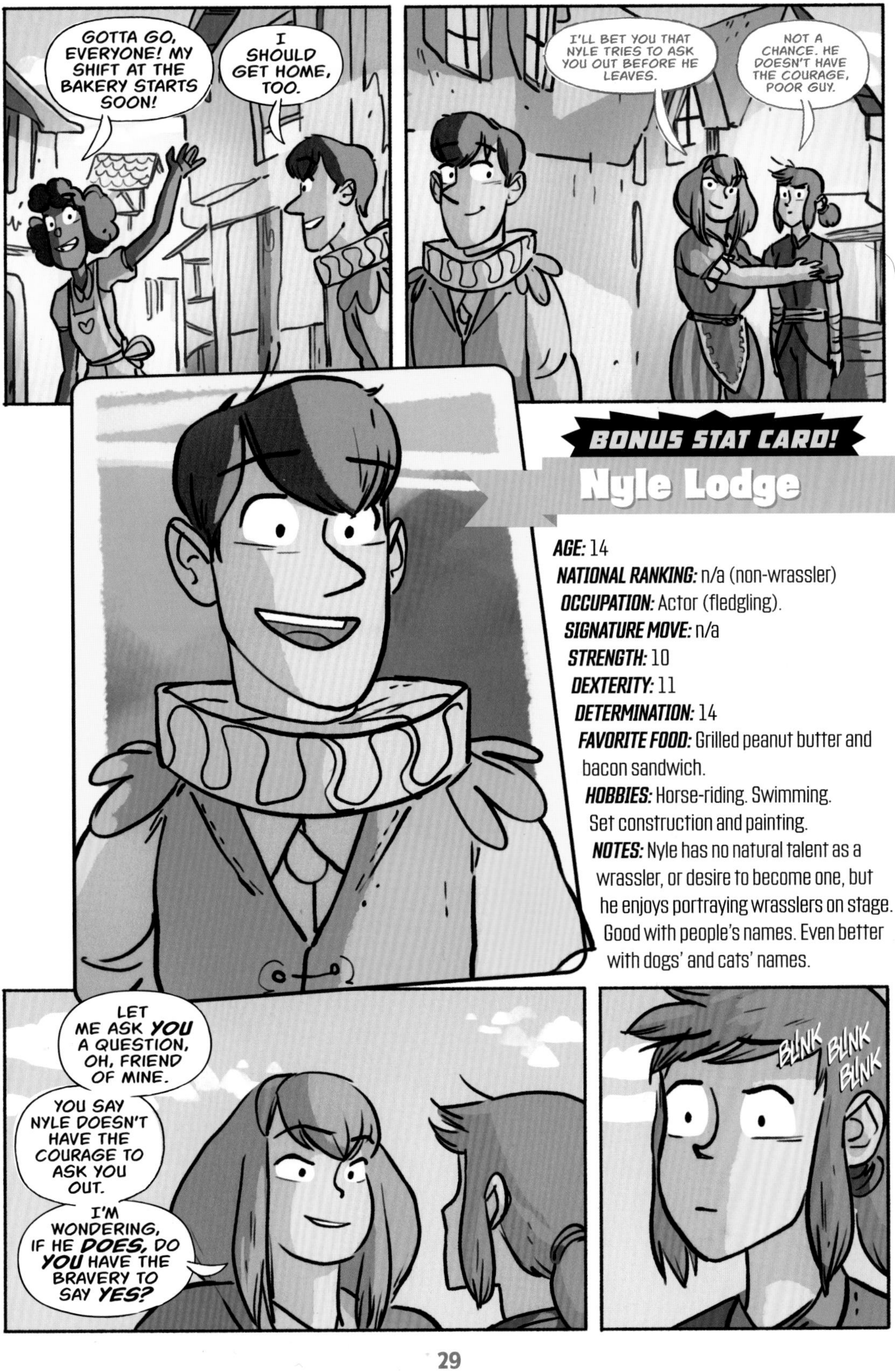
GOTTA GO, EVERYONE! MY SHIFT AT THE BAKERY STARTS SOON!
I SHOULD GET HOME, TOO.
I'LL BET YOU THAT NYLE TRIES TO ASK YOU OUT BEFORE HE LEAVES.
NOT A CHANCE. HE DOESN'T HAVE THE COURAGE, POOR GUY.
BONUS STAT CARD!
Nyle Lodge
AGE: 14
NATIONAL RANKING: n/a (non-wrassler)
OCCUPATION: Actor (fledgling).
SIGNATURE MOVE: n/a
STRENGTH: 10
DEXTERITY: 11
DETERMINATION: 14
FAVORITE FOOD: Grilled peanut butter and bacon sandwich.
HOBBIES: Horse-riding. Swimming. Set construction and painting.
NOTES: Nyle has no natural talent as a wrassler, or desire to become one, but he enjoys portraying wrasslers on stage. Good with people's names. Even better with dogs' and cats' names.
LET ME ASK YOU A QUESTION, OH, FRIEND OF MINE.
YOU SAY NYLE DOESN'T HAVE THE COURAGE TO ASK YOU OUT.
I'M WONDERING, IF HE DOES, DO YOU HAVE THE BRAVERY TO SAY YES?
BLINK BLINK BLINK

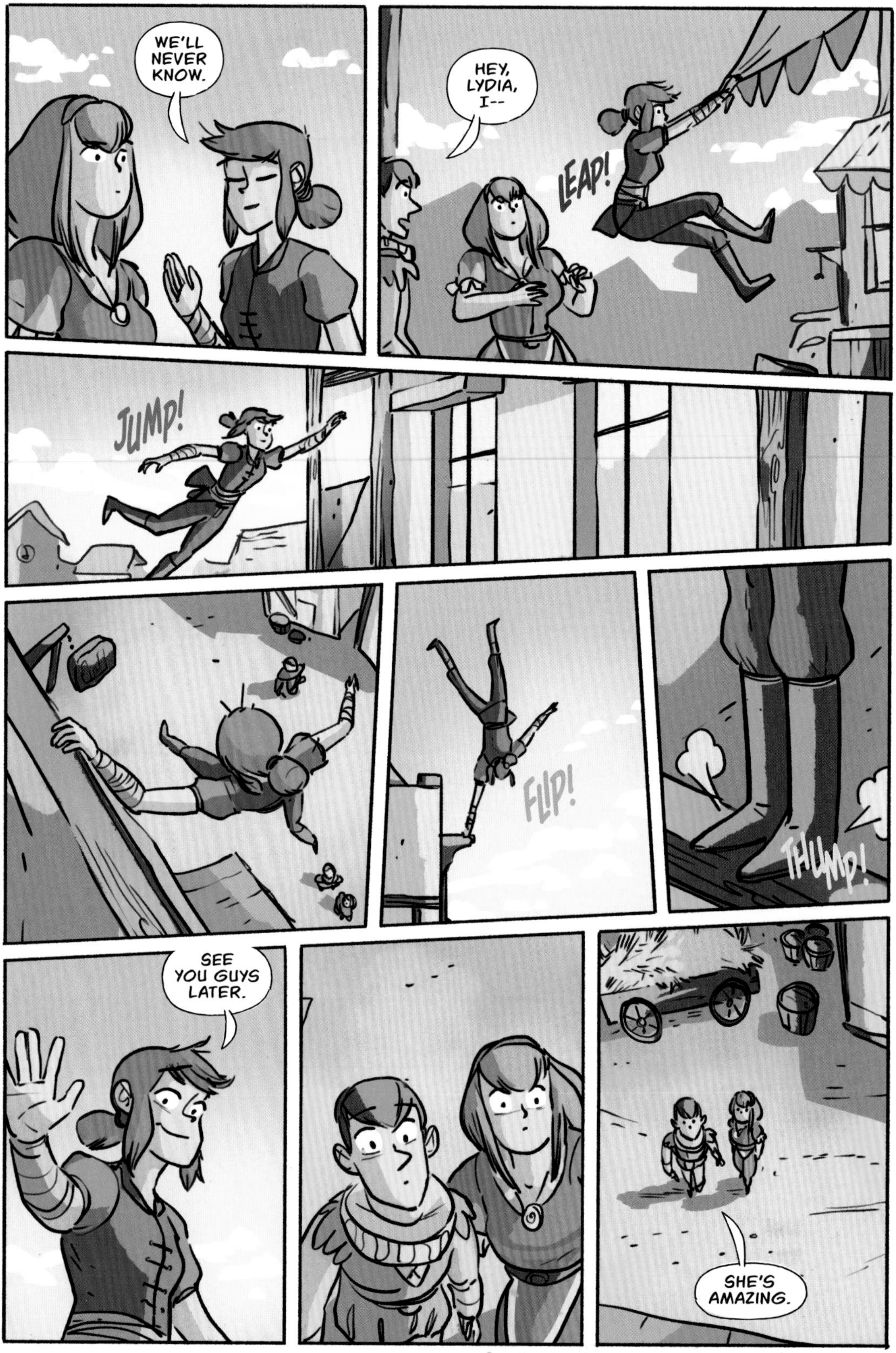

WE'LL NEVER KNOW.
HEY, LYDIA, I--
LEAP!
JUMP!
FLIP!
THUMP!
SEE YOU GUYS LATER.
SHE'S AMAZING.

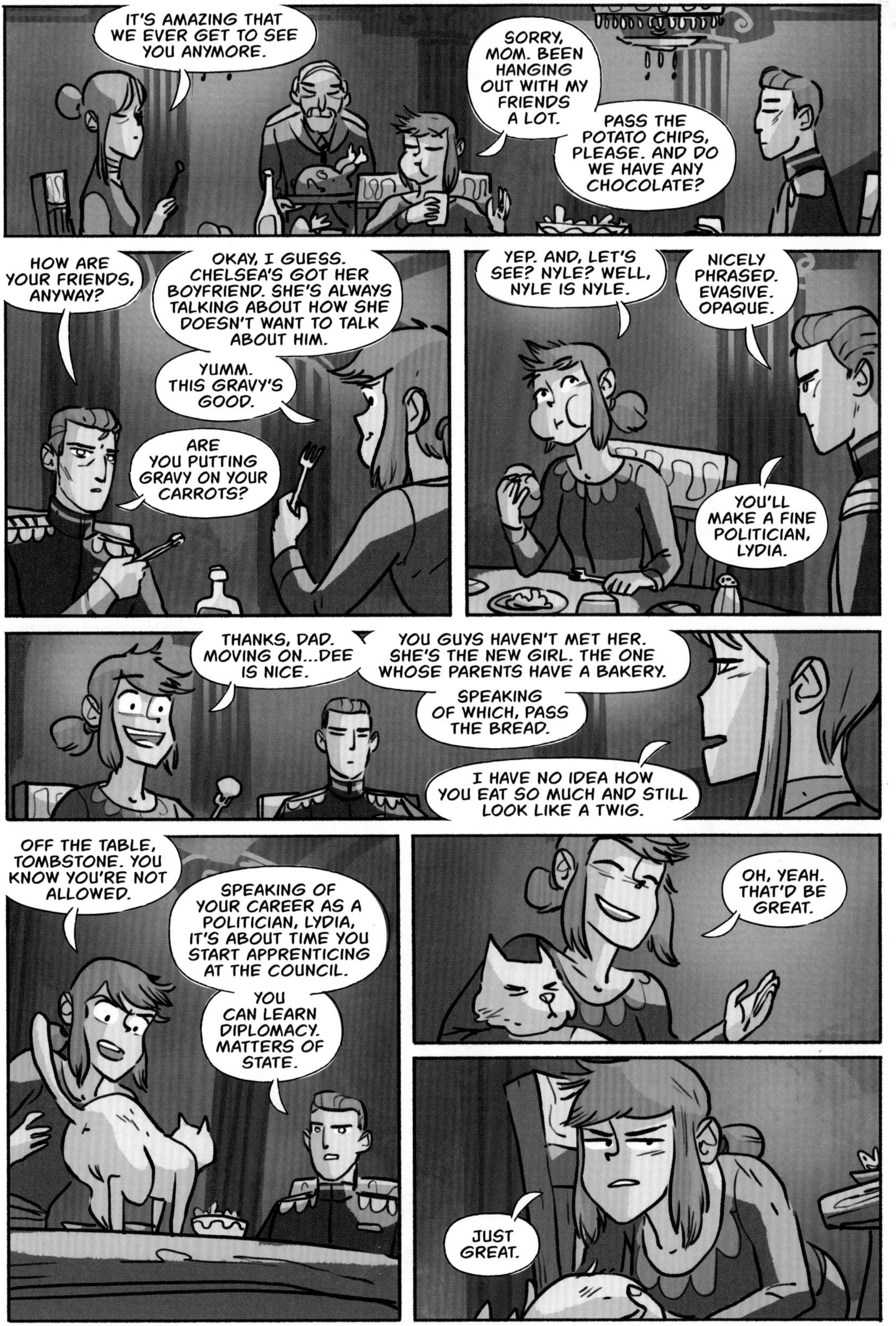
IT'S AMAZING THAT WE EVER GET TO SEE YOU ANYMORE.
SORRY, MOM. BEEN HANGING OUT WITH MY FRIENDS A LOT.
PASS THE POTATO CHIPS, PLEASE. AND DO WE HAVE ANY CHOCOLATE?
HOW ARE YOUR FRIENDS, ANYWAY?
OKAY, I GUESS. CHELSEA'S GOT HER BOYFRIEND. SHE'S ALWAYS TALKING ABOUT HOW SHE DOESN'T WANT TO TALK ABOUT HIM.
YUMM. THIS GRAVY'S GOOD.
ARE YOU PUTTING GRAVY ON YOUR CARROTS?
YEP. AND, LET'S SEE? NYLE? WELL, NYLE IS NYLE.
NICELY PHRASED. EVASIVE. OPAQUE.
YOU'LL MAKE A FINE POLITICIAN, LYDIA.
THANKS, DAD. MOVING ON...DEE IS NICE.
YOU GUYS HAVEN'T MET HER. SHE'S THE NEW GIRL. THE ONE WHOSE PARENTS HAVE A BAKERY.
SPEAKING OF WHICH, PASS THE BREAD.
I HAVE NO IDEA HOW YOU EAT SO MUCH AND STILL LOOK LIKE A TWIG.
OFF THE TABLE, TOMBSTONE. YOU KNOW YOU'RE NOT ALLOWED.
SPEAKING OF YOUR CAREER AS A POLITICIAN, LYDIA, IT'S ABOUT TIME YOU START APPRENTICING AT THE COUNCIL.
YOU CAN LEARN DIPLOMACY. MATTERS OF STATE.
OH, YEAH. THAT'D BE GREAT.
JUST GREAT.

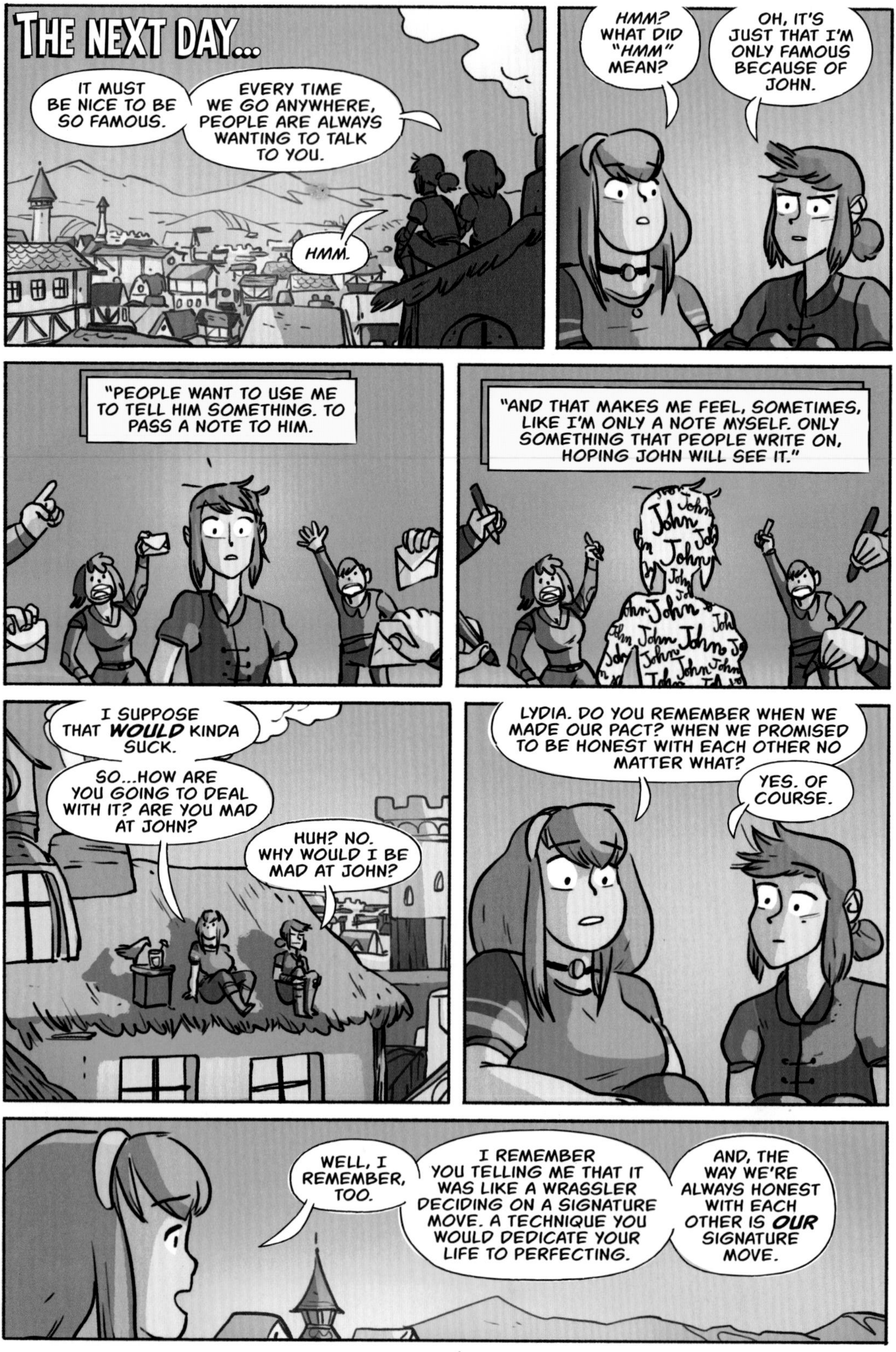
THE NEXT DAY...
IT MUST BE NICE TO BE SO FAMOUS.
EVERY TIME WE GO ANYWHERE, PEOPLE ARE ALWAYS WANTING TO TALK TO YOU.
HMM.
HMM? WHAT DID "HMM" MEAN?
OH, IT'S JUST THAT I'M ONLY FAMOUS BECAUSE OF JOHN.
"PEOPLE WANT TO USE ME TO TELL HIM SOMETHING. TO PASS A NOTE TO HIM.
"AND THAT MAKES ME FEEL, SOMETIMES, LIKE I'M ONLY A NOTE MYSELF. ONLY SOMETHING THAT PEOPLE WRITE ON, HOPING JOHN WILL SEE IT."
I SUPPOSE THAT ***WOULD*** KINDA SUCK.
SO...HOW ARE YOU GOING TO DEAL WITH IT? ARE YOU MAD AT JOHN?
HUH? NO. WHY WOULD I BE MAD AT JOHN?
LYDIA. DO YOU REMEMBER WHEN WE MADE OUR PACT? WHEN WE PROMISED TO BE HONEST WITH EACH OTHER NO MATTER WHAT?
YES. OF COURSE.
WELL, I REMEMBER, TOO.
I REMEMBER YOU TELLING ME THAT IT WAS LIKE A WRASSLER DECIDING ON A SIGNATURE MOVE. A TECHNIQUE YOU WOULD DEDICATE YOUR LIFE TO PERFECTING.
AND, THE WAY WE'RE ALWAYS HONEST WITH EACH OTHER IS ***OUR*** SIGNATURE MOVE.

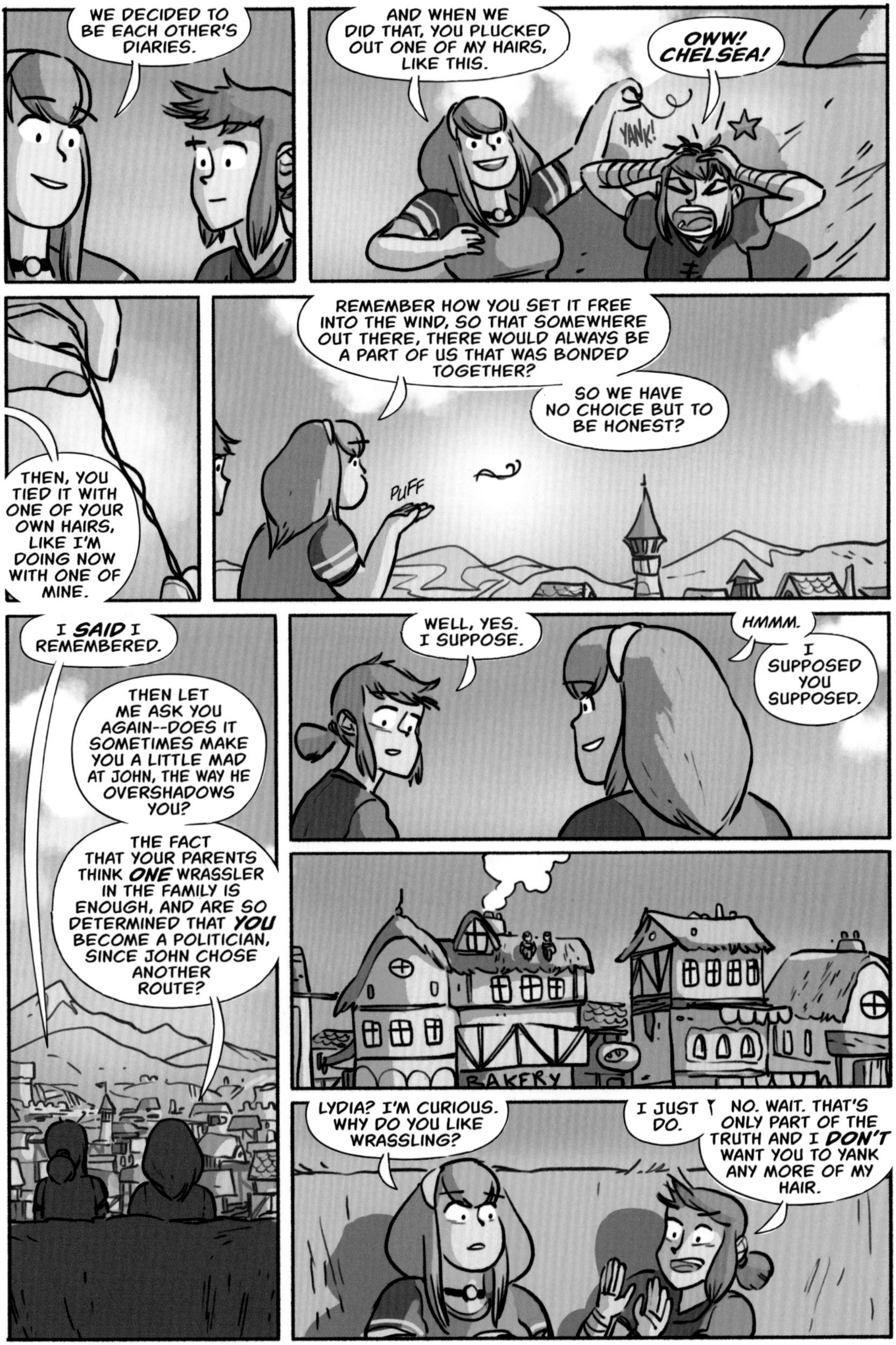
WE DECIDED TO BE EACH OTHER'S DIARIES.
AND WHEN WE DID THAT, YOU PLUCKED OUT ONE OF MY HAIRS, LIKE THIS.
YANK!
OWW! CHELSEA!
THEN, YOU TIED IT WITH ONE OF YOUR OWN HAIRS, LIKE I'M DOING NOW WITH ONE OF MINE.
REMEMBER HOW YOU SET IT FREE INTO THE WIND, SO THAT SOMEWHERE OUT THERE, THERE WOULD ALWAYS BE A PART OF US THAT WAS BONDED TOGETHER?
SO WE HAVE NO CHOICE BUT TO BE HONEST?
PUFF
I SAID I REMEMBERED.
THEN LET ME ASK YOU AGAIN--DOES IT SOMETIMES MAKE YOU A LITTLE MAD AT JOHN, THE WAY HE OVERSHADOWS YOU?
THE FACT THAT YOUR PARENTS THINK ONE WRASSLER IN THE FAMILY IS ENOUGH, AND ARE SO DETERMINED THAT YOU BECOME A POLITICIAN, SINCE JOHN CHOSE ANOTHER ROUTE?
WELL, YES. I SUPPOSE.
HMMM.
I SUPPOSED YOU SUPPOSED.
BAKERY
LYDIA? I'M CURIOUS. WHY DO YOU LIKE WRASSLING?
I JUST DO.
NO. WAIT. THAT'S ONLY PART OF THE TRUTH AND I DON'T WANT YOU TO YANK ANY MORE OF MY HAIR.

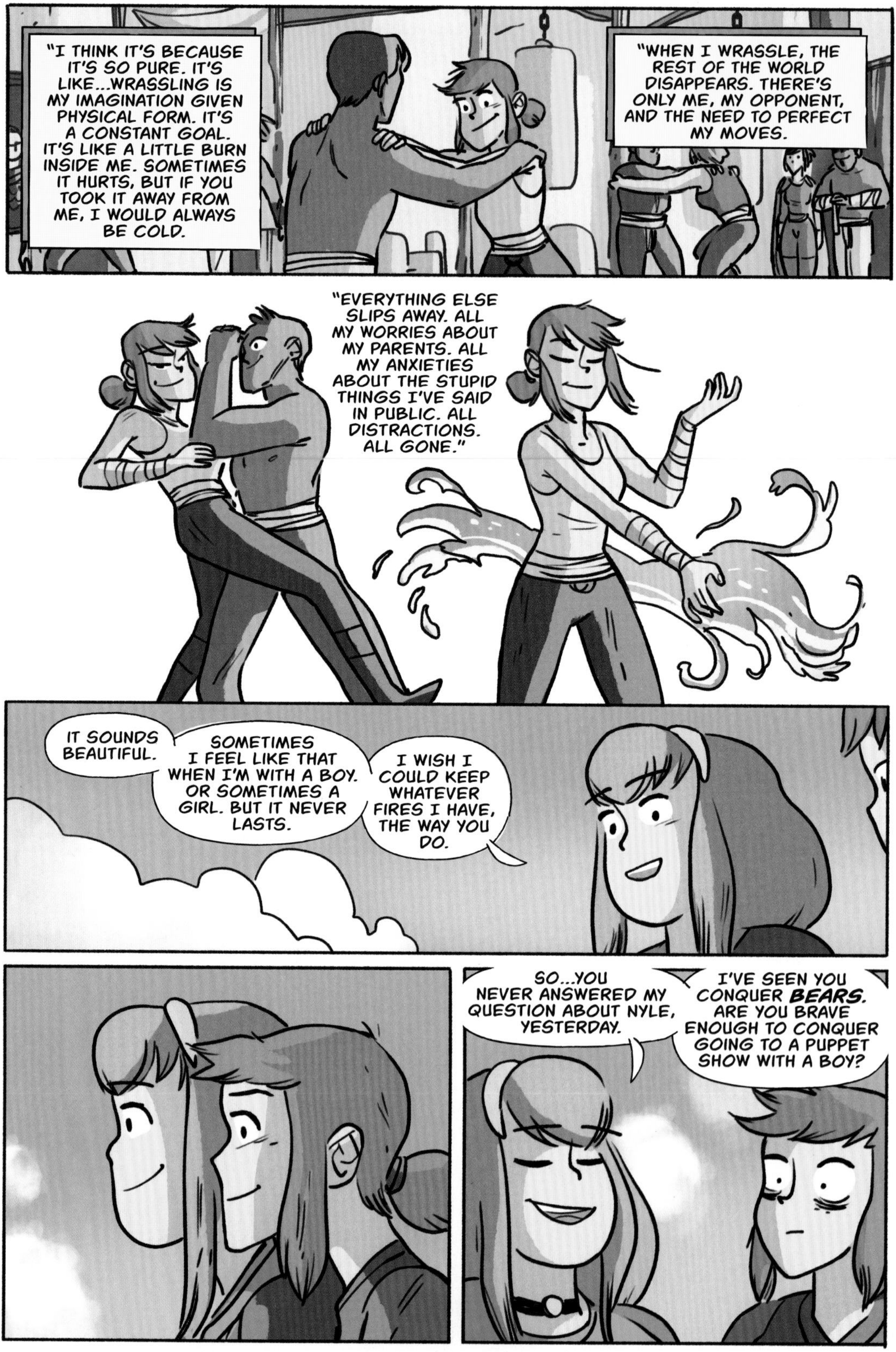
"I THINK IT'S BECAUSE IT'S SO PURE. IT'S LIKE...WRASSLING IS MY IMAGINATION GIVEN PHYSICAL FORM. IT'S A CONSTANT GOAL. IT'S LIKE A LITTLE BURN INSIDE ME. SOMETIMES IT HURTS, BUT IF YOU TOOK IT AWAY FROM ME, I WOULD ALWAYS BE COLD.
"WHEN I WRASSLE, THE REST OF THE WORLD DISAPPEARS. THERE'S ONLY ME, MY OPPONENT, AND THE NEED TO PERFECT MY MOVES.
"EVERYTHING ELSE SLIPS AWAY. ALL MY WORRIES ABOUT MY PARENTS. ALL MY ANXIETIES ABOUT THE STUPID THINGS I'VE SAID IN PUBLIC. ALL DISTRACTIONS. ALL GONE."
IT SOUNDS BEAUTIFUL.
SOMETIMES I FEEL LIKE THAT WHEN I'M WITH A BOY. OR SOMETIMES A GIRL. BUT IT NEVER LASTS.
I WISH I COULD KEEP WHATEVER FIRES I HAVE, THE WAY YOU DO.
SO...YOU NEVER ANSWERED MY QUESTION ABOUT NYLE, YESTERDAY.
I'VE SEEN YOU CONQUER **BEARS.** ARE YOU BRAVE ENOUGH TO CONQUER GOING TO A PUPPET SHOW WITH A BOY?

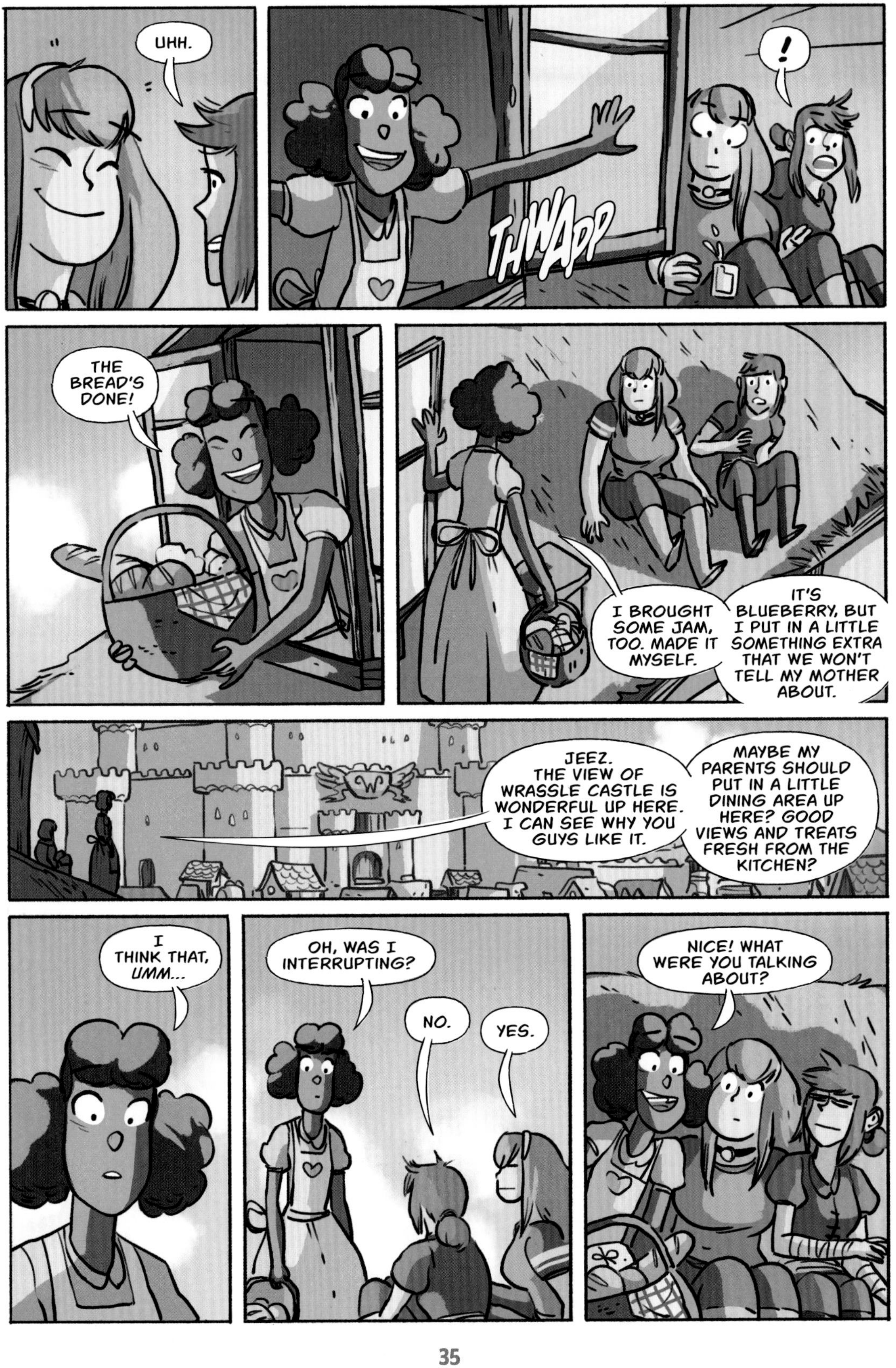
UHH.
!
THWAPP
THE BREAD'S DONE!
I BROUGHT SOME JAM, TOO. MADE IT MYSELF.
IT'S BLUEBERRY, BUT I PUT IN A LITTLE SOMETHING EXTRA THAT WE WON'T TELL MY MOTHER ABOUT.
JEEZ. THE VIEW OF WRASSLE CASTLE IS WONDERFUL UP HERE. I CAN SEE WHY YOU GUYS LIKE IT.
MAYBE MY PARENTS SHOULD PUT IN A LITTLE DINING AREA UP HERE? GOOD VIEWS AND TREATS FRESH FROM THE KITCHEN?
I THINK THAT, UMM...
OH, WAS I INTERRUPTING?
NO.
YES.
NICE! WHAT WERE YOU TALKING ABOUT?

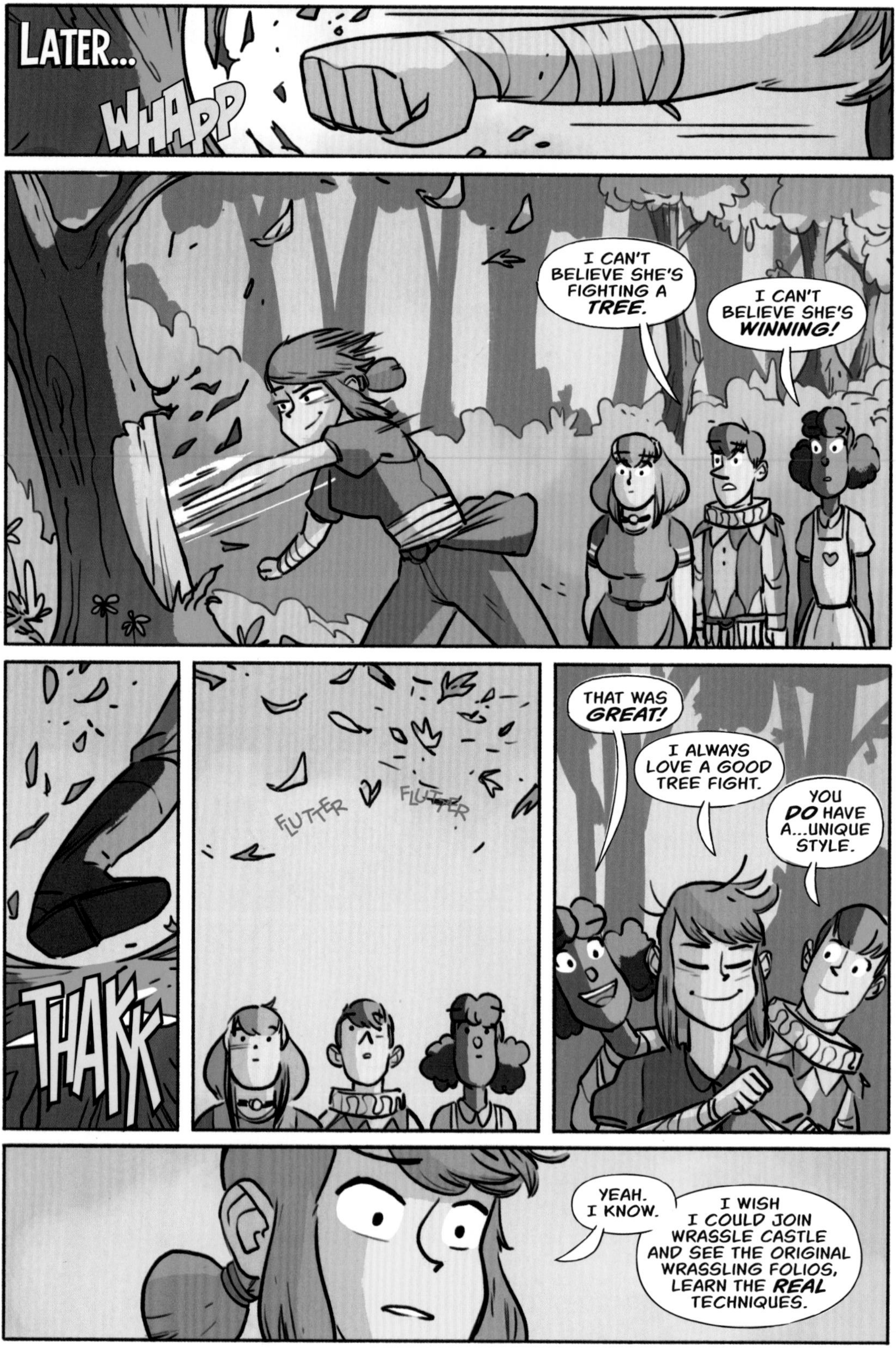
LATER...
WHAPP
I CAN'T BELIEVE SHE'S FIGHTING A TREE.
I CAN'T BELIEVE SHE'S WINNING!
THAKK
FLUTTER
FLUTTER
THAT WAS GREAT!
I ALWAYS LOVE A GOOD TREE FIGHT.
YOU DO HAVE A...UNIQUE STYLE.
YEAH. I KNOW.
I WISH I COULD JOIN WRASSLE CASTLE AND SEE THE ORIGINAL WRASSLING FOLIOS, LEARN THE REAL TECHNIQUES.

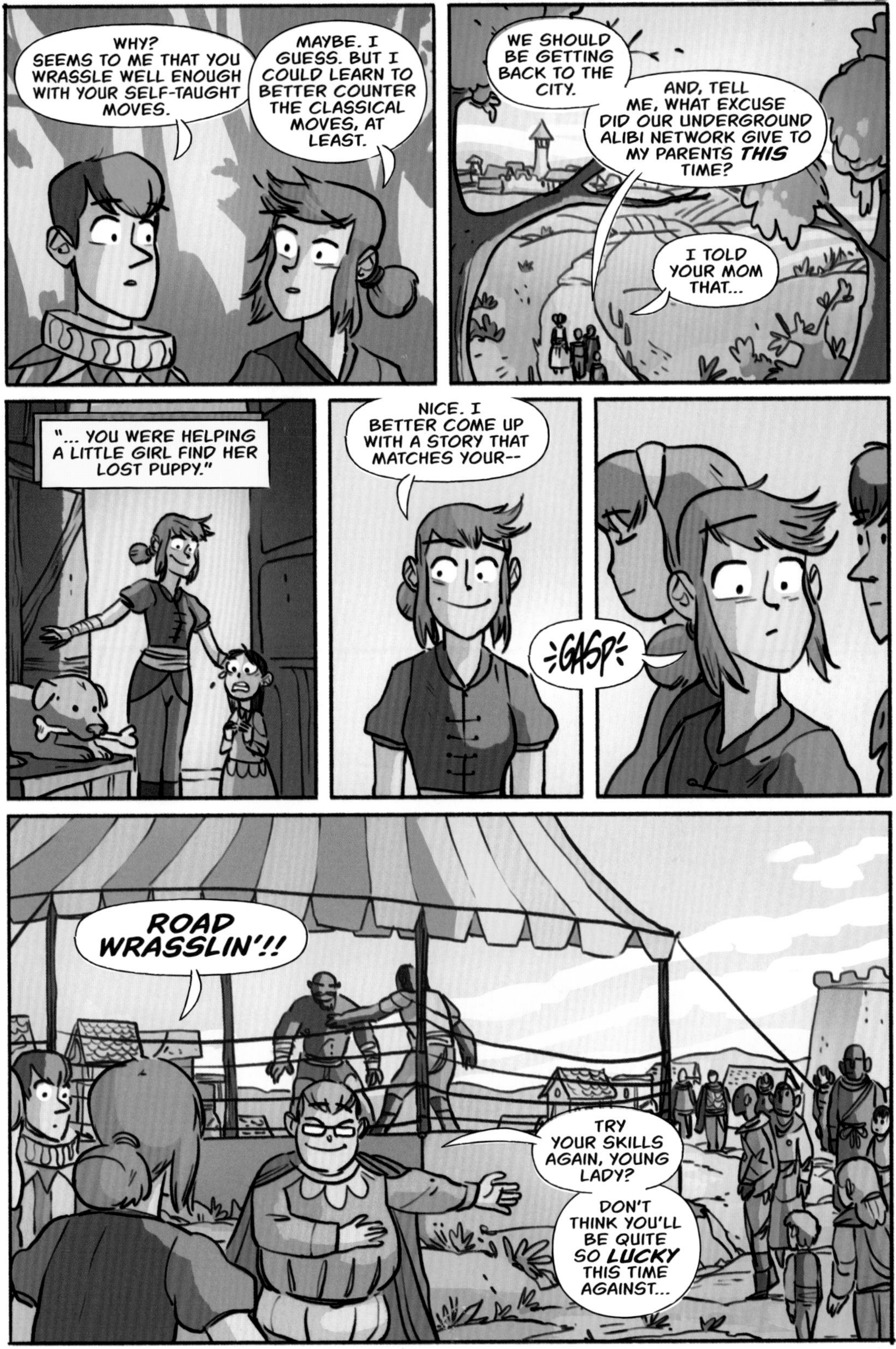
WHY? SEEMS TO ME THAT YOU WRASSLE WELL ENOUGH WITH YOUR SELF-TAUGHT MOVES.
MAYBE. I GUESS. BUT I COULD LEARN TO BETTER COUNTER THE CLASSICAL MOVES, AT LEAST.
WE SHOULD BE GETTING BACK TO THE CITY.
AND, TELL ME, WHAT EXCUSE DID OUR UNDERGROUND ALIBI NETWORK GIVE TO MY PARENTS *THIS* TIME?
I TOLD YOUR MOM THAT...
"... YOU WERE HELPING A LITTLE GIRL FIND HER LOST PUPPY."
NICE. I BETTER COME UP WITH A STORY THAT MATCHES YOUR--
GASP
ROAD WRASSLIN'!!
TRY YOUR SKILLS AGAIN, YOUNG LADY?
DON'T THINK YOU'LL BE QUITE SO *LUCKY* THIS TIME AGAINST...

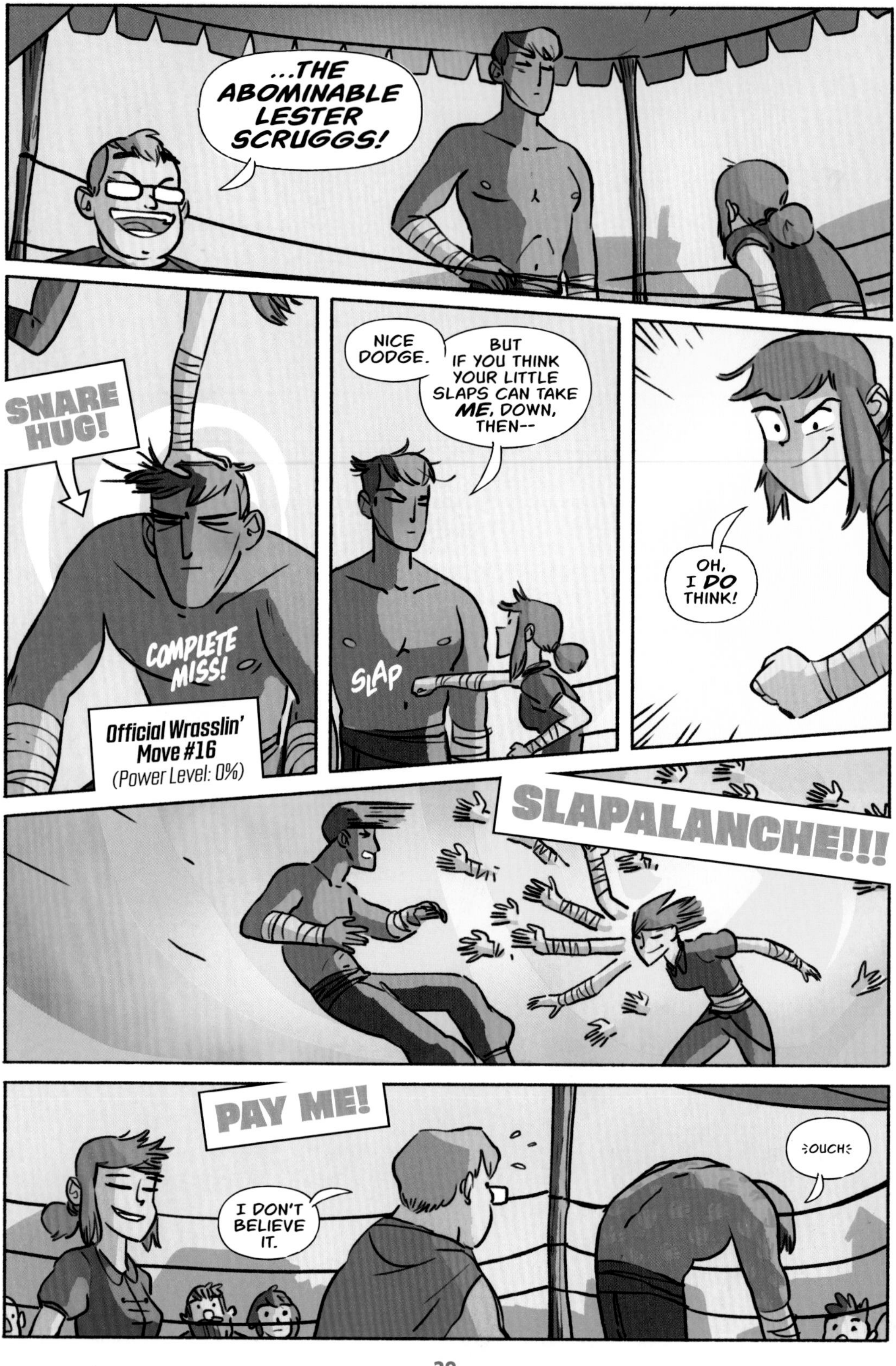
...THE ABOMINABLE LESTER SCRUGGS!
SNARE HUG!
COMPLETE MISS!
Official Wrasslin' Move #16
(Power Level: 0%)
NICE DODGE.
BUT IF YOU THINK YOUR LITTLE SLAPS CAN TAKE ME, DOWN, THEN--
SLAP
OH, I DO THINK!
SLAPALANCHE!!!
PAY ME!
I DON'T BELIEVE IT.
OUCH

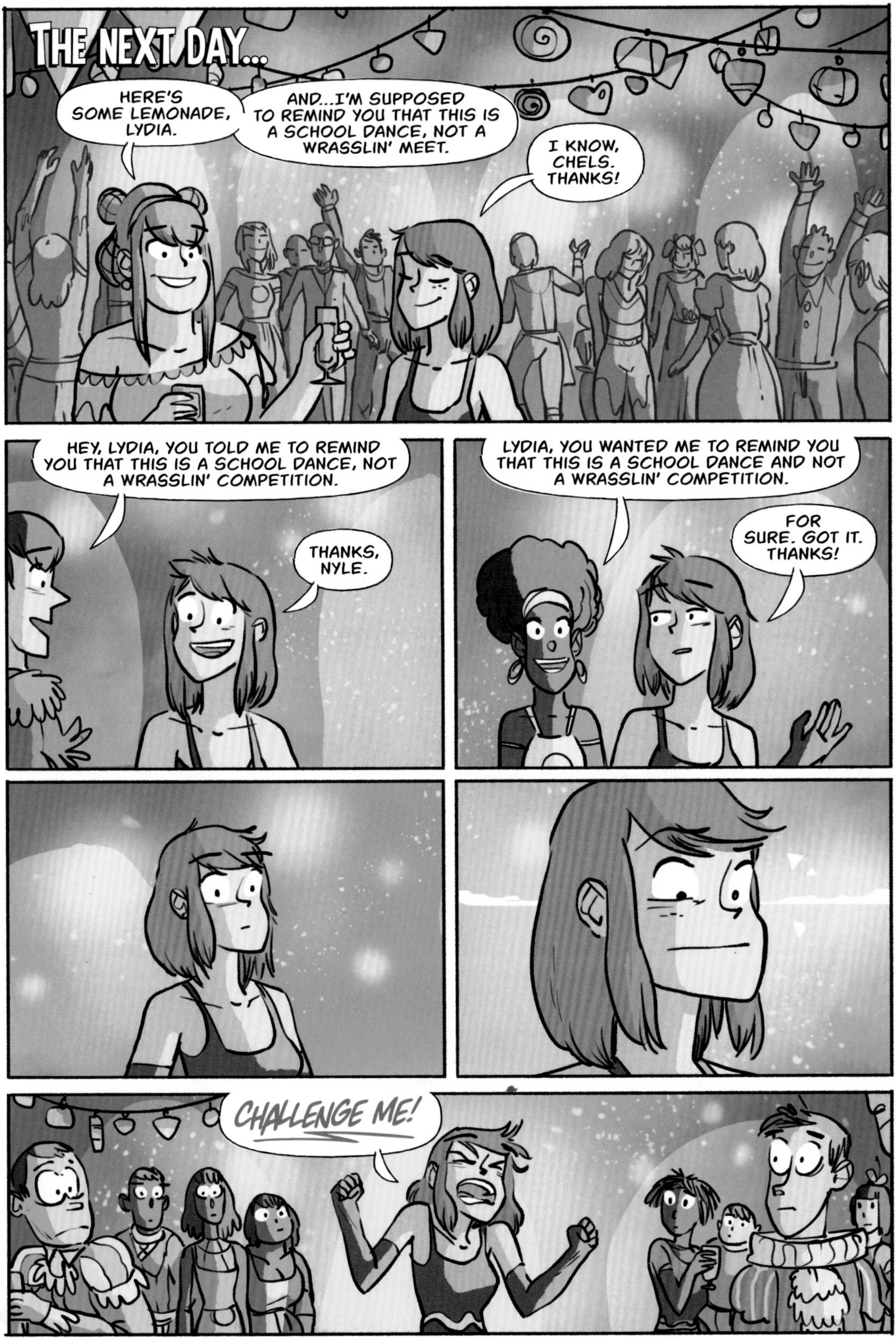

THE NEXT DAY...
HERE'S SOME LEMONADE, LYDIA.
AND...I'M SUPPOSED TO REMIND YOU THAT THIS IS A SCHOOL DANCE, NOT A WRASSLIN' MEET.
I KNOW, CHELS. THANKS!
HEY, LYDIA, YOU TOLD ME TO REMIND YOU THAT THIS IS A SCHOOL DANCE, NOT A WRASSLIN' COMPETITION.
THANKS, NYLE.
LYDIA, YOU WANTED ME TO REMIND YOU THAT THIS IS A SCHOOL DANCE AND NOT A WRASSLIN' COMPETITION.
FOR SURE. GOT IT. THANKS!
CHALLENGE ME!

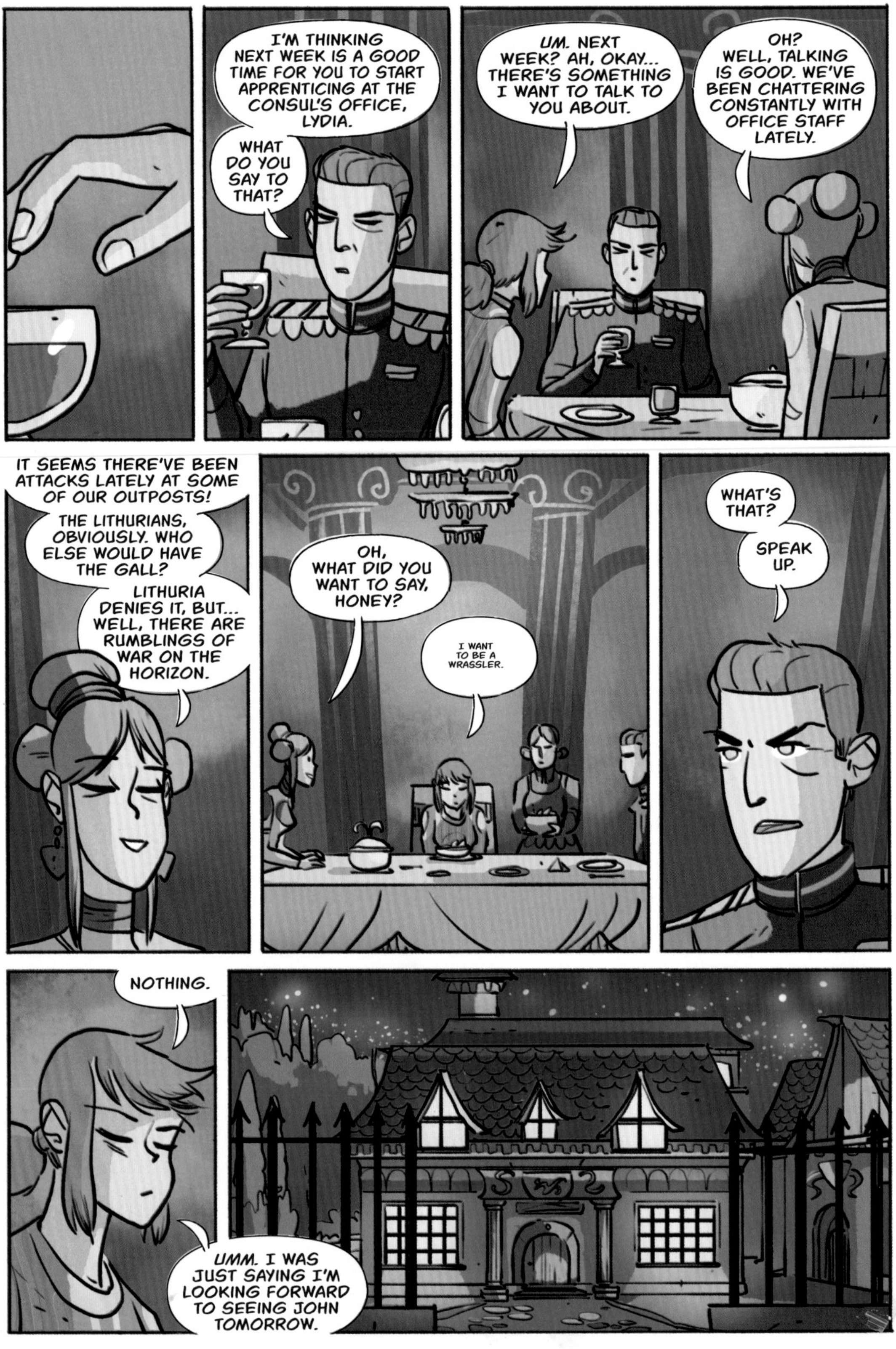
I'M THINKING NEXT WEEK IS A GOOD TIME FOR YOU TO START APPRENTICING AT THE CONSUL'S OFFICE, LYDIA.
WHAT DO YOU SAY TO THAT?
UM. NEXT WEEK? AH, OKAY... THERE'S SOMETHING I WANT TO TALK TO YOU ABOUT.
OH? WELL, TALKING IS GOOD. WE'VE BEEN CHATTERING CONSTANTLY WITH OFFICE STAFF LATELY.
IT SEEMS THERE'VE BEEN ATTACKS LATELY AT SOME OF OUR OUTPOSTS!
THE LITHURIANS, OBVIOUSLY. WHO ELSE WOULD HAVE THE GALL?
LITHURIA DENIES IT, BUT... WELL, THERE ARE RUMBLINGS OF WAR ON THE HORIZON.
OH, WHAT DID YOU WANT TO SAY, HONEY?
I WANT TO BE A WRASSLER.
WHAT'S THAT?
SPEAK UP.
NOTHING.
UMM. I WAS JUST SAYING I'M LOOKING FORWARD TO SEEING JOHN TOMORROW.

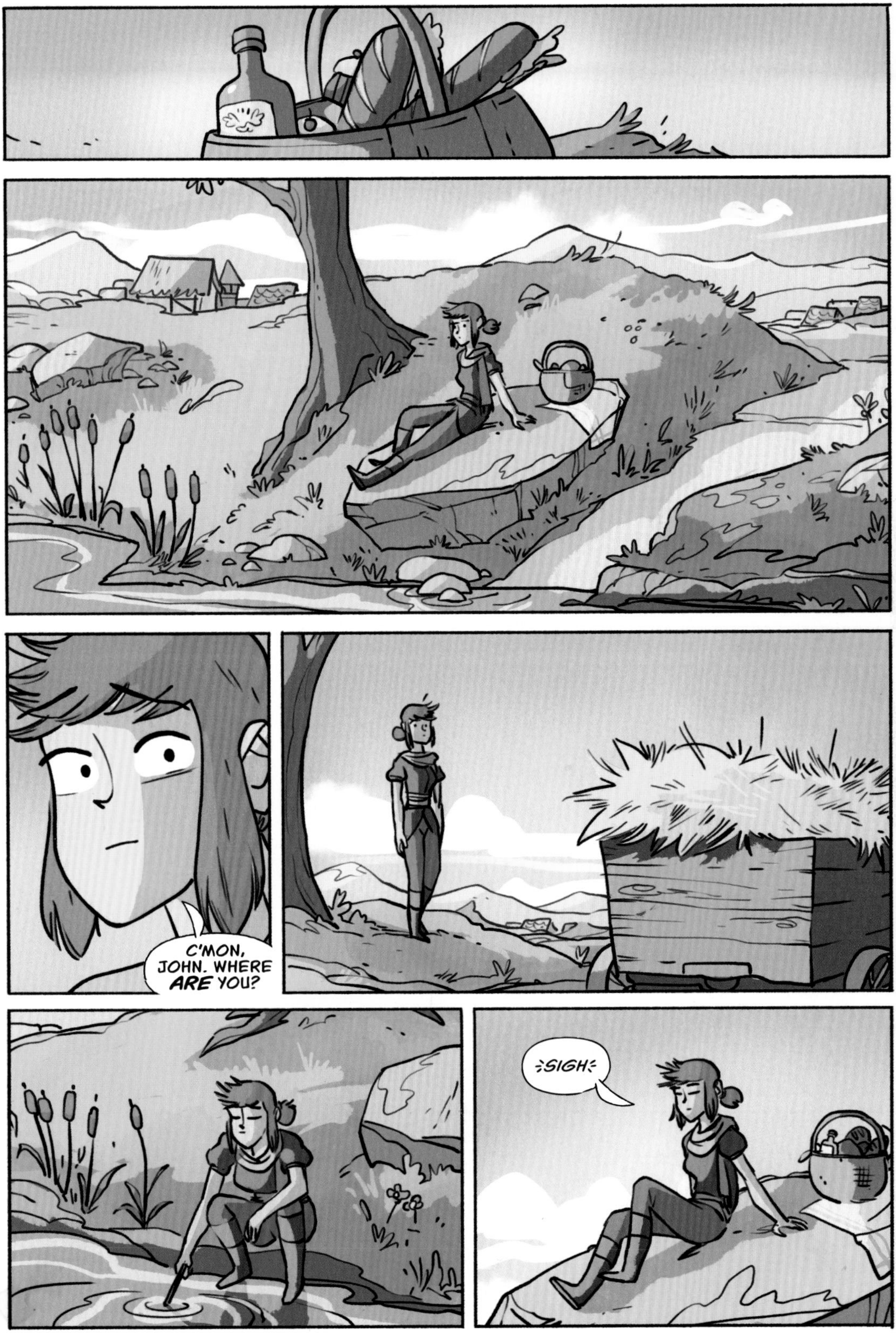
C'MON, JOHN. WHERE ARE YOU?
SIGH

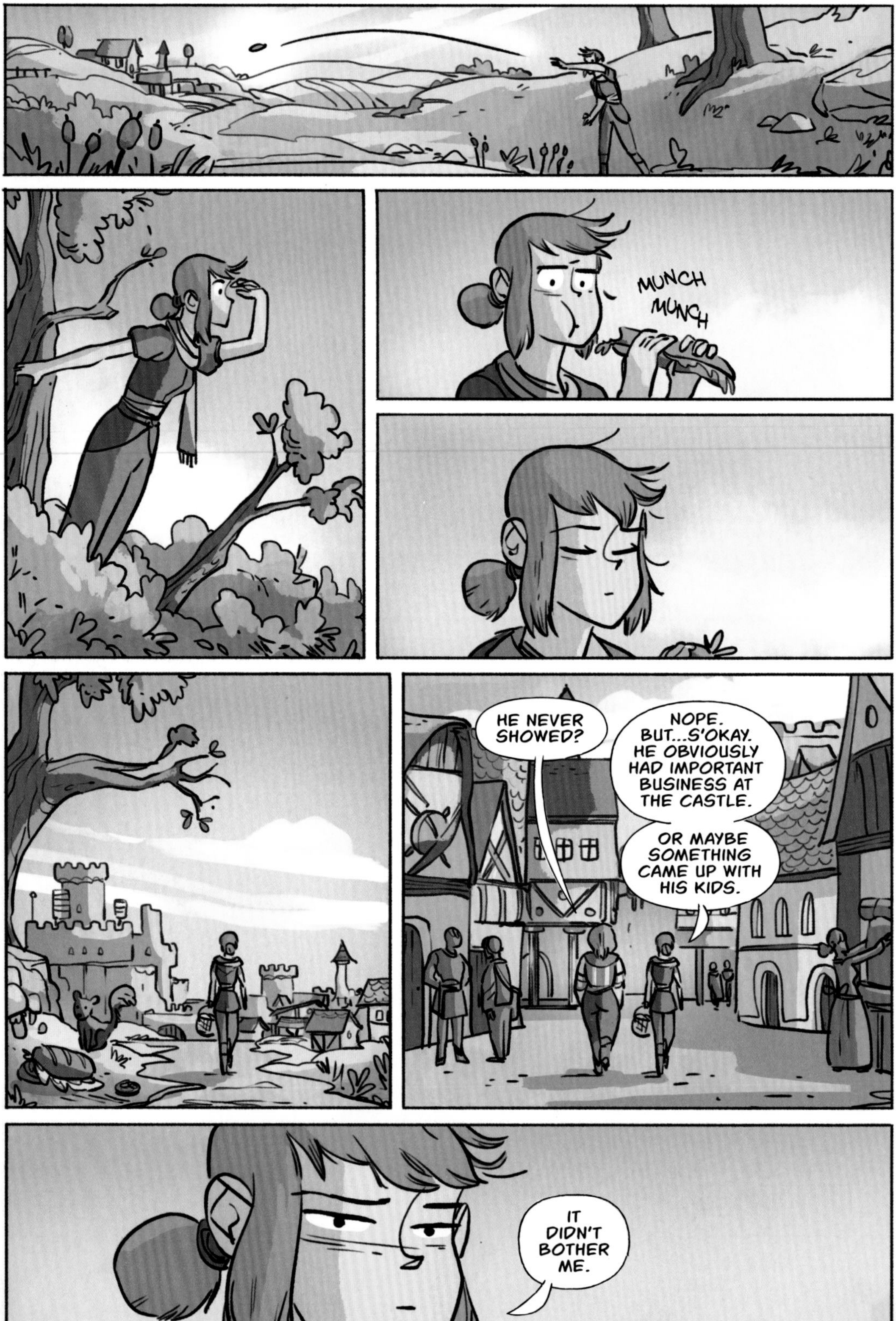
MUNCH
MUNCH
HE NEVER SHOWED?
NOPE. BUT...S'OKAY. HE OBVIOUSLY HAD IMPORTANT BUSINESS AT THE CASTLE.
OR MAYBE SOMETHING CAME UP WITH HIS KIDS.
IT DIDN'T BOTHER ME.

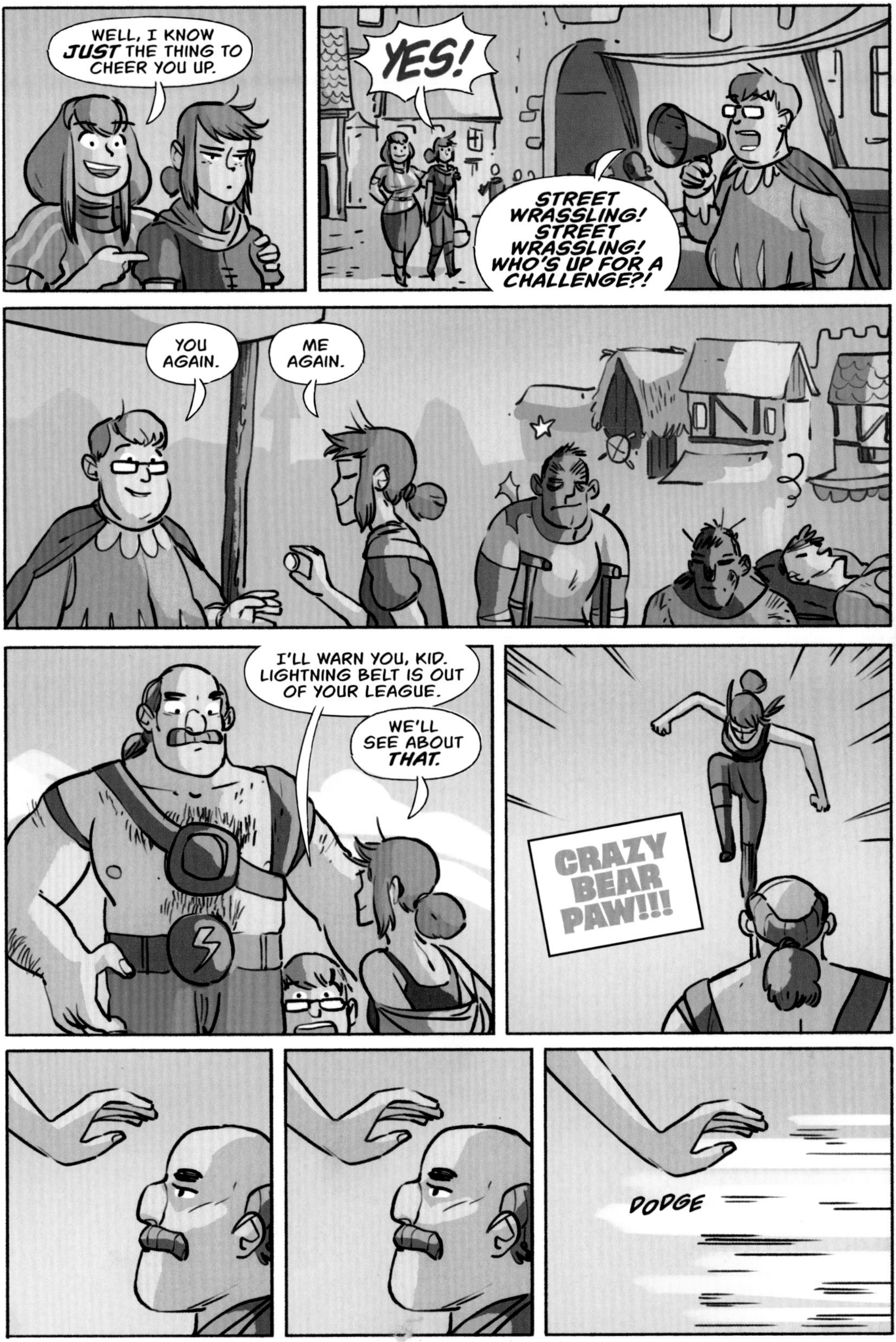
WELL, I KNOW JUST THE THING TO CHEER YOU UP.
YES!
STREET WRASSLING! STREET WRASSLING! WHO'S UP FOR A CHALLENGE?!
YOU AGAIN.
ME AGAIN.
I'LL WARN YOU, KID. LIGHTNING BELT IS OUT OF YOUR LEAGUE.
WE'LL SEE ABOUT THAT.
CRAZY BEAR PAW!!!
DODGE

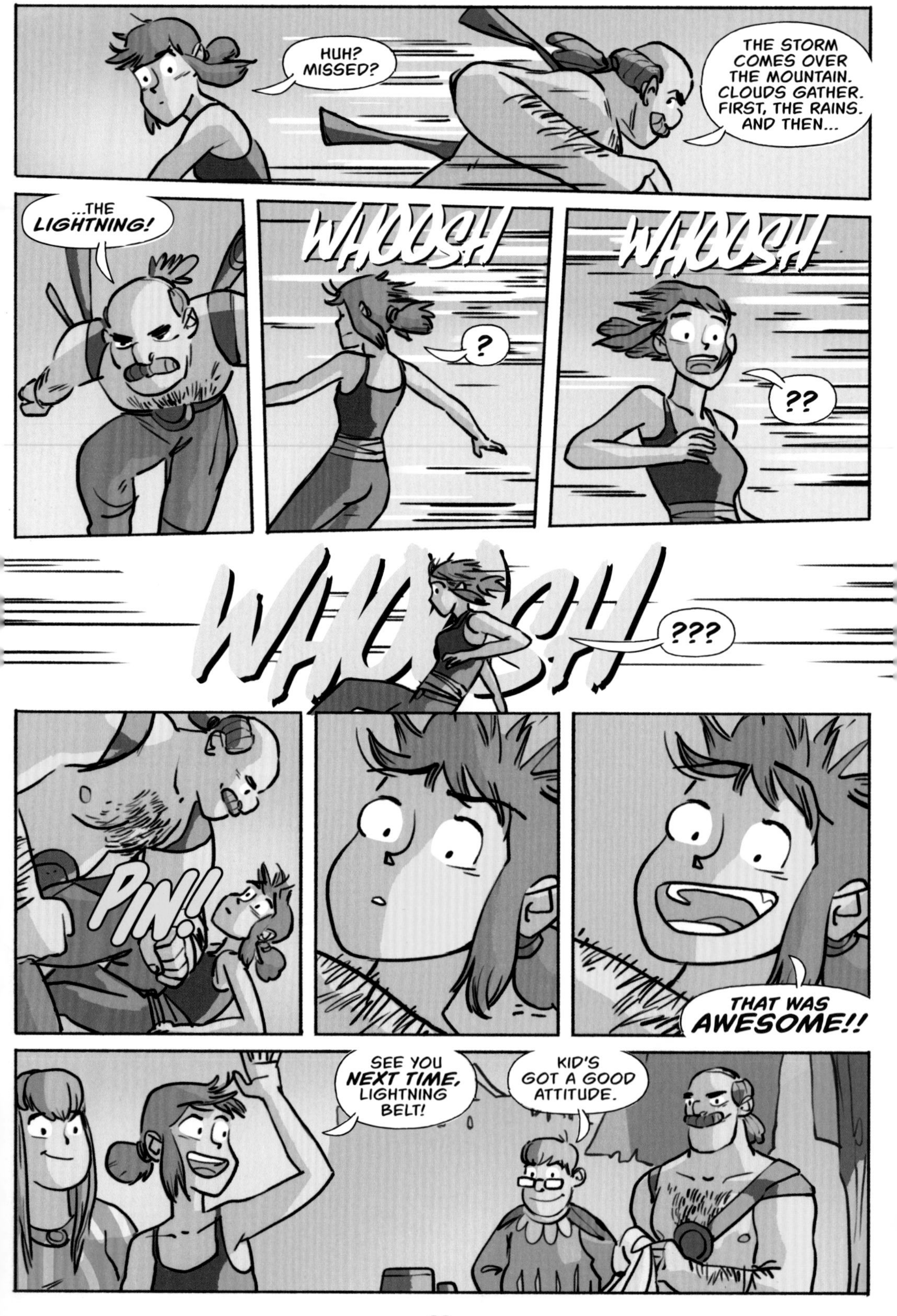
HUH? MISSED?
THE STORM COMES OVER THE MOUNTAIN. CLOUDS GATHER. FIRST, THE RAINS. AND THEN...
...THE LIGHTNING!
WHOOSH
?
WHOOSH
??
WHOOSH
???
PIN!
THAT WAS AWESOME!!
SEE YOU NEXT TIME, LIGHTNING BELT!
KID'S GOT A GOOD ATTITUDE.

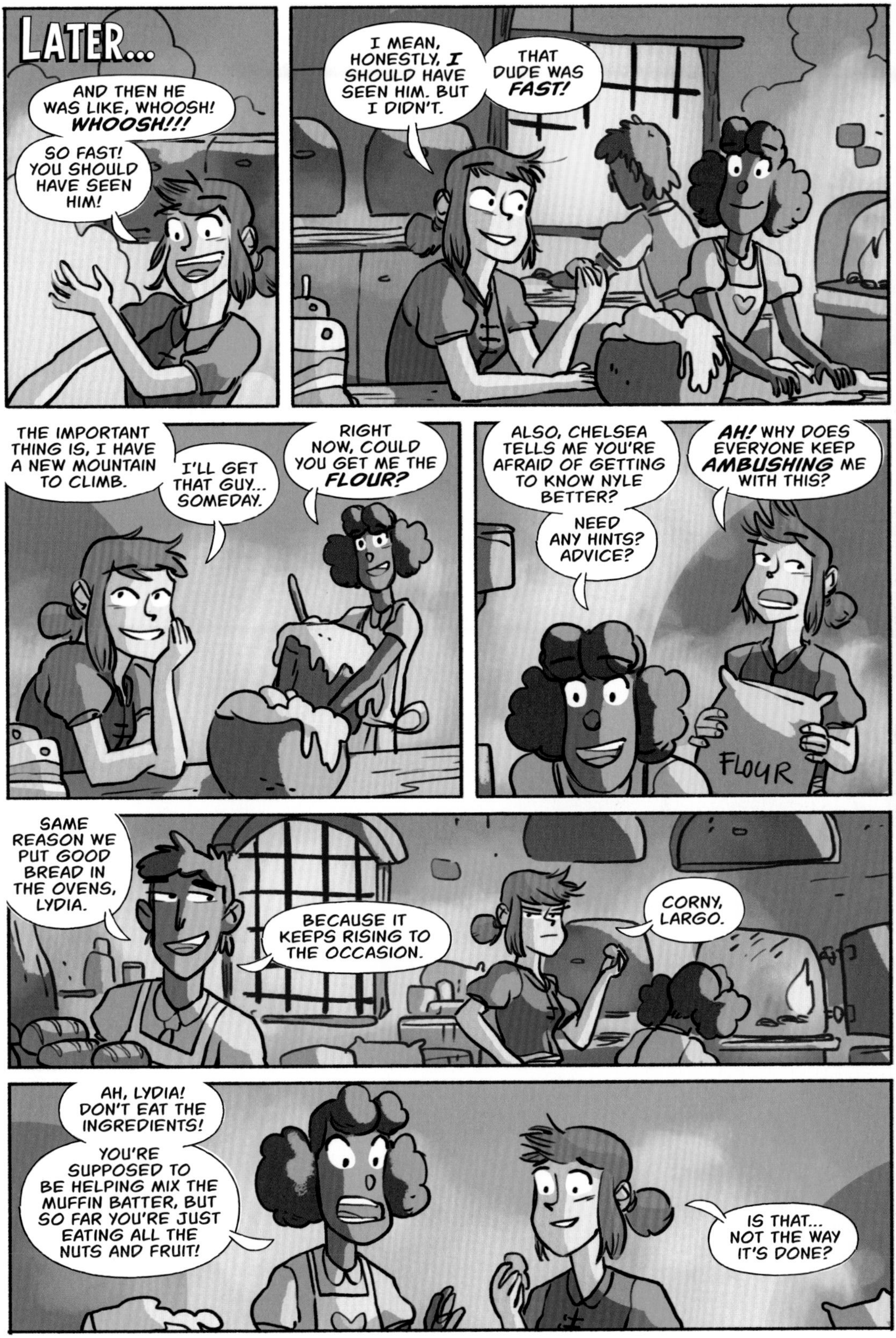
LATER...
AND THEN HE WAS LIKE, WHOOSH! WHOOSH!!!
SO FAST! YOU SHOULD HAVE SEEN HIM!
I MEAN, HONESTLY, I SHOULD HAVE SEEN HIM. BUT I DIDN'T.
THAT DUDE WAS FAST!
THE IMPORTANT THING IS, I HAVE A NEW MOUNTAIN TO CLIMB.
I'LL GET THAT GUY... SOMEDAY.
RIGHT NOW, COULD YOU GET ME THE FLOUR?
ALSO, CHELSEA TELLS ME YOU'RE AFRAID OF GETTING TO KNOW NYLE BETTER?
NEED ANY HINTS? ADVICE?
AH! WHY DOES EVERYONE KEEP AMBUSHING ME WITH THIS?
FLOUR
SAME REASON WE PUT GOOD BREAD IN THE OVENS, LYDIA.
BECAUSE IT KEEPS RISING TO THE OCCASION.
CORNY, LARGO.
AH, LYDIA! DON'T EAT THE INGREDIENTS!
YOU'RE SUPPOSED TO BE HELPING MIX THE MUFFIN BATTER, BUT SO FAR YOU'RE JUST EATING ALL THE NUTS AND FRUIT!
IS THAT... NOT THE WAY IT'S DONE?

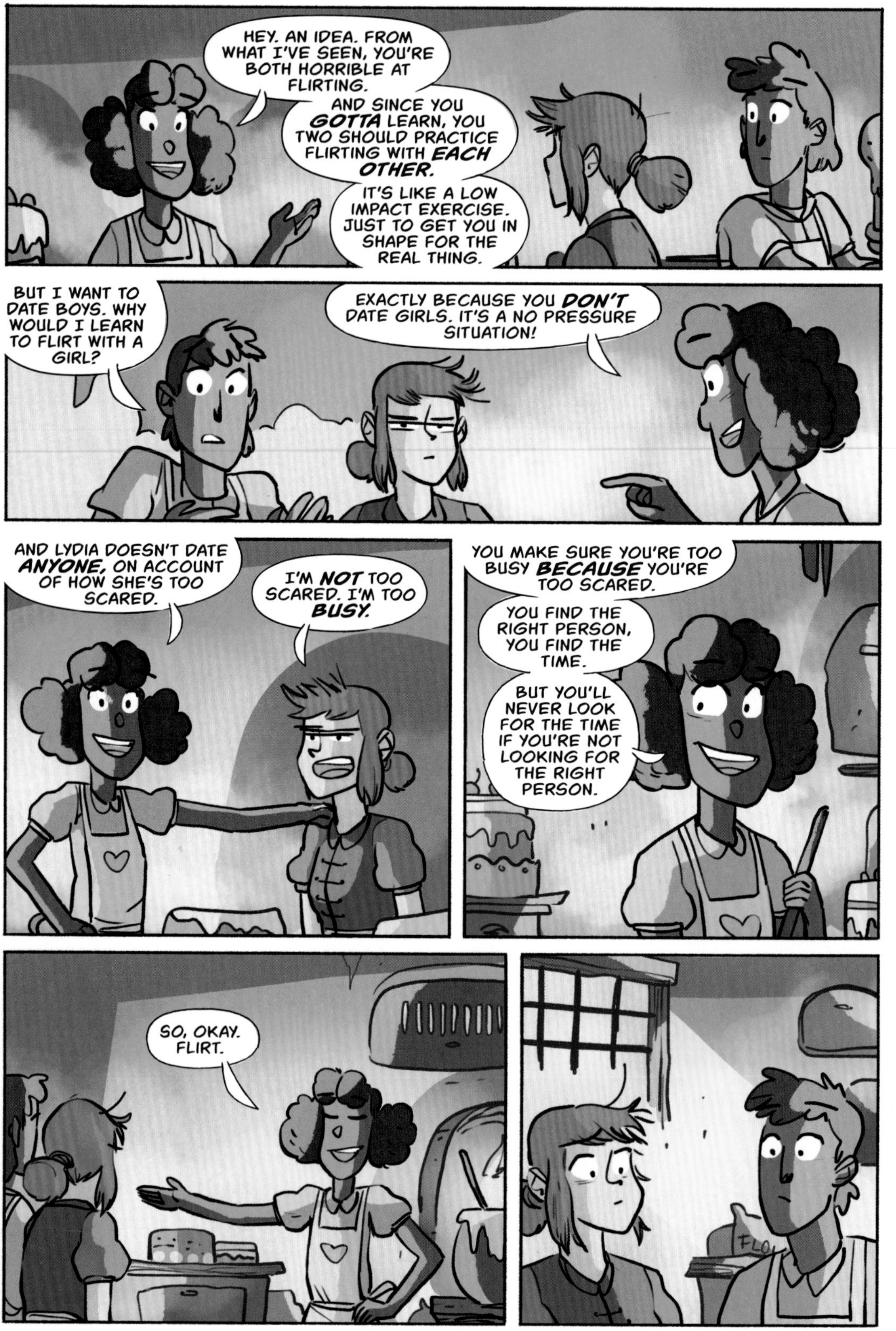
HEY. AN IDEA. FROM WHAT I'VE SEEN, YOU'RE BOTH HORRIBLE AT FLIRTING.
AND SINCE YOU GOTTA LEARN, YOU TWO SHOULD PRACTICE FLIRTING WITH EACH OTHER.
IT'S LIKE A LOW IMPACT EXERCISE. JUST TO GET YOU IN SHAPE FOR THE REAL THING.
BUT I WANT TO DATE BOYS. WHY WOULD I LEARN TO FLIRT WITH A GIRL?
EXACTLY BECAUSE YOU DON'T DATE GIRLS. IT'S A NO PRESSURE SITUATION!
AND LYDIA DOESN'T DATE ANYONE, ON ACCOUNT OF HOW SHE'S TOO SCARED.
I'M NOT TOO SCARED. I'M TOO BUSY.
YOU MAKE SURE YOU'RE TOO BUSY BECAUSE YOU'RE TOO SCARED.
YOU FIND THE RIGHT PERSON, YOU FIND THE TIME.
BUT YOU'LL NEVER LOOK FOR THE TIME IF YOU'RE NOT LOOKING FOR THE RIGHT PERSON.
SO, OKAY. FLIRT.

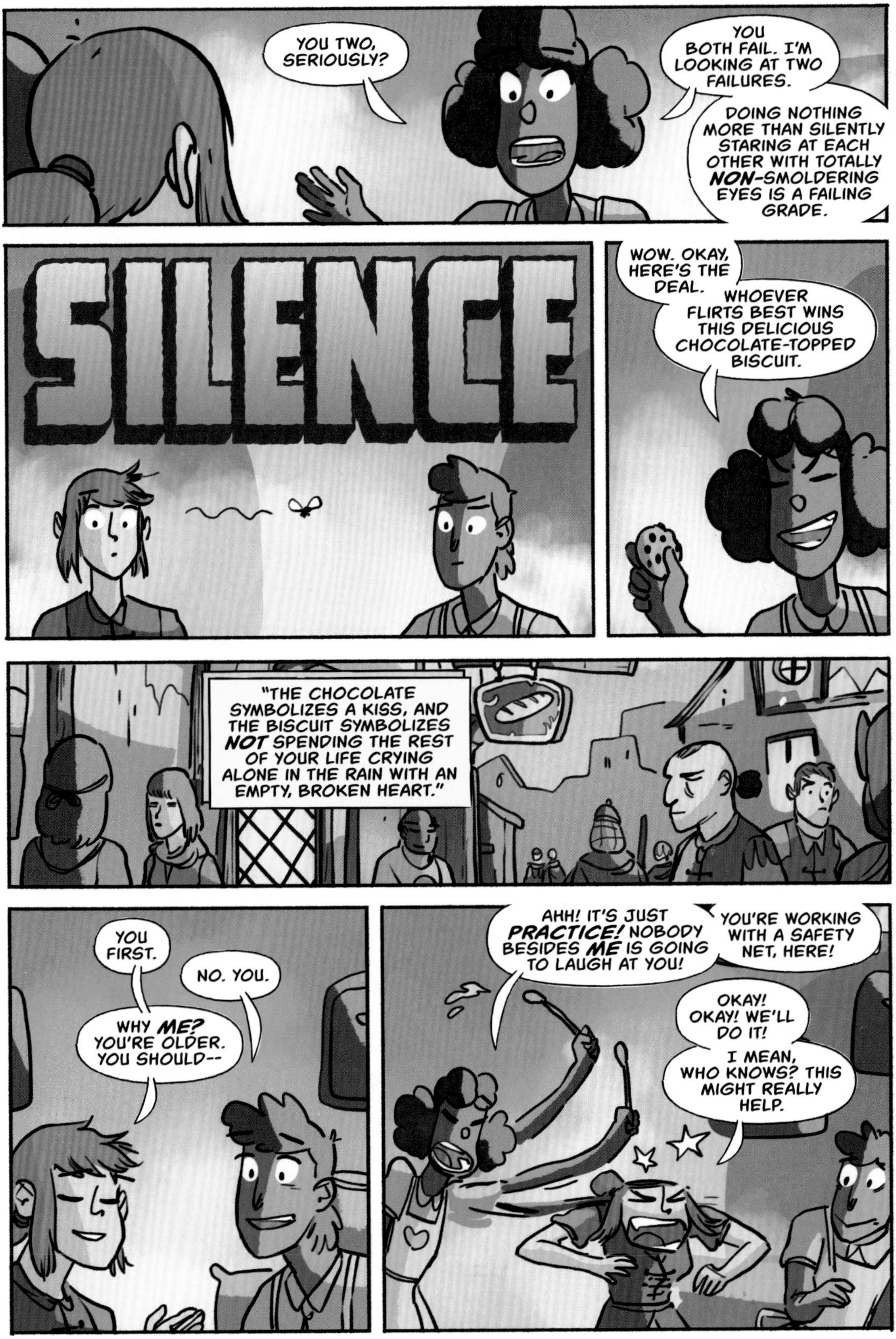
YOU TWO, SERIOUSLY?
YOU BOTH FAIL. I'M LOOKING AT TWO FAILURES.
DOING NOTHING MORE THAN SILENTLY STARING AT EACH OTHER WITH TOTALLY NON-SMOLDERING EYES IS A FAILING GRADE.
SILENCE
WOW. OKAY, HERE'S THE DEAL.
WHOEVER FLIRTS BEST WINS THIS DELICIOUS CHOCOLATE-TOPPED BISCUIT.
"THE CHOCOLATE SYMBOLIZES A KISS, AND THE BISCUIT SYMBOLIZES NOT SPENDING THE REST OF YOUR LIFE CRYING ALONE IN THE RAIN WITH AN EMPTY, BROKEN HEART."
YOU FIRST.
NO. YOU.
WHY ME? YOU'RE OLDER. YOU SHOULD--
AHH! IT'S JUST PRACTICE! NOBODY BESIDES ME IS GOING TO LAUGH AT YOU!
YOU'RE WORKING WITH A SAFETY NET, HERE!
OKAY! OKAY! WE'LL DO IT!
I MEAN, WHO KNOWS? THIS MIGHT REALLY HELP.

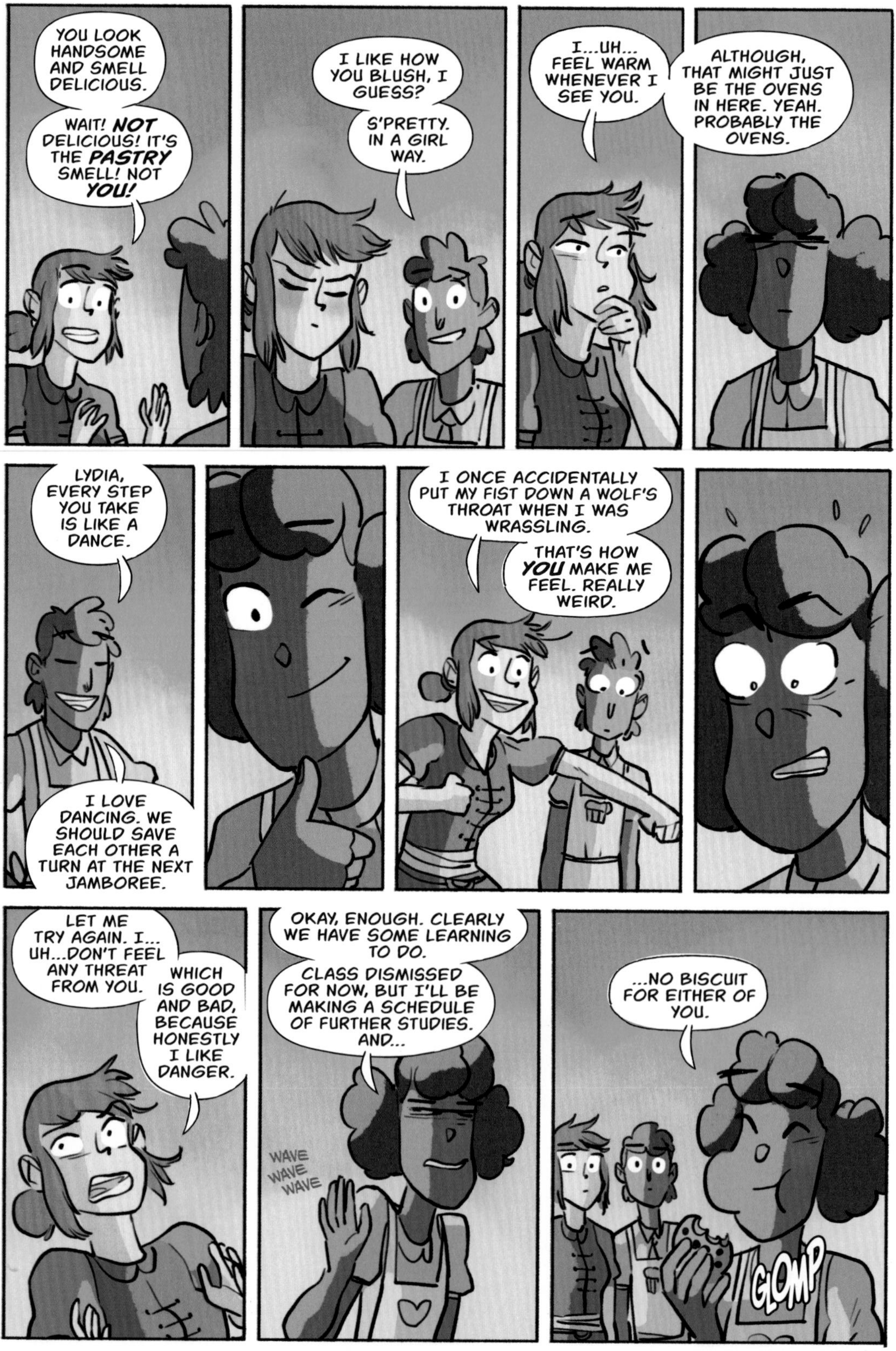
YOU LOOK HANDSOME AND SMELL DELICIOUS.
WAIT! NOT DELICIOUS! IT'S THE PASTRY SMELL! NOT YOU!
I LIKE HOW YOU BLUSH, I GUESS?
S'PRETTY. IN A GIRL WAY.
I...UH... FEEL WARM WHENEVER I SEE YOU.
ALTHOUGH, THAT MIGHT JUST BE THE OVENS IN HERE. YEAH. PROBABLY THE OVENS.
LYDIA, EVERY STEP YOU TAKE IS LIKE A DANCE.
I LOVE DANCING. WE SHOULD SAVE EACH OTHER A TURN AT THE NEXT JAMBOREE.
I ONCE ACCIDENTALLY PUT MY FIST DOWN A WOLF'S THROAT WHEN I WAS WRASSLING.
THAT'S HOW YOU MAKE ME FEEL. REALLY WEIRD.
LET ME TRY AGAIN. I... UH...DON'T FEEL ANY THREAT FROM YOU.
WHICH IS GOOD AND BAD, BECAUSE HONESTLY I LIKE DANGER.
OKAY, ENOUGH. CLEARLY WE HAVE SOME LEARNING TO DO.
CLASS DISMISSED FOR NOW, BUT I'LL BE MAKING A SCHEDULE OF FURTHER STUDIES. AND...
WAVE WAVE WAVE
...NO BISCUIT FOR EITHER OF YOU.
GLOMP

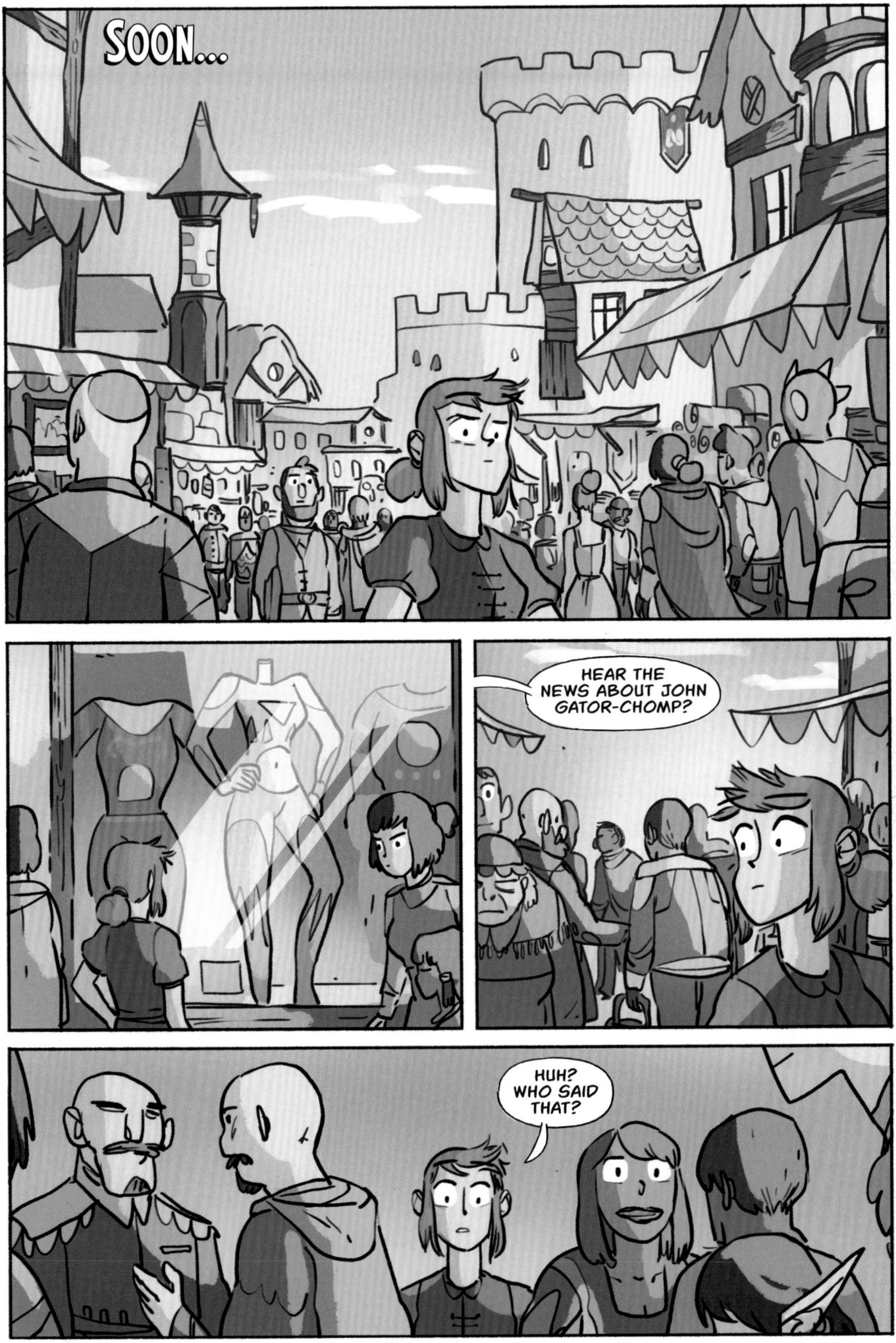
SOON...
HEAR THE NEWS ABOUT JOHN GATOR-CHOMP?
HUH? WHO SAID THAT?

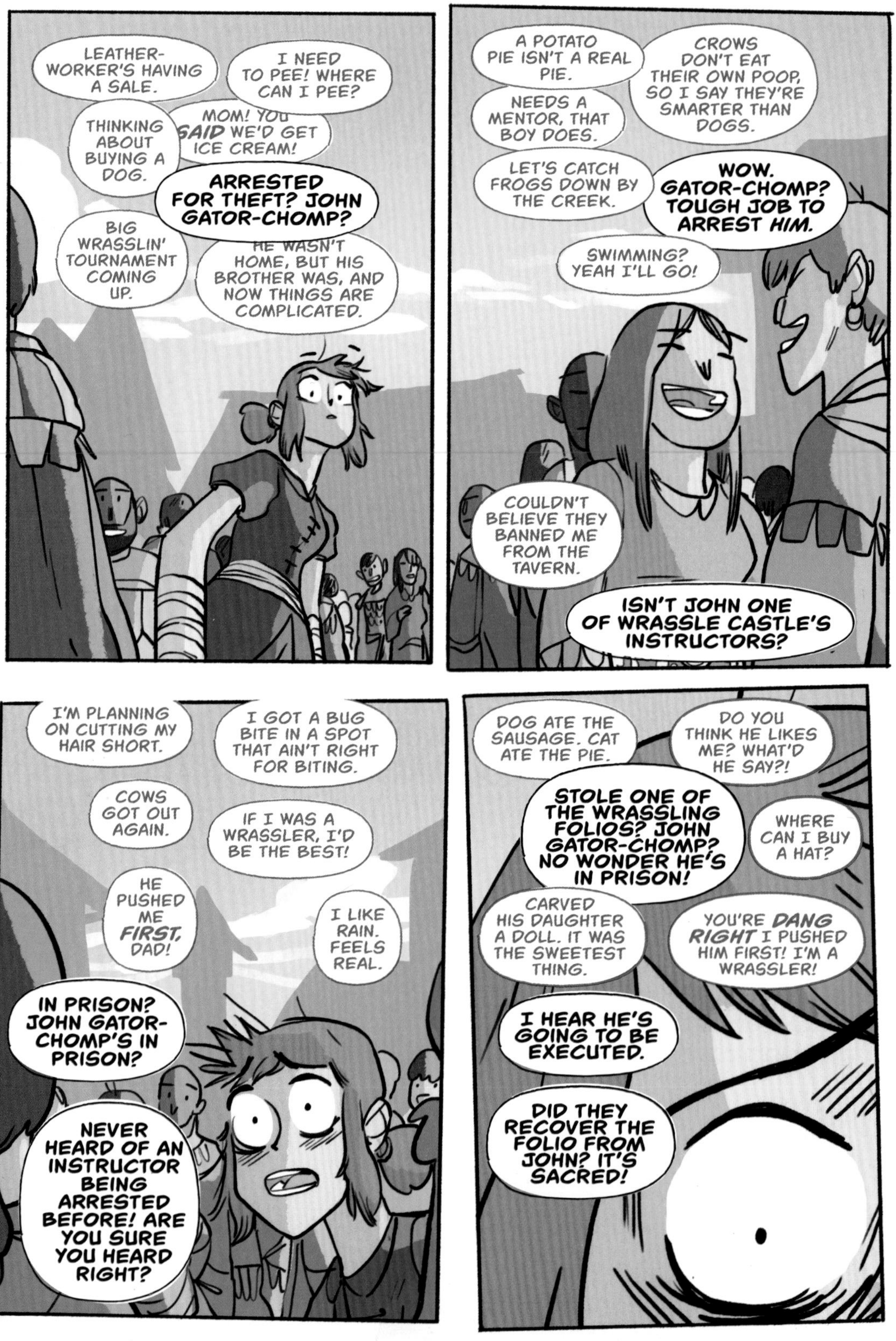
LEATHER-WORKER'S HAVING A SALE.
I NEED TO PEE! WHERE CAN I PEE?
THINKING ABOUT BUYING A DOG.
MOM! YOU SAID WE'D GET ICE CREAM!
ARRESTED FOR THEFT? JOHN GATOR-CHOMP?
BIG WRASSLIN' TOURNAMENT COMING UP.
HE WASN'T HOME, BUT HIS BROTHER WAS, AND NOW THINGS ARE COMPLICATED.
A POTATO PIE ISN'T A REAL PIE.
CROWS DON'T EAT THEIR OWN POOP, SO I SAY THEY'RE SMARTER THAN DOGS.
NEEDS A MENTOR, THAT BOY DOES.
LET'S CATCH FROGS DOWN BY THE CREEK.
WOW. GATOR-CHOMP? TOUGH JOB TO ARREST HIM.
SWIMMING? YEAH I'LL GO!
COULDN'T BELIEVE THEY BANNED ME FROM THE TAVERN.
ISN'T JOHN ONE OF WRASSLE CASTLE'S INSTRUCTORS?
I'M PLANNING ON CUTTING MY HAIR SHORT.
I GOT A BUG BITE IN A SPOT THAT AIN'T RIGHT FOR BITING.
COWS GOT OUT AGAIN.
IF I WAS A WRASSLER, I'D BE THE BEST!
HE PUSHED ME FIRST, DAD!
I LIKE RAIN. FEELS REAL.
IN PRISON? JOHN GATOR-CHOMP'S IN PRISON?
NEVER HEARD OF AN INSTRUCTOR BEING ARRESTED BEFORE! ARE YOU SURE YOU HEARD RIGHT?
DOG ATE THE SAUSAGE. CAT ATE THE PIE.
DO YOU THINK HE LIKES ME? WHAT'D HE SAY?!
STOLE ONE OF THE WRASSLING FOLIOS? JOHN GATOR-CHOMP? NO WONDER HE'S IN PRISON!
WHERE CAN I BUY A HAT?
CARVED HIS DAUGHTER A DOLL. IT WAS THE SWEETEST THING.
YOU'RE DANG RIGHT I PUSHED HIM FIRST! I'M A WRASSLER!
I HEAR HE'S GOING TO BE EXECUTED.
DID THEY RECOVER THE FOLIO FROM JOHN? IT'S SACRED!

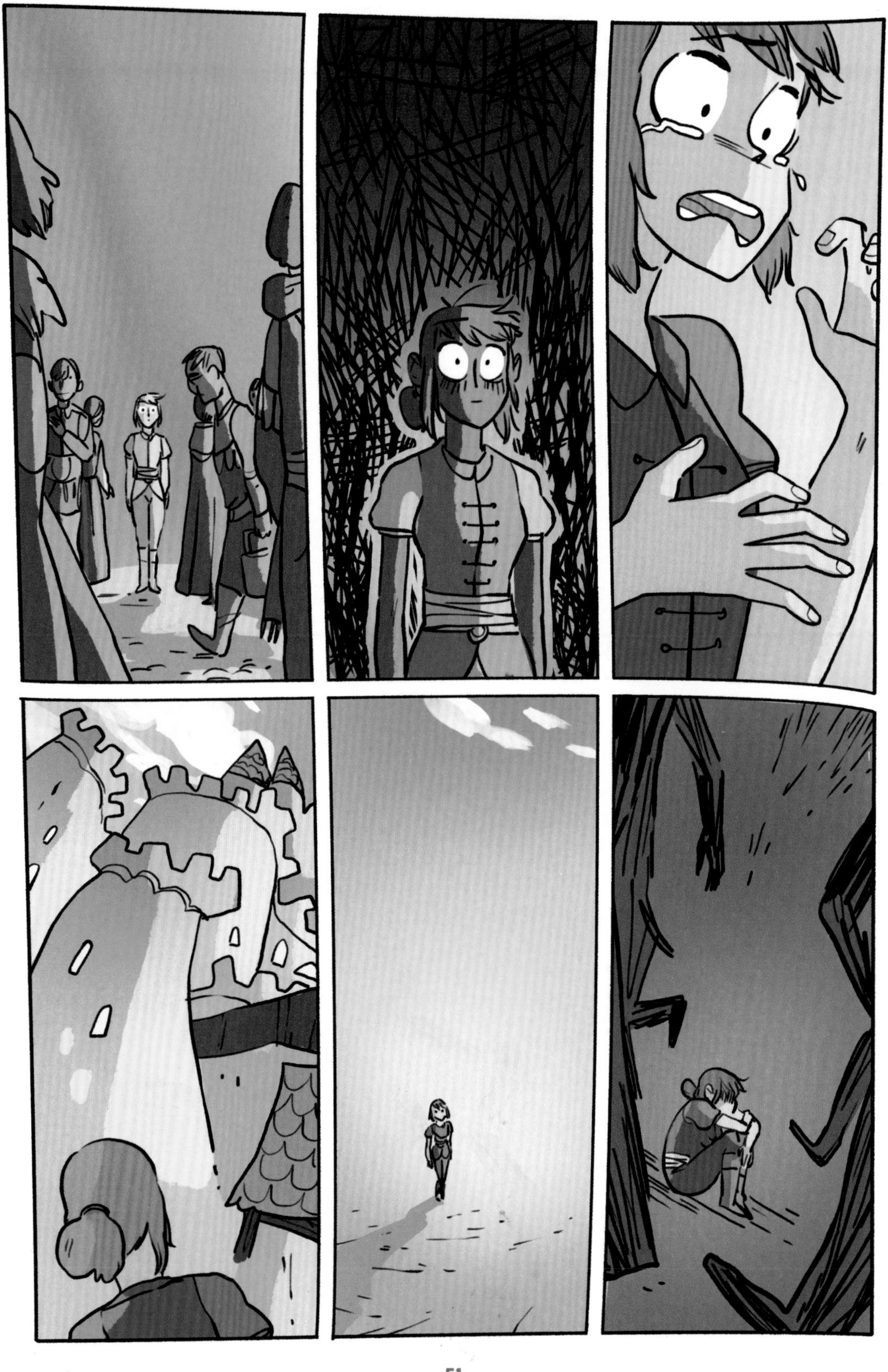

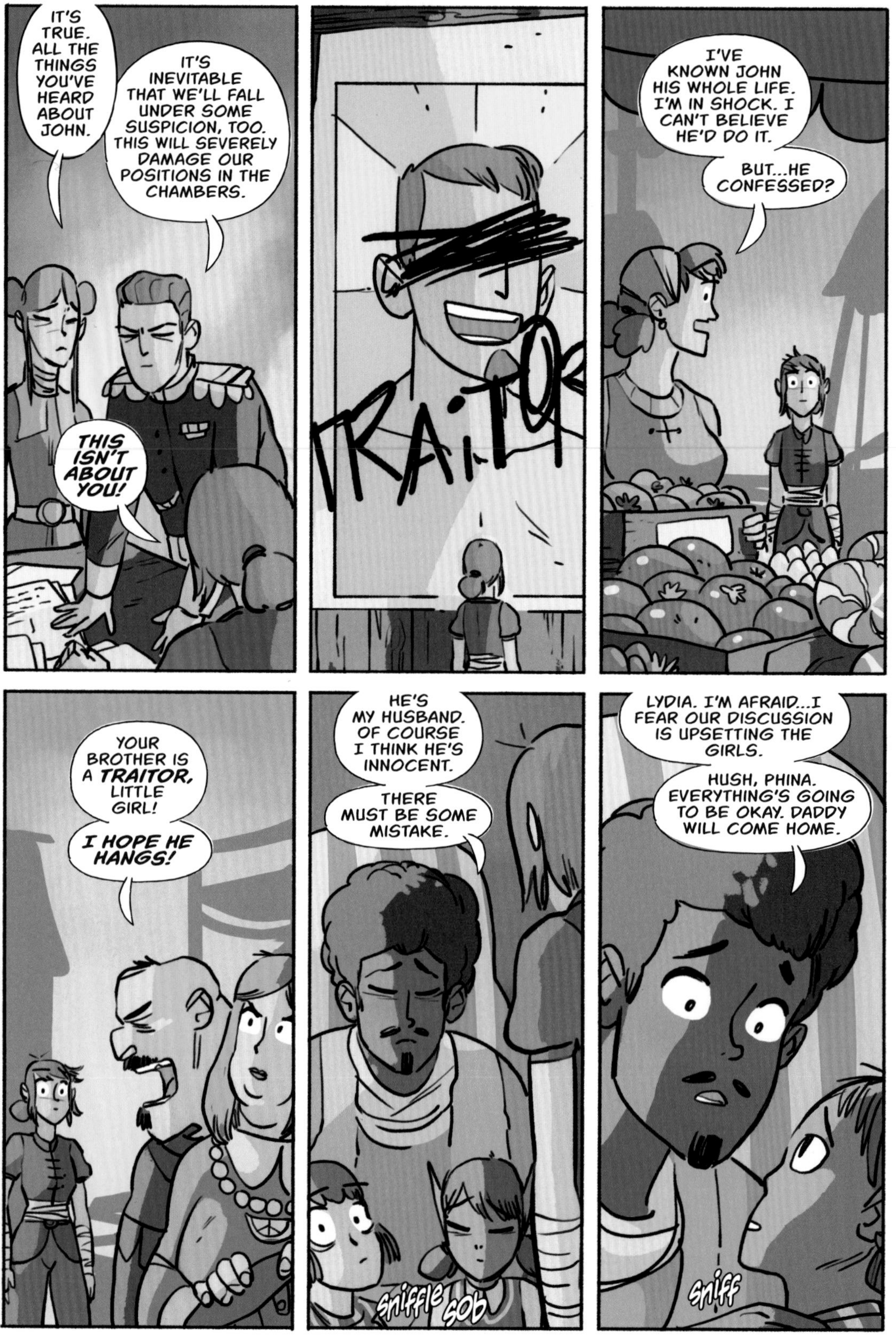
IT'S TRUE. ALL THE THINGS YOU'VE HEARD ABOUT JOHN.
IT'S INEVITABLE THAT WE'LL FALL UNDER SOME SUSPICION, TOO. THIS WILL SEVERELY DAMAGE OUR POSITIONS IN THE CHAMBERS.
THIS ISN'T ABOUT YOU!
TRAITOR
I'VE KNOWN JOHN HIS WHOLE LIFE. I'M IN SHOCK. I CAN'T BELIEVE HE'D DO IT.
BUT...HE CONFESSED?
YOUR BROTHER IS A TRAITOR, LITTLE GIRL!
I HOPE HE HANGS!
HE'S MY HUSBAND. OF COURSE I THINK HE'S INNOCENT.
THERE MUST BE SOME MISTAKE.
sniffle
sob
LYDIA. I'M AFRAID...I FEAR OUR DISCUSSION IS UPSETTING THE GIRLS.
HUSH, PHINA. EVERYTHING'S GOING TO BE OKAY. DADDY WILL COME HOME.
sniff

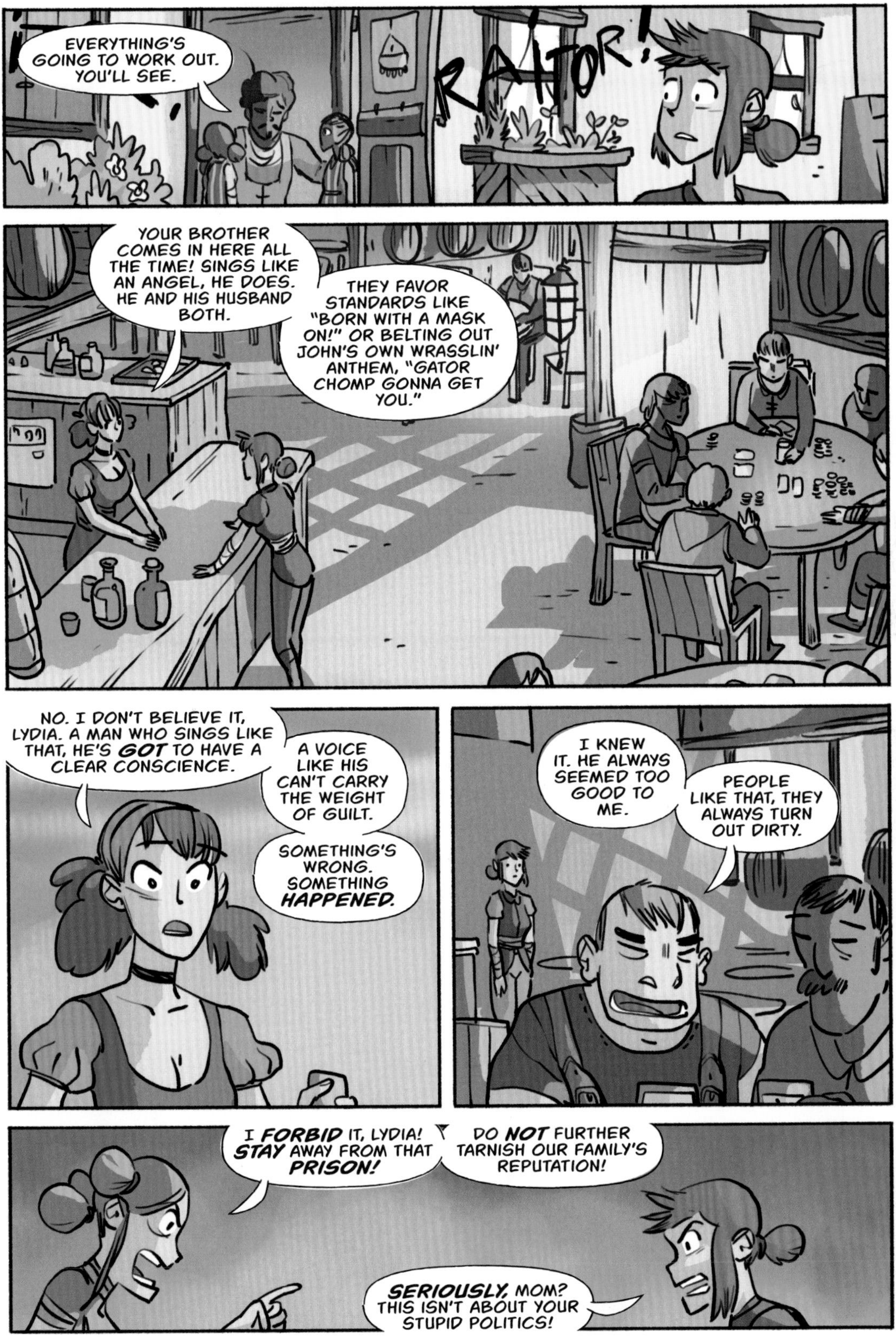
EVERYTHING'S GOING TO WORK OUT. YOU'LL SEE.
RAITOR!
YOUR BROTHER COMES IN HERE ALL THE TIME! SINGS LIKE AN ANGEL, HE DOES. HE AND HIS HUSBAND BOTH.
THEY FAVOR STANDARDS LIKE "BORN WITH A MASK ON!" OR BELTING OUT JOHN'S OWN WRASSLIN' ANTHEM, "GATOR CHOMP GONNA GET YOU."
NO. I DON'T BELIEVE IT, LYDIA. A MAN WHO SINGS LIKE THAT, HE'S GOT TO HAVE A CLEAR CONSCIENCE.
A VOICE LIKE HIS CAN'T CARRY THE WEIGHT OF GUILT.
SOMETHING'S WRONG. SOMETHING HAPPENED.
I KNEW IT. HE ALWAYS SEEMED TOO GOOD TO ME.
PEOPLE LIKE THAT, THEY ALWAYS TURN OUT DIRTY.
I FORBID IT, LYDIA! STAY AWAY FROM THAT PRISON!
DO NOT FURTHER TARNISH OUR FAMILY'S REPUTATION!
SERIOUSLY, MOM? THIS ISN'T ABOUT YOUR STUPID POLITICS!

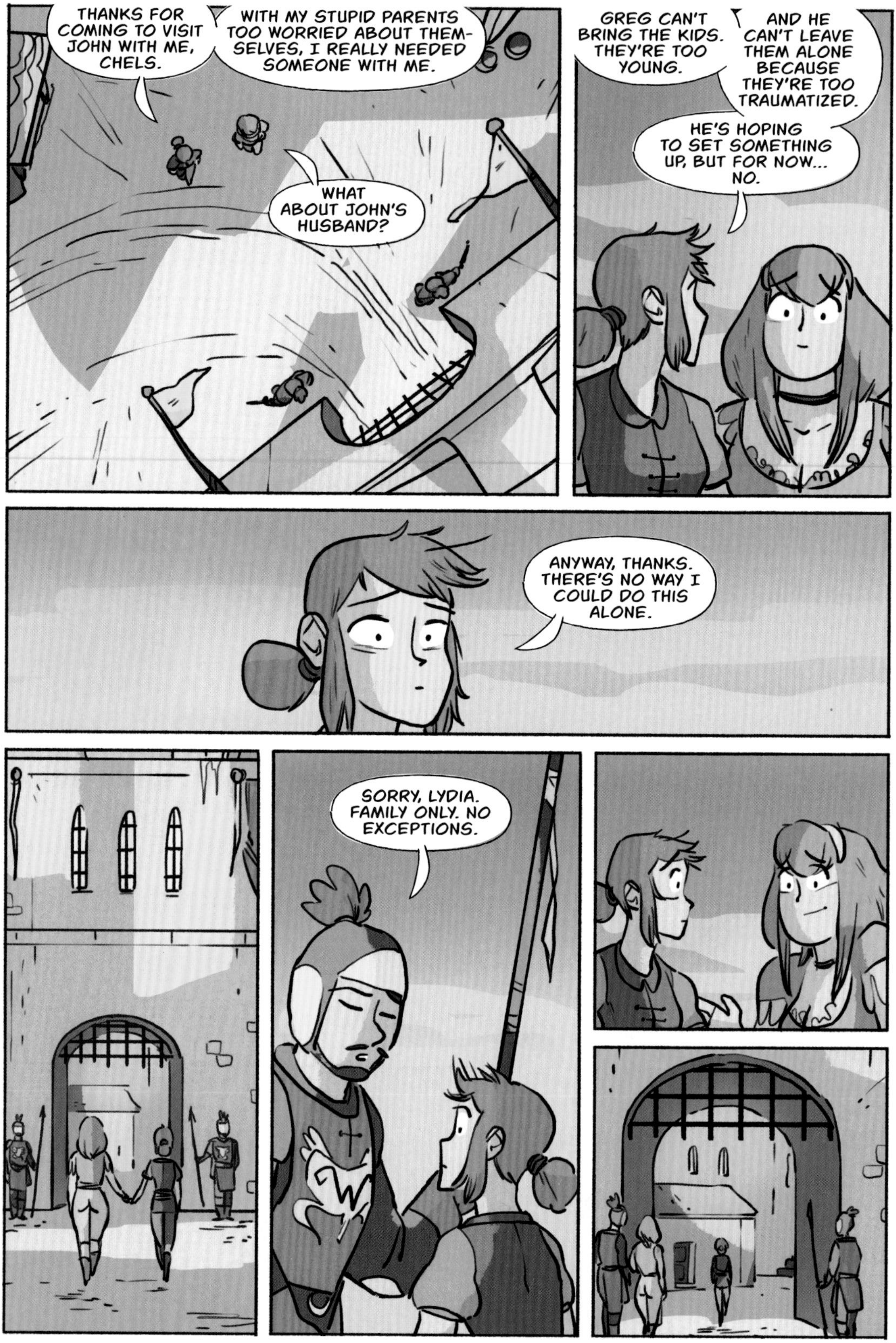
THANKS FOR COMING TO VISIT JOHN WITH ME, CHELS.
WITH MY STUPID PARENTS TOO WORRIED ABOUT THEMSELVES, I REALLY NEEDED SOMEONE WITH ME.
WHAT ABOUT JOHN'S HUSBAND?
GREG CAN'T BRING THE KIDS. THEY'RE TOO YOUNG.
AND HE CAN'T LEAVE THEM ALONE BECAUSE THEY'RE TOO TRAUMATIZED.
HE'S HOPING TO SET SOMETHING UP, BUT FOR NOW... NO.
ANYWAY, THANKS. THERE'S NO WAY I COULD DO THIS ALONE.
SORRY, LYDIA. FAMILY ONLY. NO EXCEPTIONS.

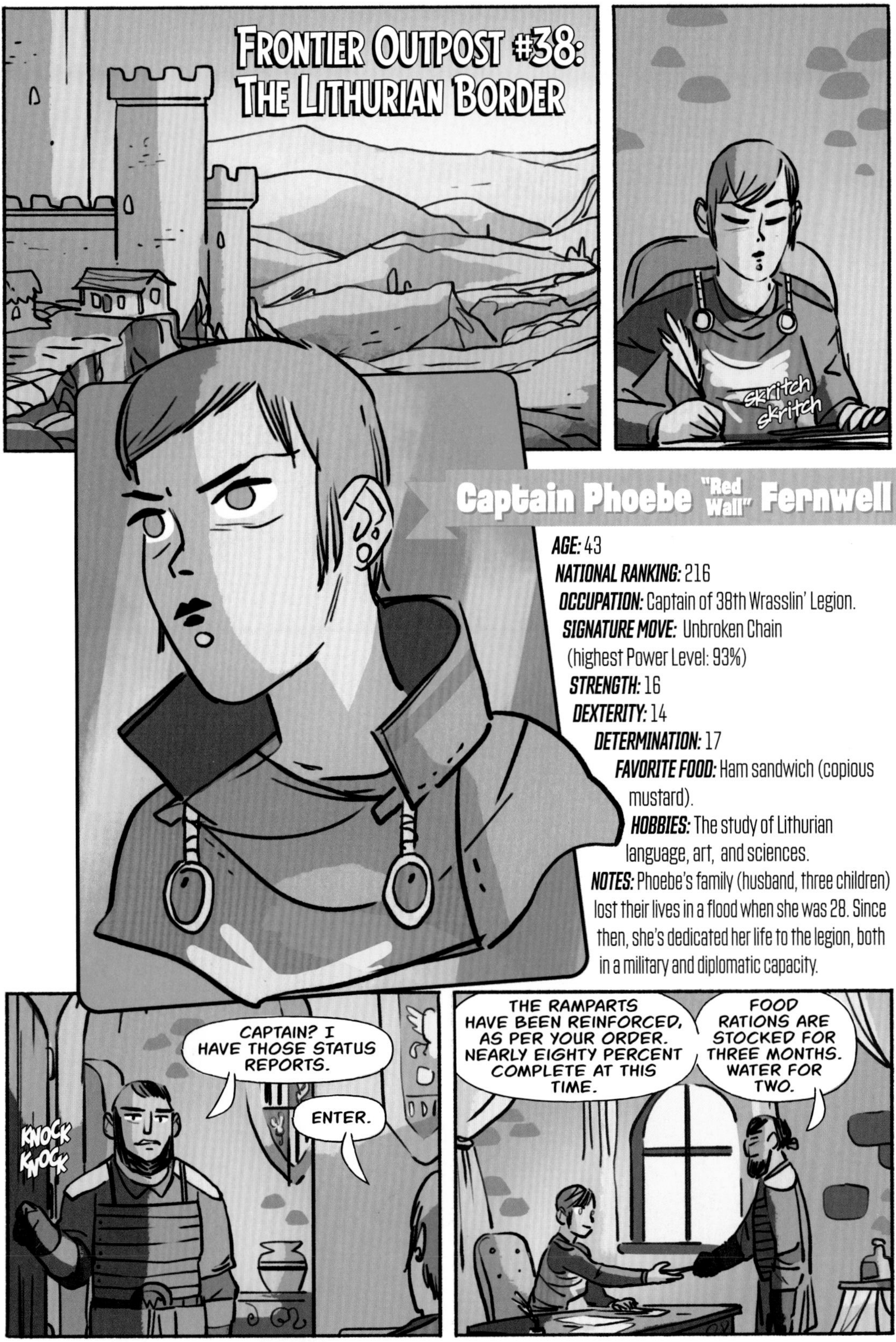
FRONTIER OUTPOST #38:
THE LITHURIAN BORDER
skritch skritch
Captain Phoebe "Red Wall" Fernwell
AGE: 43
NATIONAL RANKING: 216
OCCUPATION: Captain of 38th Wrasslin' Legion.
SIGNATURE MOVE: Unbroken Chain (highest Power Level: 93%)
STRENGTH: 16
DEXTERITY: 14
DETERMINATION: 17
FAVORITE FOOD: Ham sandwich (copious mustard).
HOBBIES: The study of Lithurian language, art, and sciences.
NOTES: Phoebe's family (husband, three children) lost their lives in a flood when she was 28. Since then, she's dedicated her life to the legion, both in a military and diplomatic capacity.
KNOCK KNOCK
CAPTAIN? I HAVE THOSE STATUS REPORTS.
ENTER.
THE RAMPARTS HAVE BEEN REINFORCED, AS PER YOUR ORDER. NEARLY EIGHTY PERCENT COMPLETE AT THIS TIME.
FOOD RATIONS ARE STOCKED FOR THREE MONTHS. WATER FOR TWO.

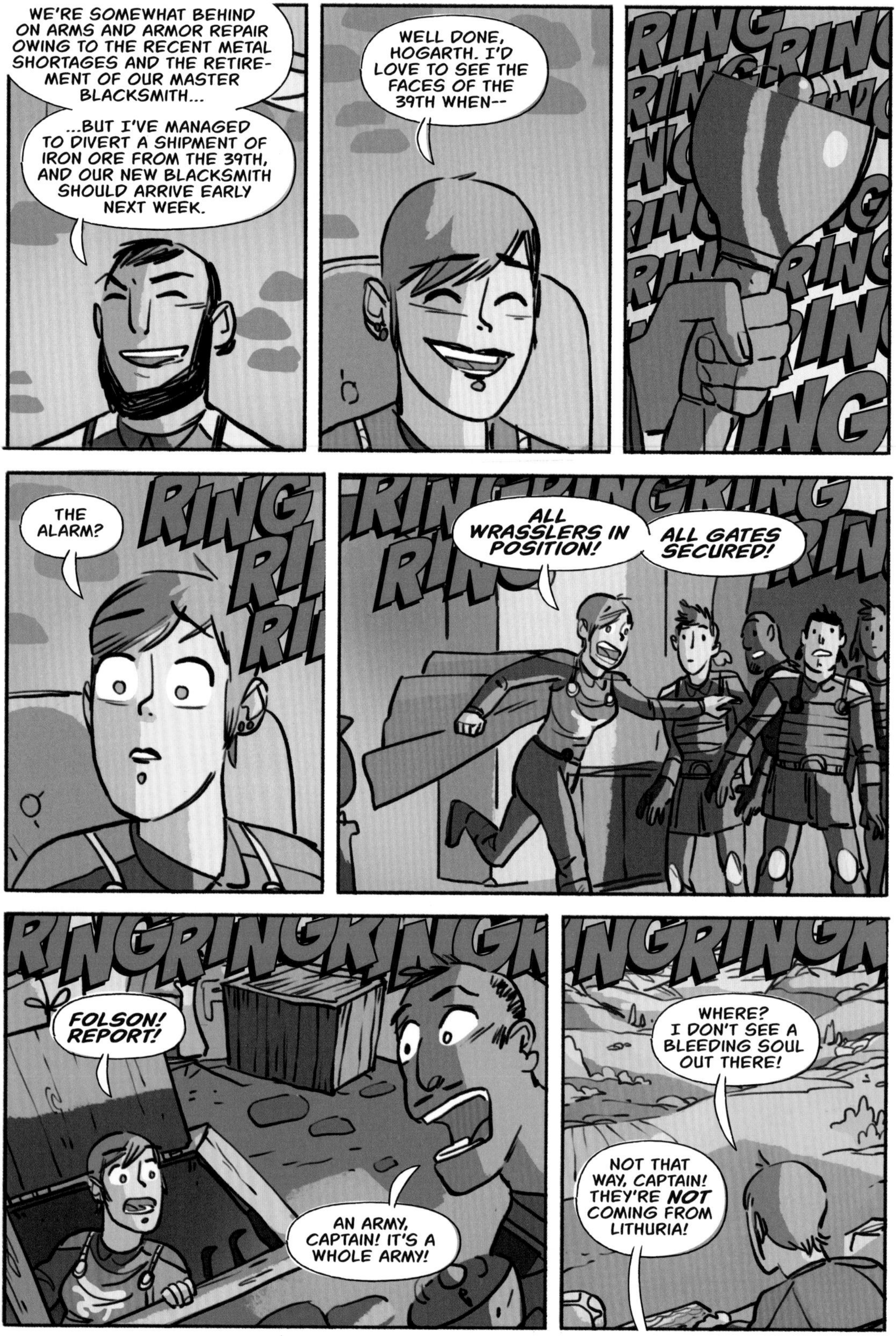

WE'RE SOMEWHAT BEHIND ON ARMS AND ARMOR REPAIR OWING TO THE RECENT METAL SHORTAGES AND THE RETIREMENT OF OUR MASTER BLACKSMITH...
...BUT I'VE MANAGED TO DIVERT A SHIPMENT OF IRON ORE FROM THE 39TH, AND OUR NEW BLACKSMITH SHOULD ARRIVE EARLY NEXT WEEK.
WELL DONE, HOGARTH. I'D LOVE TO SEE THE FACES OF THE 39TH WHEN--
RING RING RING RING RING RING RING RING RING RING
RING RING RING
THE ALARM?
RING RING RING RING
ALL WRASSLERS IN POSITION!
ALL GATES SECURED!
RING RING RING
FOLSON! REPORT!
AN ARMY, CAPTAIN! IT'S A WHOLE ARMY!
RING RING
WHERE? I DON'T SEE A BLEEDING SOUL OUT THERE!
NOT THAT WAY, CAPTAIN! THEY'RE NOT COMING FROM LITHURIA!

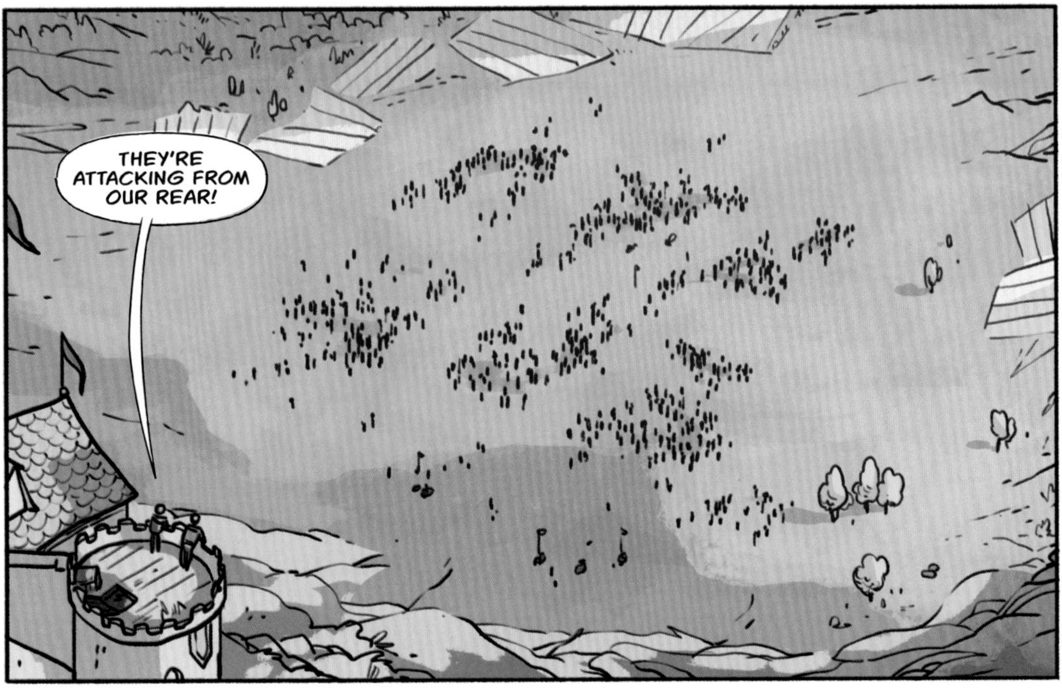
THEY'RE ATTACKING FROM OUR REAR!

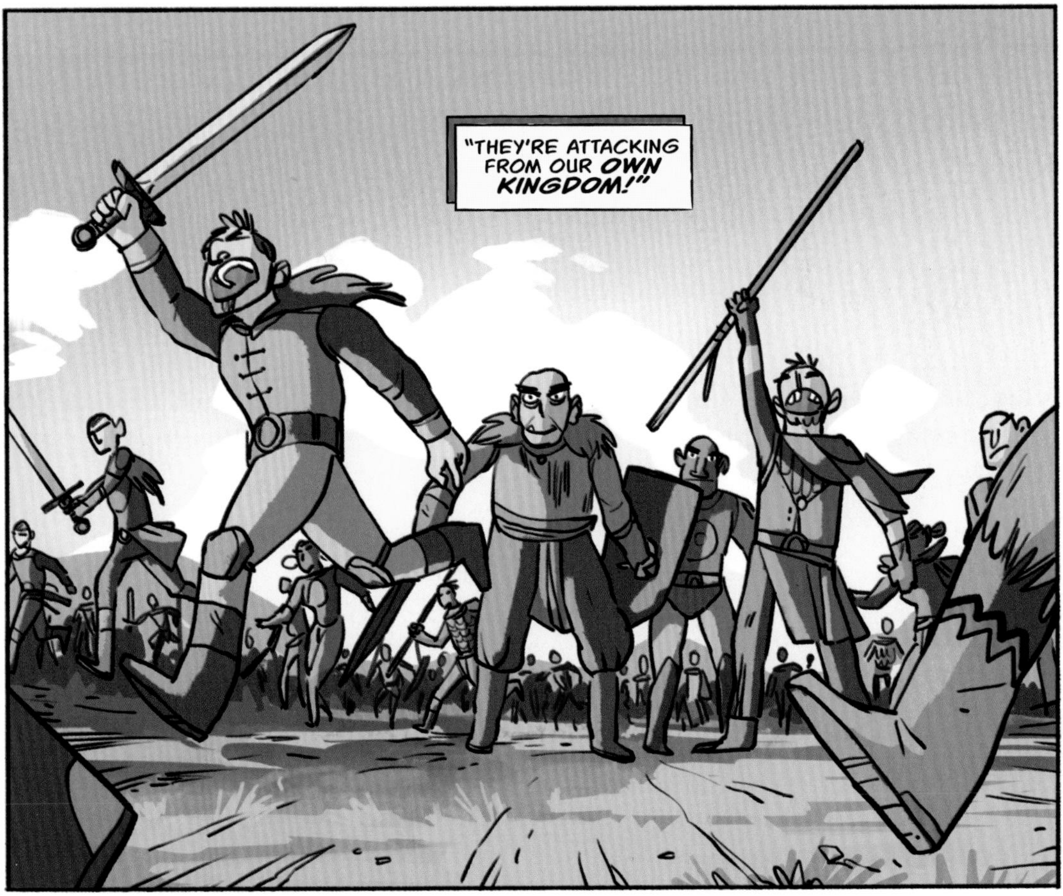
"THEY'RE ATTACKING FROM OUR OWN KINGDOM!"

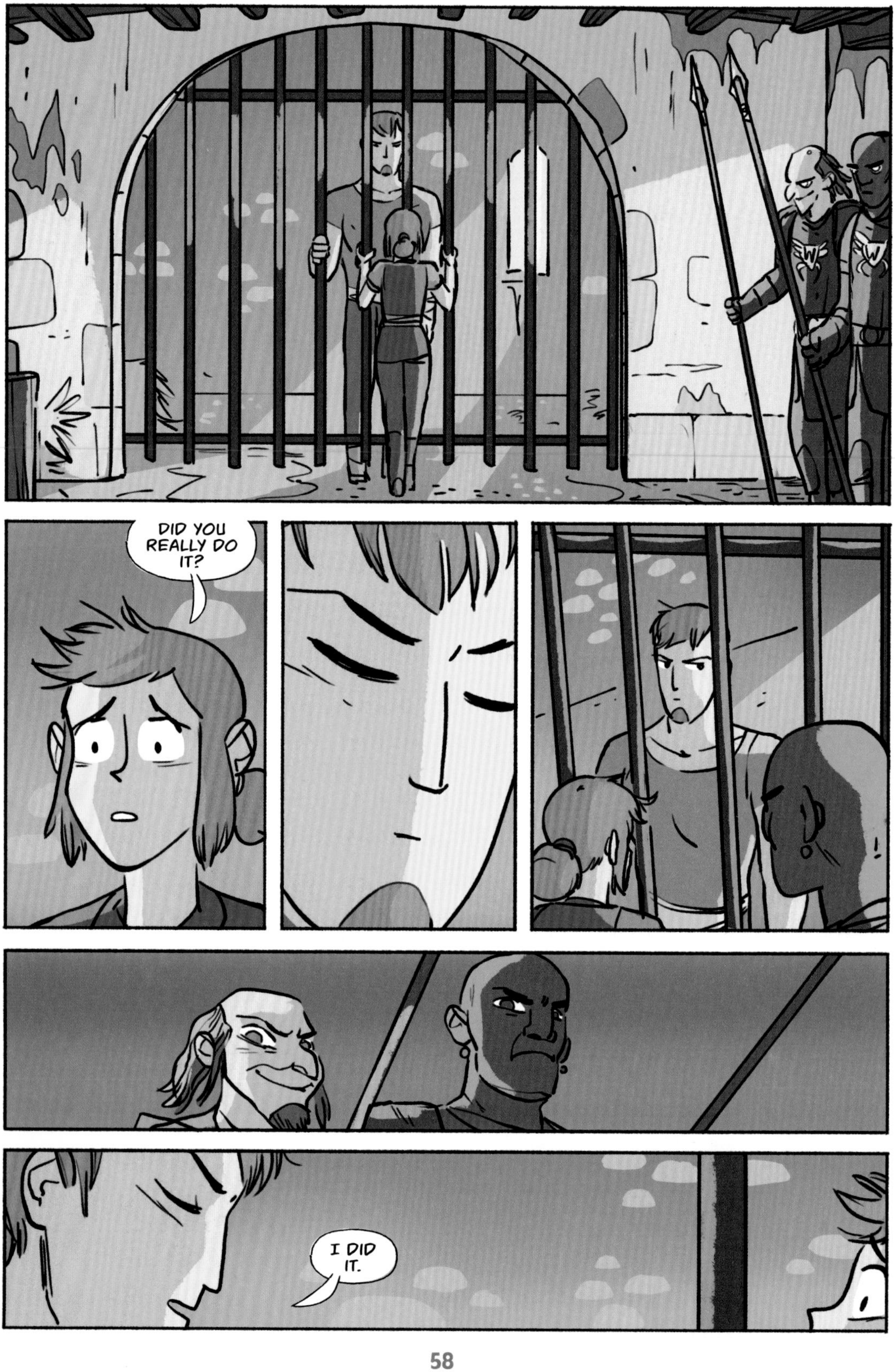
DID YOU REALLY DO IT?
I DID IT.

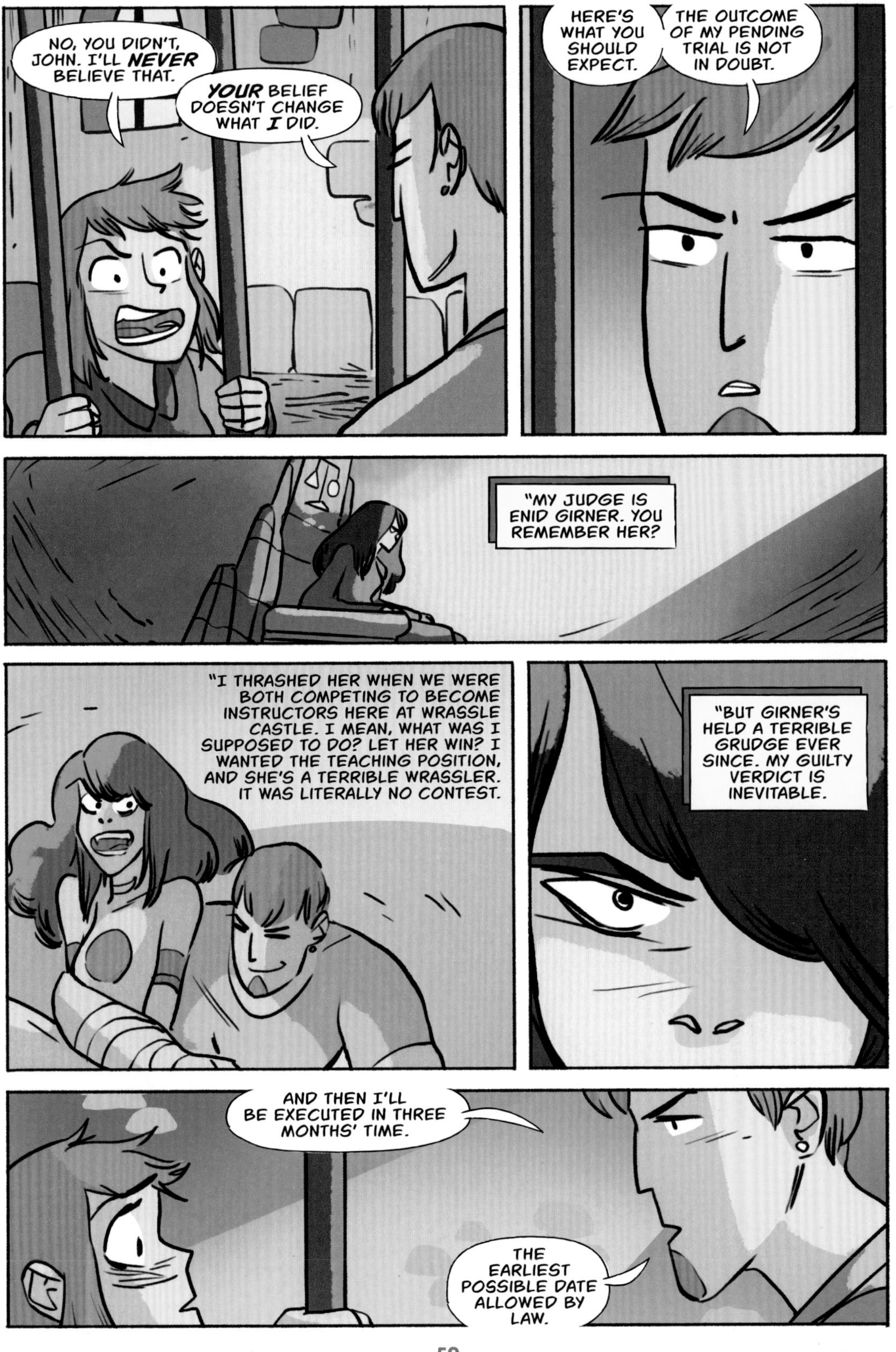

NO, YOU DIDN'T, JOHN. I'LL NEVER BELIEVE THAT.
YOUR BELIEF DOESN'T CHANGE WHAT I DID.
HERE'S WHAT YOU SHOULD EXPECT.
THE OUTCOME OF MY PENDING TRIAL IS NOT IN DOUBT.
"MY JUDGE IS ENID GIRNER. YOU REMEMBER HER?
"I THRASHED HER WHEN WE WERE BOTH COMPETING TO BECOME INSTRUCTORS HERE AT WRASSLE CASTLE. I MEAN, WHAT WAS I SUPPOSED TO DO? LET HER WIN? I WANTED THE TEACHING POSITION, AND SHE'S A TERRIBLE WRASSLER. IT WAS LITERALLY NO CONTEST.
"BUT GIRNER'S HELD A TERRIBLE GRUDGE EVER SINCE. MY GUILTY VERDICT IS INEVITABLE.
AND THEN I'LL BE EXECUTED IN THREE MONTHS' TIME.
THE EARLIEST POSSIBLE DATE ALLOWED BY LAW.

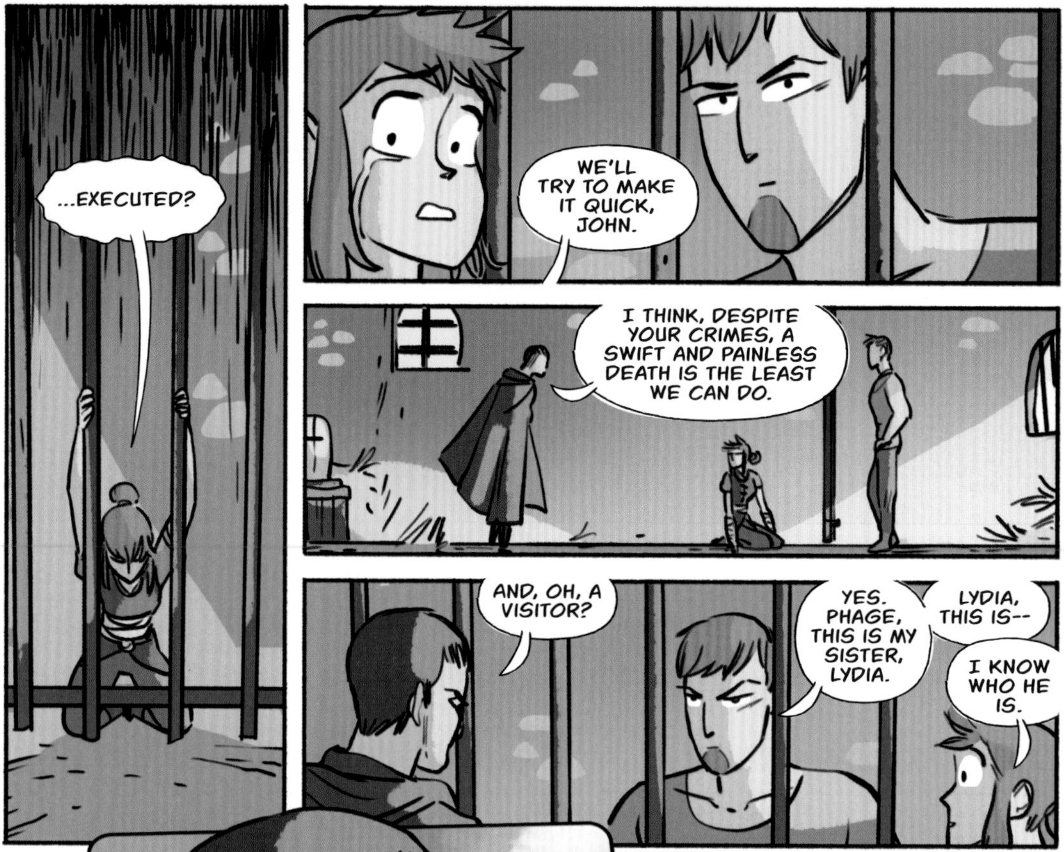
...EXECUTED?
WE'LL TRY TO MAKE IT QUICK, JOHN.
I THINK, DESPITE YOUR CRIMES, A SWIFT AND PAINLESS DEATH IS THE LEAST WE CAN DO.
AND, OH, A VISITOR?
YES. PHAGE, THIS IS MY SISTER, LYDIA.
LYDIA, THIS IS--
I KNOW WHO HE IS.

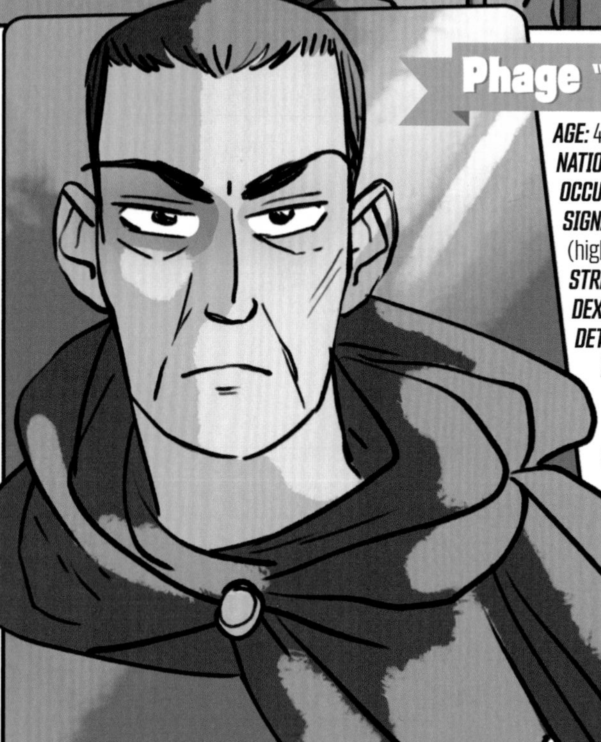

Phage "Swordfist" Leffengan

AGE: 49
NATIONAL RANKING: 1
OCCUPATION: Second in command of Wrassle Castle.
SIGNATURE MOVE: Swordfist (highest Power Level: 98%)
STRENGTH: 16
DEXTERITY: 19
DETERMINATION: 19
FAVORITE FOOD: Liver and tomato soup.
HOBBIES: Rabbit hunting.
NOTES: Phage was orphaned in a tragic accident when he was fifteen, and adopted and raised by the offices of Wrassle Castle. Tragedy begat success, as Phage is now responsible for the construction and upkeep of all Pinnland's territorial outposts, as well as all aspects of the Wrassling Outreach Program, sending out emissaries to peaceable foreign nations and hosting their wrasslers in return.

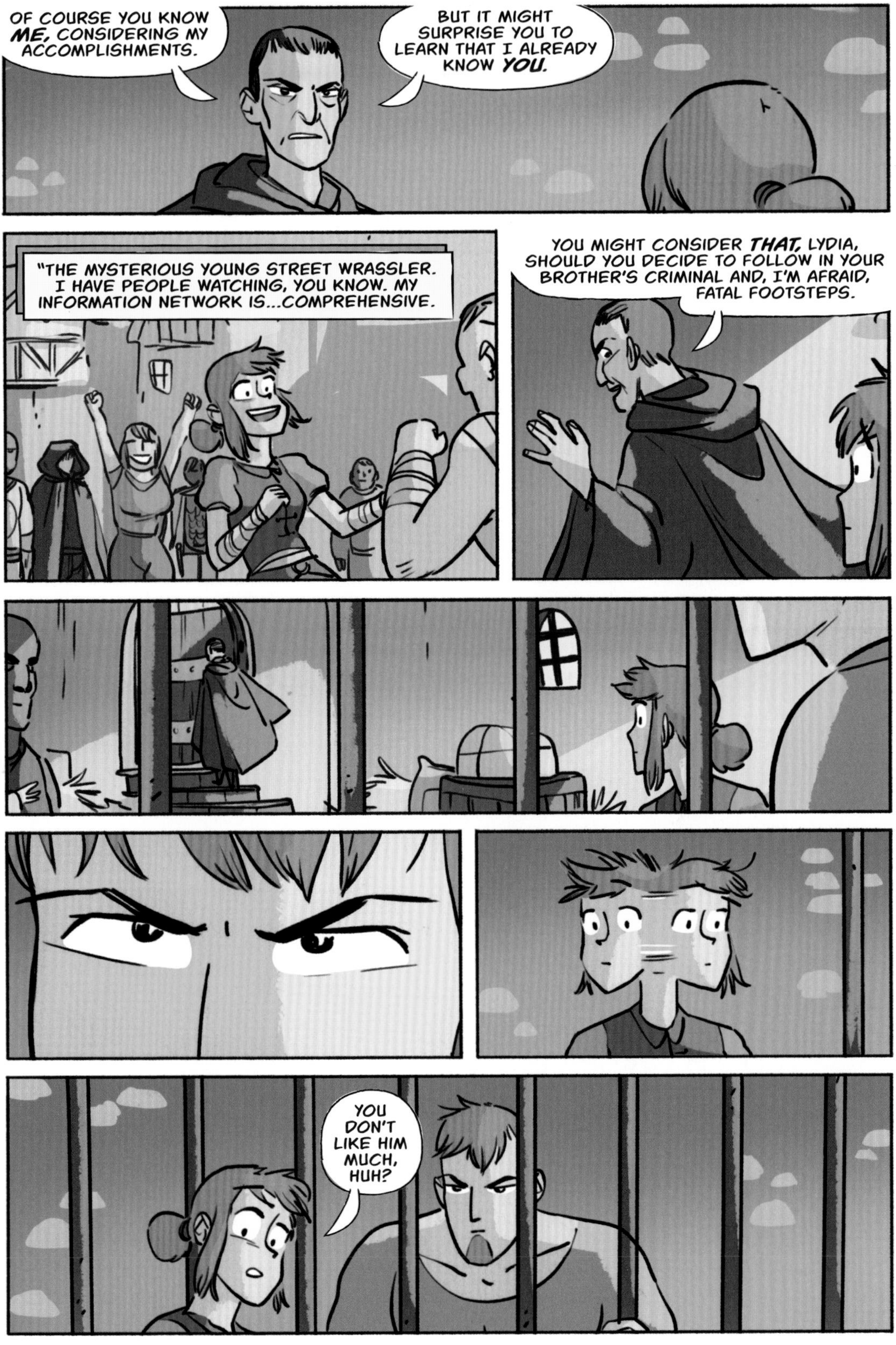
OF COURSE YOU KNOW *ME,* CONSIDERING MY ACCOMPLISHMENTS.
BUT IT MIGHT SURPRISE YOU TO LEARN THAT I ALREADY KNOW *YOU.*
"THE MYSTERIOUS YOUNG STREET WRASSLER. I HAVE PEOPLE WATCHING, YOU KNOW. MY INFORMATION NETWORK IS...COMPREHENSIVE.
YOU MIGHT CONSIDER *THAT,* LYDIA, SHOULD YOU DECIDE TO FOLLOW IN YOUR BROTHER'S CRIMINAL AND, I'M AFRAID, FATAL FOOTSTEPS.
YOU DON'T LIKE HIM MUCH, HUH?

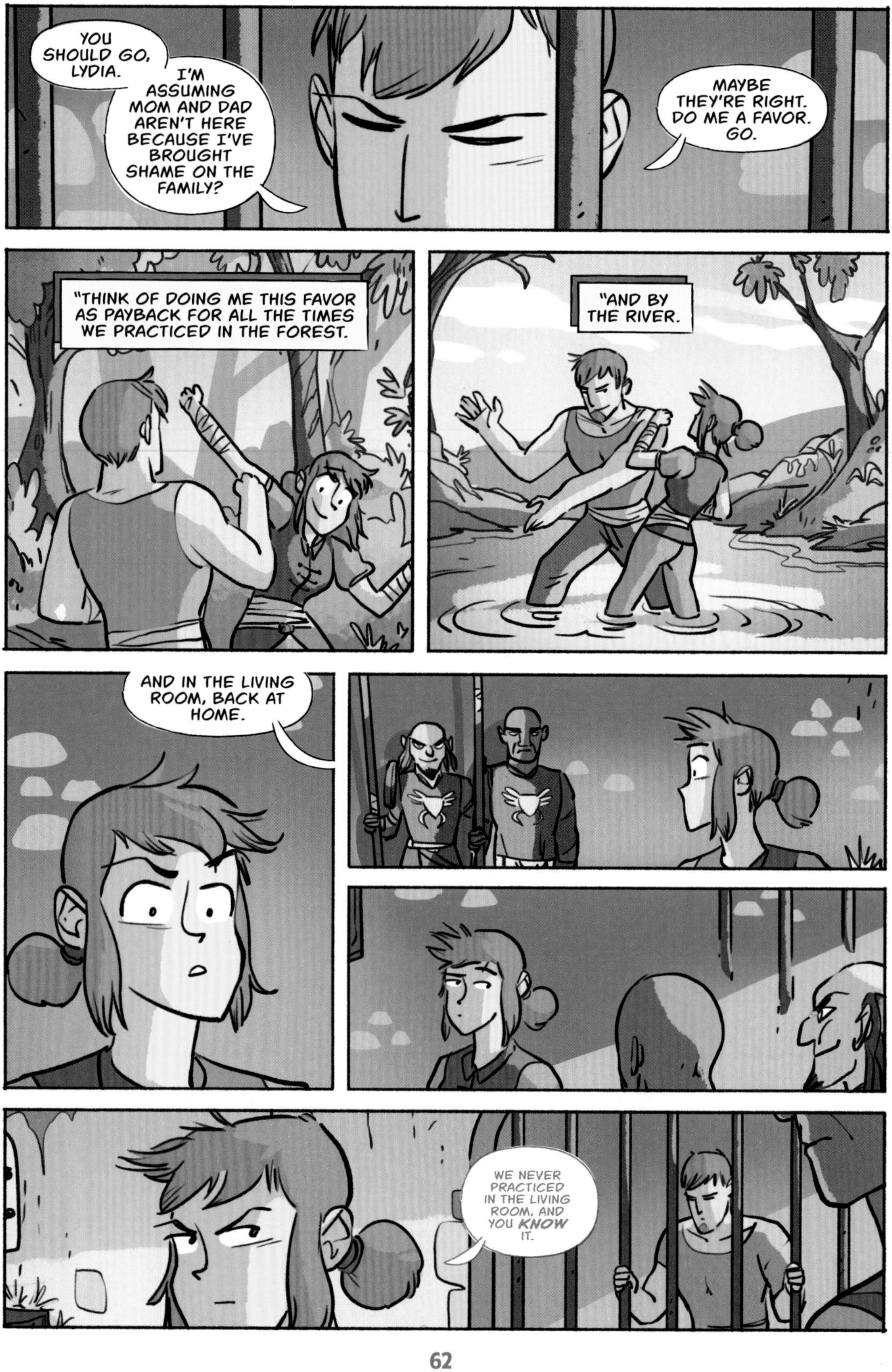
YOU SHOULD GO, LYDIA.
I'M ASSUMING MOM AND DAD AREN'T HERE BECAUSE I'VE BROUGHT SHAME ON THE FAMILY?
MAYBE THEY'RE RIGHT. DO ME A FAVOR. GO.
"THINK OF DOING ME THIS FAVOR AS PAYBACK FOR ALL THE TIMES WE PRACTICED IN THE FOREST.
"AND BY THE RIVER.
AND IN THE LIVING ROOM, BACK AT HOME.
WE NEVER PRACTICED IN THE LIVING ROOM, AND YOU *KNOW* IT.

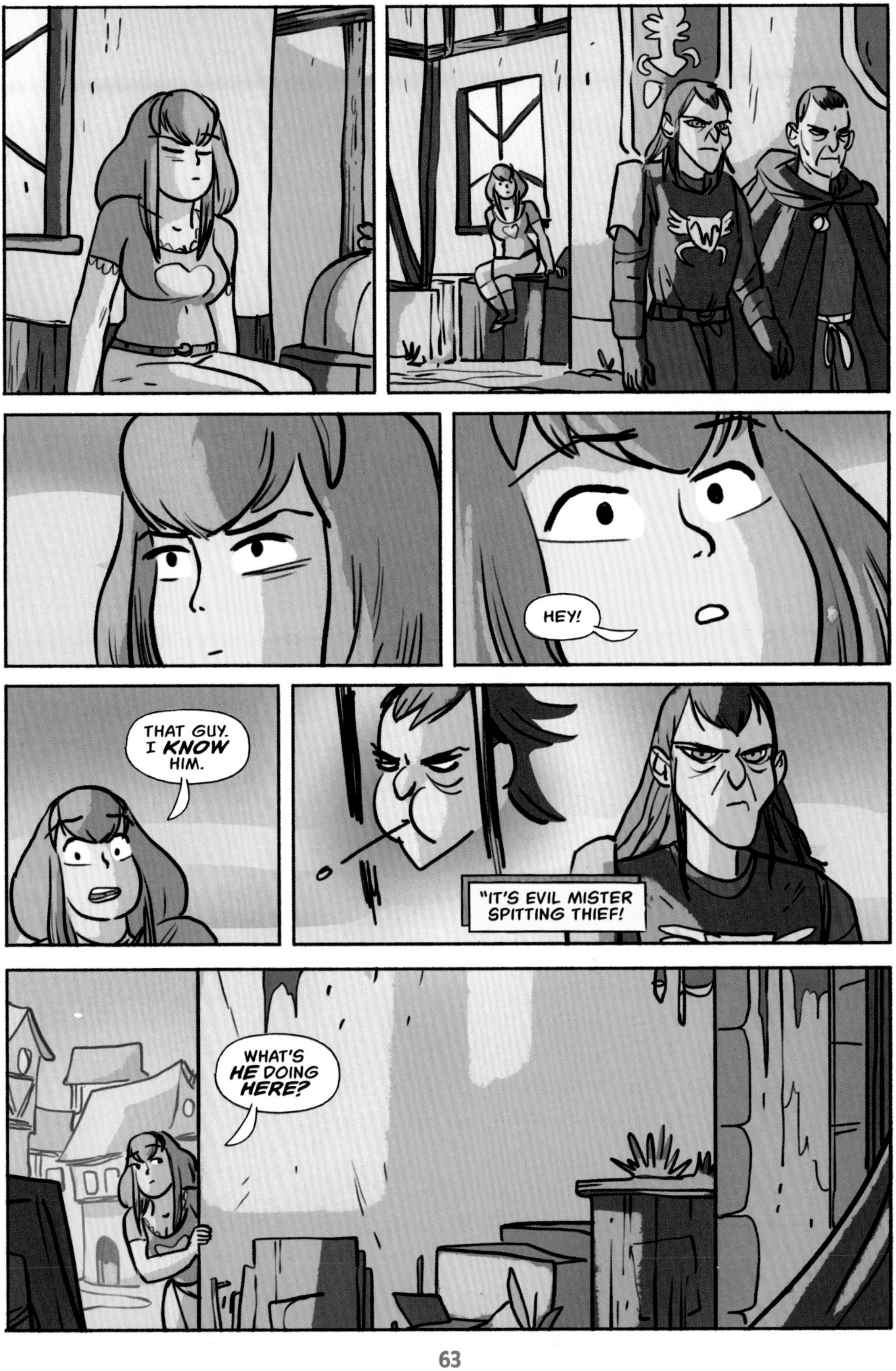
HEY!
THAT GUY. I KNOW HIM.
"IT'S EVIL MISTER SPITTING THIEF!
WHAT'S HE DOING HERE?

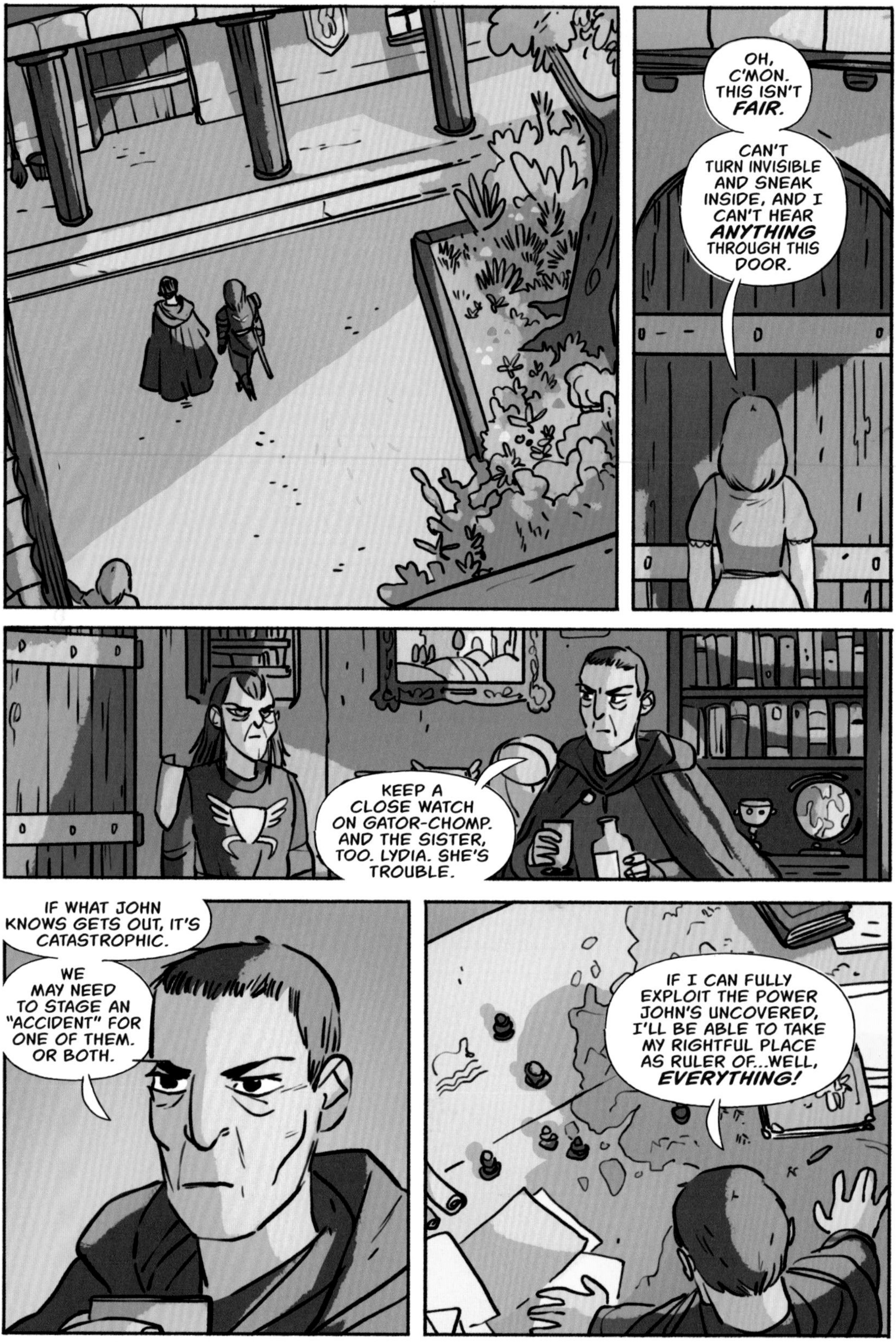
OH, C'MON. THIS ISN'T FAIR.
CAN'T TURN INVISIBLE AND SNEAK INSIDE, AND I CAN'T HEAR ANYTHING THROUGH THIS DOOR.
KEEP A CLOSE WATCH ON GATOR-CHOMP. AND THE SISTER, TOO. LYDIA. SHE'S TROUBLE.
IF WHAT JOHN KNOWS GETS OUT, IT'S CATASTROPHIC.
WE MAY NEED TO STAGE AN "ACCIDENT" FOR ONE OF THEM. OR BOTH.
IF I CAN FULLY EXPLOIT THE POWER JOHN'S UNCOVERED, I'LL BE ABLE TO TAKE MY RIGHTFUL PLACE AS RULER OF...WELL, EVERYTHING!

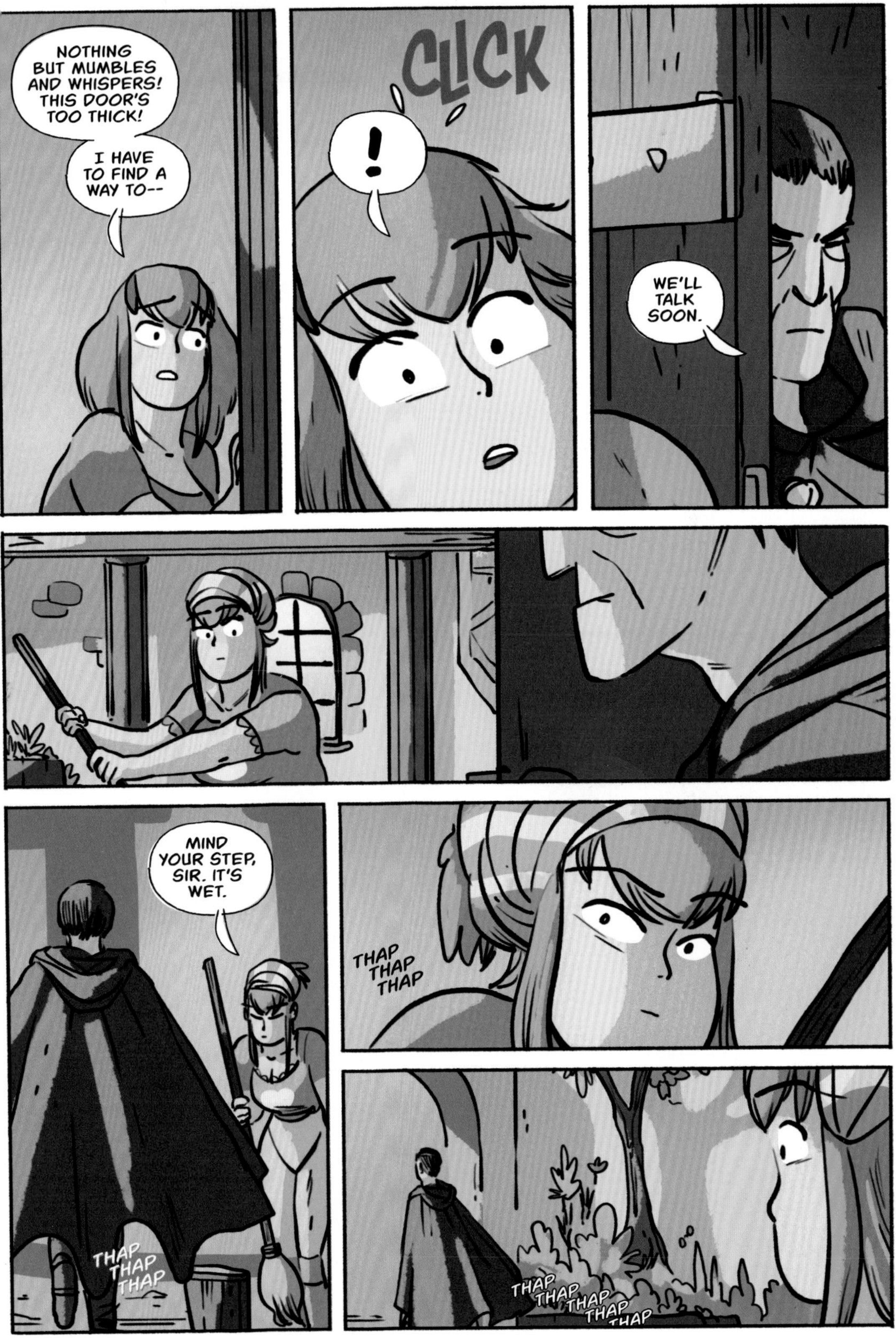
NOTHING BUT MUMBLES AND WHISPERS! THIS DOOR'S TOO THICK!
I HAVE TO FIND A WAY TO--
CLICK
!
WE'LL TALK SOON.
MIND YOUR STEP, SIR. IT'S WET.
THAP THAP THAP
THAP THAP THAP
THAP THAP THAP THAP THAP

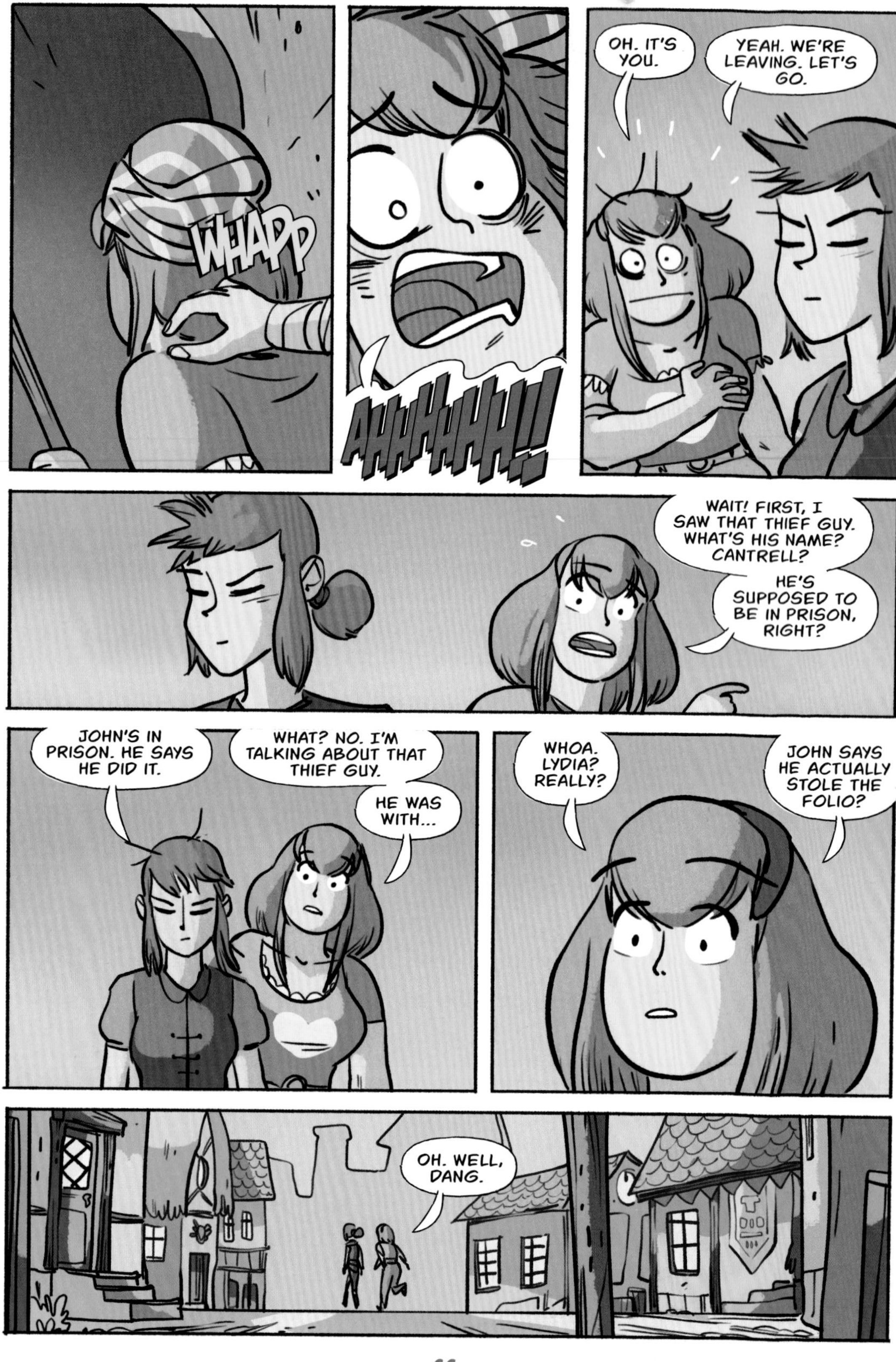
WHAPP
AHHHHHH!!
OH. IT'S YOU.
YEAH. WE'RE LEAVING. LET'S GO.
WAIT! FIRST, I SAW THAT THIEF GUY. WHAT'S HIS NAME? CANTRELL?
HE'S SUPPOSED TO BE IN PRISON, RIGHT?
JOHN'S IN PRISON. HE SAYS HE DID IT.
WHAT? NO. I'M TALKING ABOUT THAT THIEF GUY.
HE WAS WITH...
WHOA. LYDIA? REALLY?
JOHN SAYS HE ACTUALLY STOLE THE FOLIO?
OH. WELL, DANG.

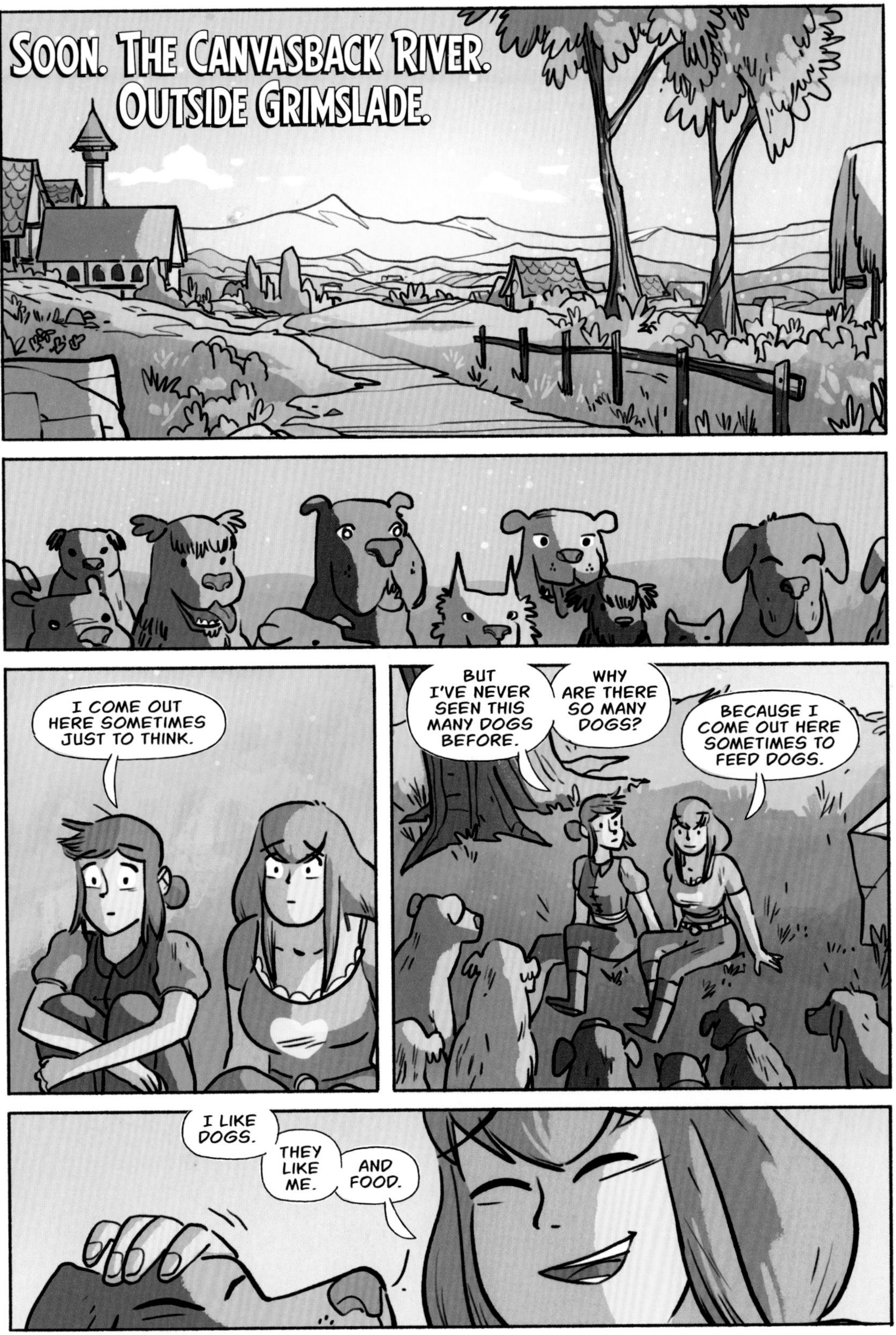

SOON. THE CANVASBACK RIVER. OUTSIDE GRIMSLADE.
I COME OUT HERE SOMETIMES JUST TO THINK.
BUT I'VE NEVER SEEN THIS MANY DOGS BEFORE.
WHY ARE THERE SO MANY DOGS?
BECAUSE I COME OUT HERE SOMETIMES TO FEED DOGS.
I LIKE DOGS.
THEY LIKE ME.
AND FOOD.

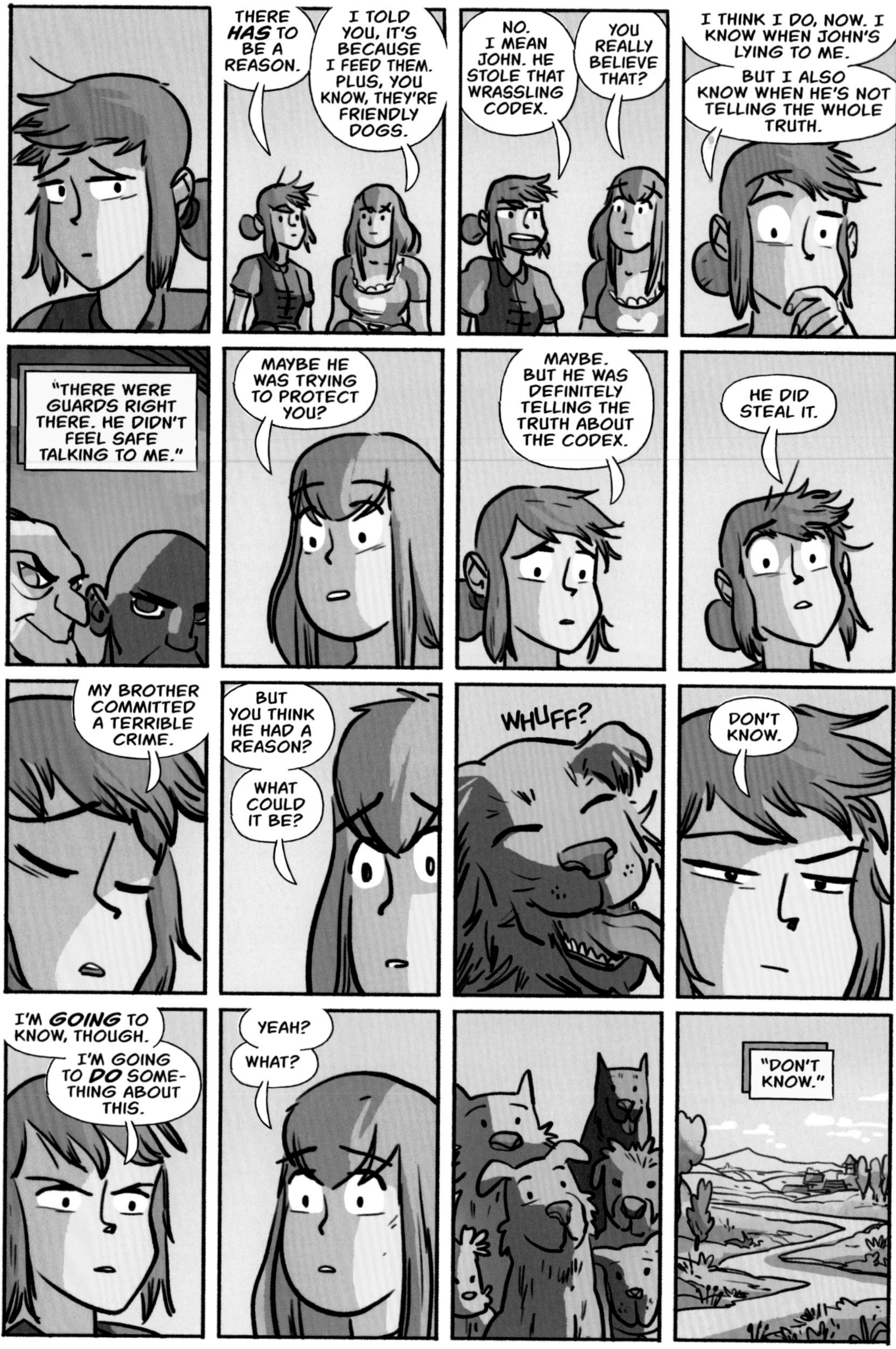
THERE HAS TO BE A REASON.
I TOLD YOU, IT'S BECAUSE I FEED THEM. PLUS, YOU KNOW, THEY'RE FRIENDLY DOGS.
NO. I MEAN JOHN. HE STOLE THAT WRASSLING CODEX.
YOU REALLY BELIEVE THAT?
I THINK I DO, NOW. I KNOW WHEN JOHN'S LYING TO ME.
BUT I ALSO KNOW WHEN HE'S NOT TELLING THE WHOLE TRUTH.
"THERE WERE GUARDS RIGHT THERE. HE DIDN'T FEEL SAFE TALKING TO ME."
MAYBE HE WAS TRYING TO PROTECT YOU?
MAYBE. BUT HE WAS DEFINITELY TELLING THE TRUTH ABOUT THE CODEX.
HE DID STEAL IT.
MY BROTHER COMMITTED A TERRIBLE CRIME.
BUT YOU THINK HE HAD A REASON?
WHAT COULD IT BE?
WHUFF?
DON'T KNOW.
I'M GOING TO KNOW, THOUGH.
I'M GOING TO DO SOMETHING ABOUT THIS.
YEAH?
WHAT?
"DON'T KNOW."

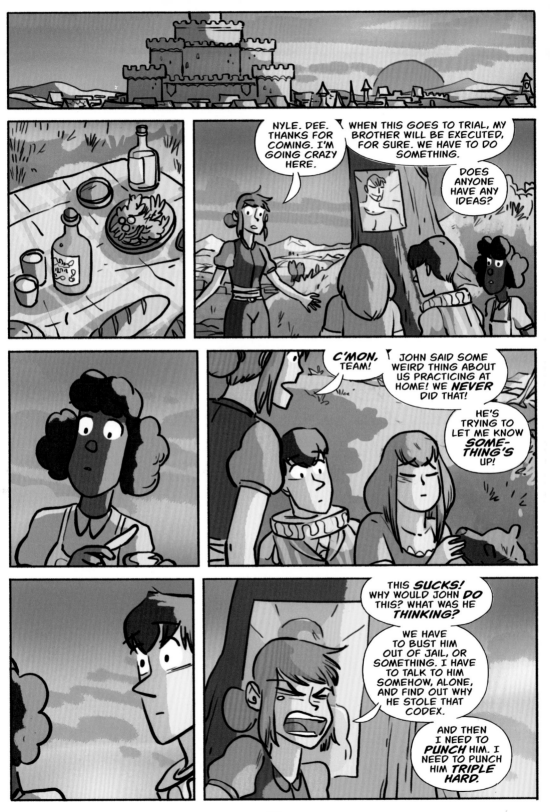

NYLE. DEE. THANKS FOR COMING. I'M GOING CRAZY HERE.

WHEN THIS GOES TO TRIAL, MY BROTHER WILL BE EXECUTED, FOR SURE. WE HAVE TO DO SOMETHING.

DOES ANYONE HAVE ANY IDEAS?

C'MON, TEAM!

JOHN SAID SOME WEIRD THING ABOUT US PRACTICING AT HOME! WE *NEVER* DID THAT!

HE'S TRYING TO LET ME KNOW *SOME-THING'S* UP!

THIS *SUCKS!* WHY WOULD JOHN *DO* THIS? WHAT WAS HE *THINKING?*

WE HAVE TO BUST HIM OUT OF JAIL, OR SOMETHING. I HAVE TO TALK TO HIM SOMEHOW, ALONE, AND FIND OUT WHY HE STOLE THAT CODEX.

AND THEN I NEED TO *PUNCH* HIM. I NEED TO PUNCH HIM *TRIPLE HARD.*

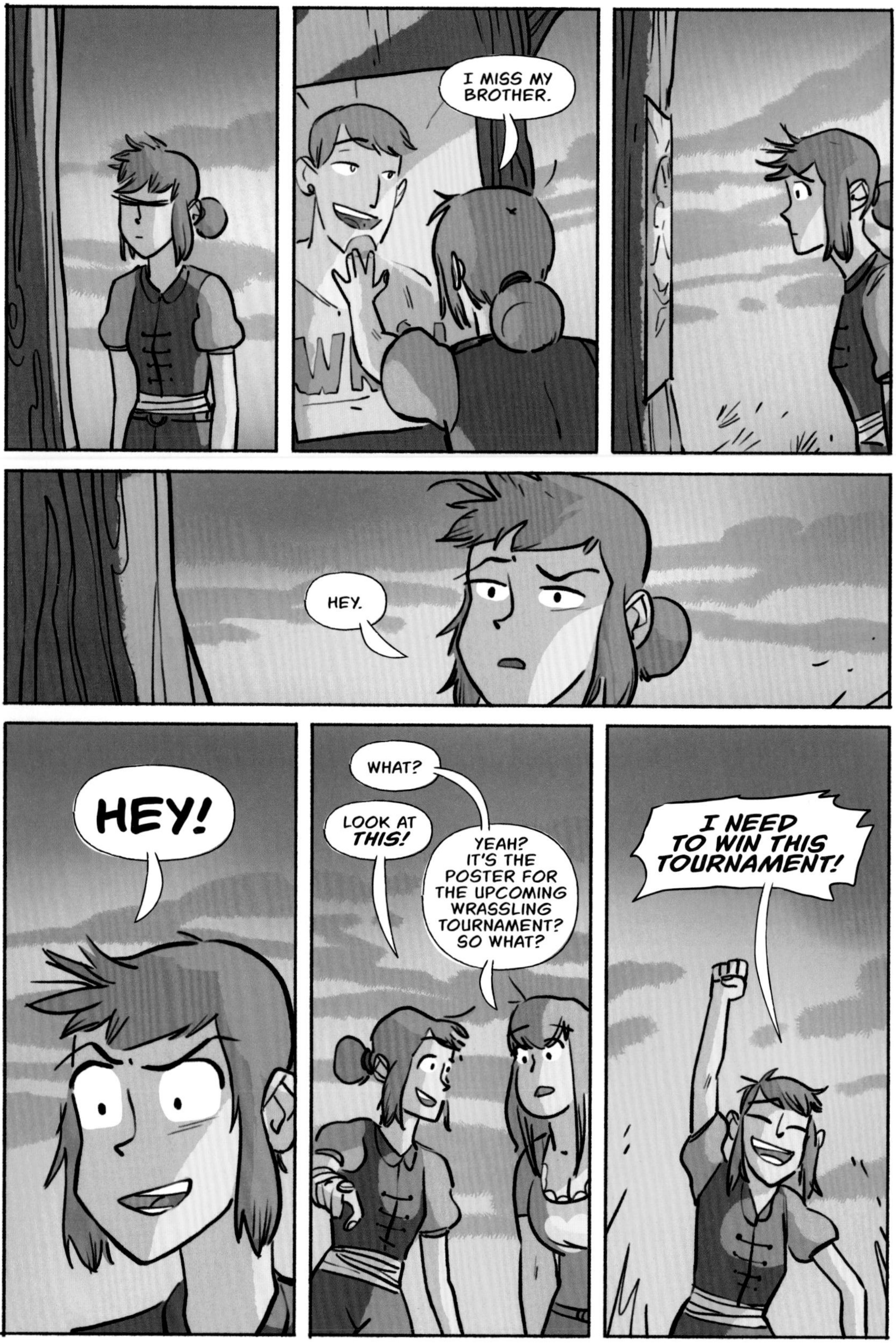

I MISS MY BROTHER.
HEY.
HEY!
WHAT?
LOOK AT THIS!
YEAH? IT'S THE POSTER FOR THE UPCOMING WRASSLING TOURNAMENT? SO WHAT?
I NEED TO WIN THIS TOURNAMENT!

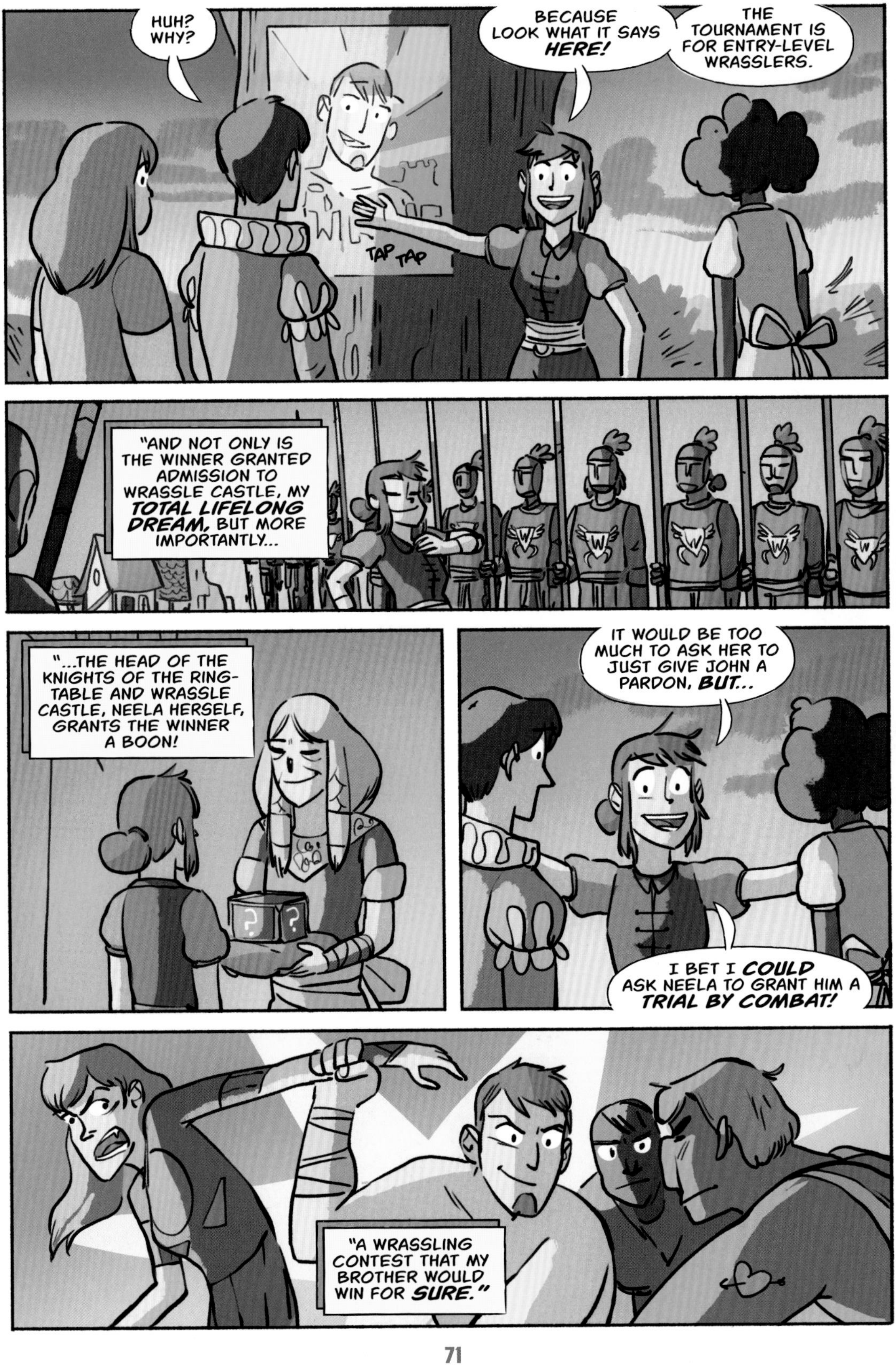
HUH? WHY?
BECAUSE LOOK WHAT IT SAYS HERE!
THE TOURNAMENT IS FOR ENTRY-LEVEL WRASSLERS.
TAP TAP
"AND NOT ONLY IS THE WINNER GRANTED ADMISSION TO WRASSLE CASTLE, MY TOTAL LIFELONG DREAM, BUT MORE IMPORTANTLY...
"...THE HEAD OF THE KNIGHTS OF THE RING-TABLE AND WRASSLE CASTLE, NEELA HERSELF, GRANTS THE WINNER A BOON!
IT WOULD BE TOO MUCH TO ASK HER TO JUST GIVE JOHN A PARDON, BUT...
I BET I COULD ASK NEELA TO GRANT HIM A TRIAL BY COMBAT!
"A WRASSLING CONTEST THAT MY BROTHER WOULD WIN FOR SURE."

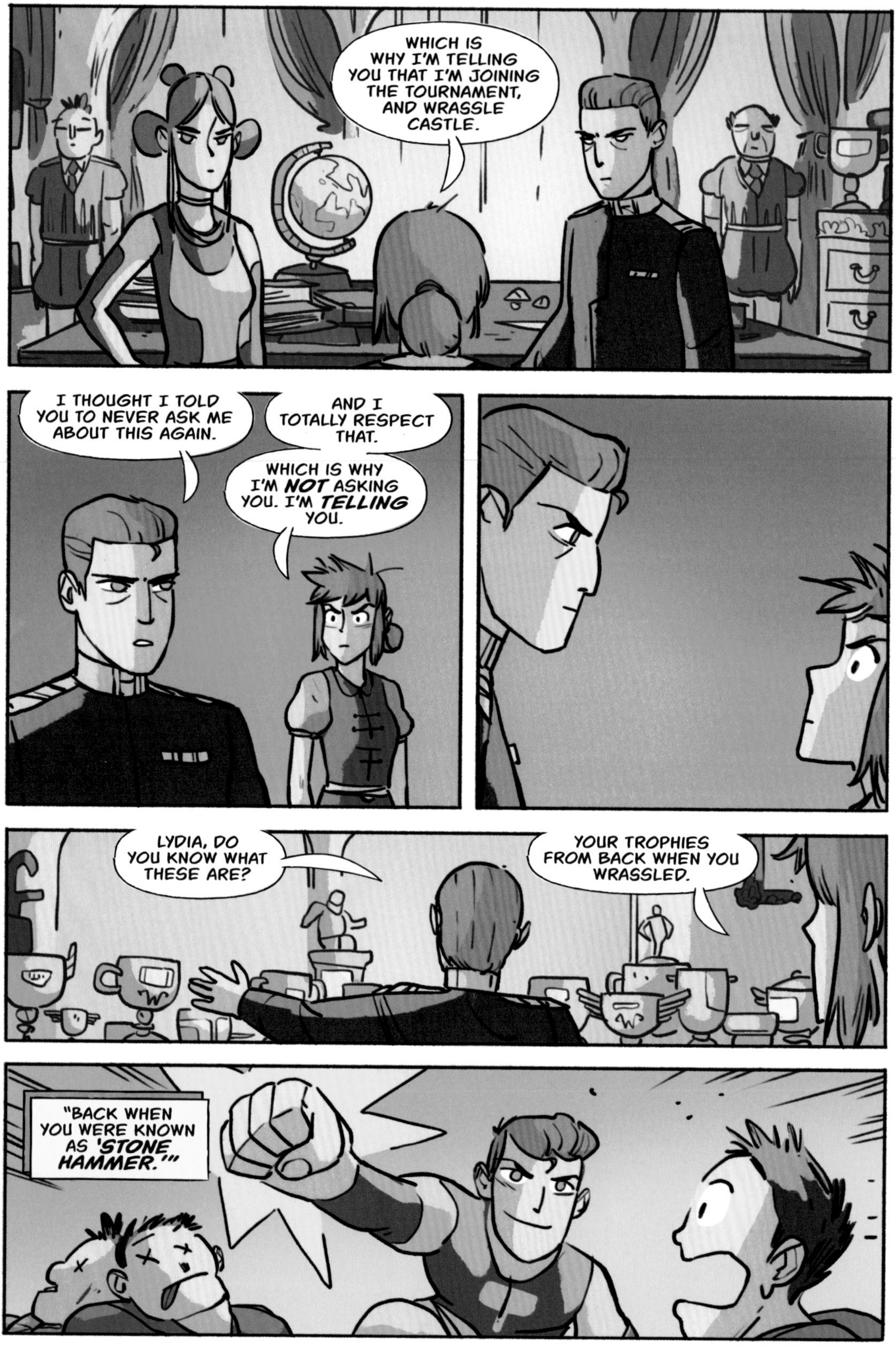
WHICH IS WHY I'M TELLING YOU THAT I'M JOINING THE TOURNAMENT, AND WRASSLE CASTLE.
I THOUGHT I TOLD YOU TO NEVER ASK ME ABOUT THIS AGAIN.
AND I TOTALLY RESPECT THAT.
WHICH IS WHY I'M **NOT** ASKING YOU. I'M **TELLING** YOU.
LYDIA, DO YOU KNOW WHAT THESE ARE?
YOUR TROPHIES FROM BACK WHEN YOU WRASSLED.
"BACK WHEN YOU WERE KNOWN AS '**STONE HAMMER**.'"

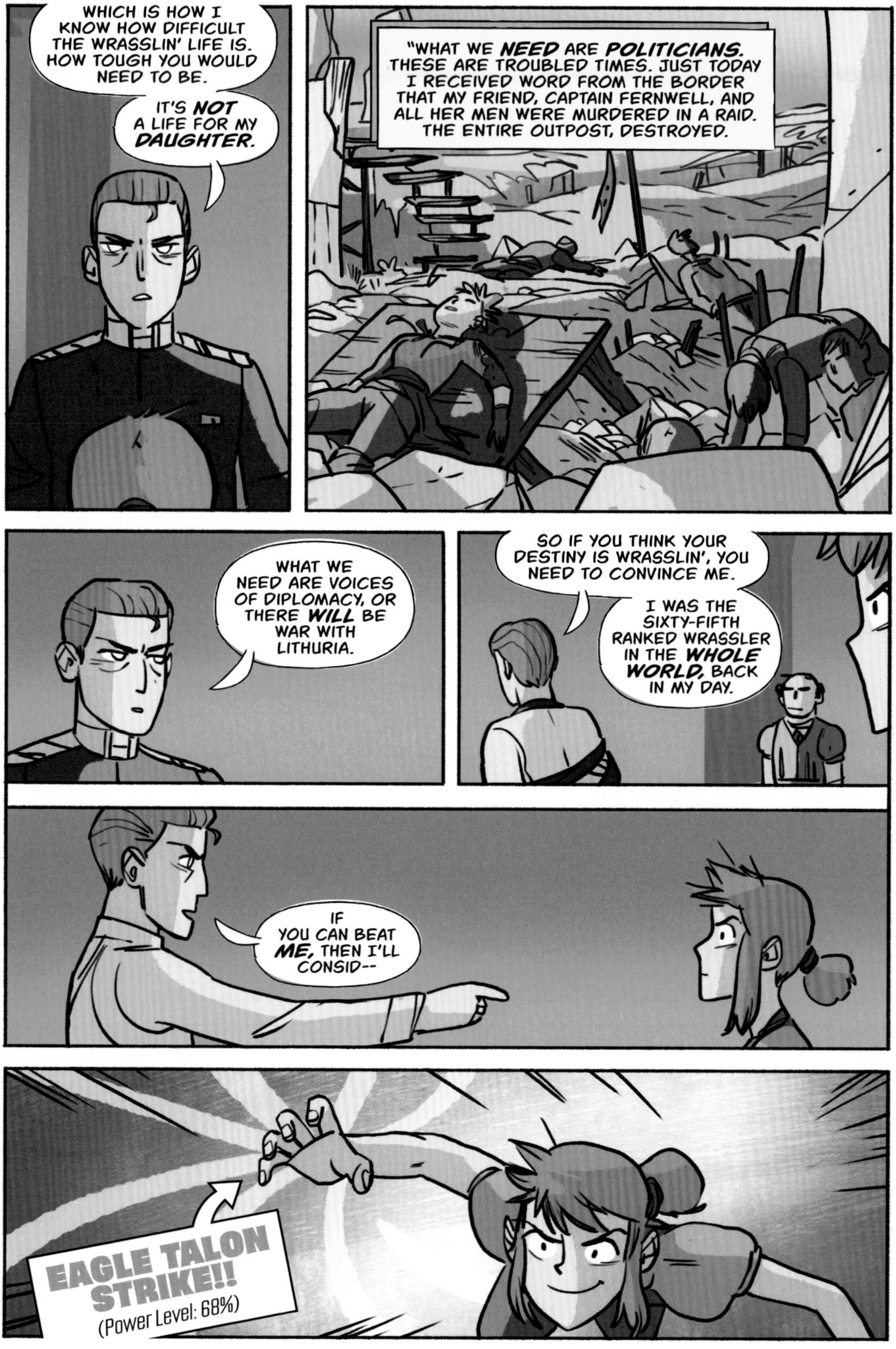

WHICH IS HOW I KNOW HOW DIFFICULT THE WRASSLIN' LIFE IS. HOW TOUGH YOU WOULD NEED TO BE.
IT'S **NOT** A LIFE FOR MY **DAUGHTER**.
"WHAT WE **NEED** ARE **POLITICIANS.** THESE ARE TROUBLED TIMES. JUST TODAY I RECEIVED WORD FROM THE BORDER THAT MY FRIEND, CAPTAIN FERNWELL, AND ALL HER MEN WERE MURDERED IN A RAID. THE ENTIRE OUTPOST, DESTROYED.
WHAT WE NEED ARE VOICES OF DIPLOMACY, OR THERE **WILL** BE WAR WITH LITHURIA.
SO IF YOU THINK YOUR DESTINY IS WRASSLIN', YOU NEED TO CONVINCE ME.
I WAS THE SIXTY-FIFTH RANKED WRASSLER IN THE **WHOLE WORLD,** BACK IN MY DAY.
IF YOU CAN BEAT **ME,** THEN I'LL CONSID--
EAGLE TALON STRIKE!!
(Power Level: 68%)

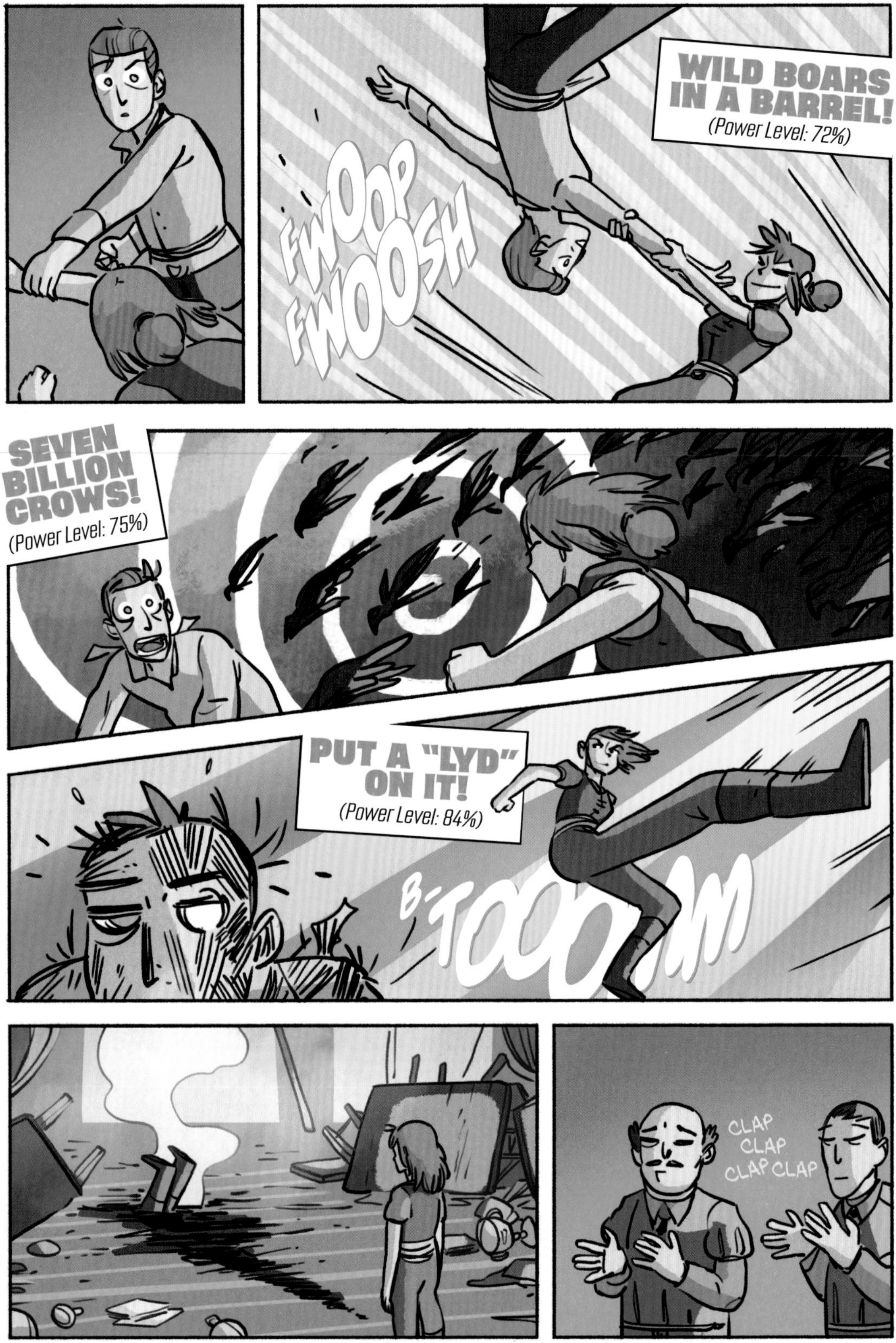
WILD BOARS IN A BARREL!
(Power Level: 72%)
FWOOP
FWOOSH
SEVEN BILLION CROWS!
(Power Level: 75%)
PUT A "LYD" ON IT!
(Power Level: 84%)
B-TOOOOM
CLAP
CLAP
CLAP CLAP

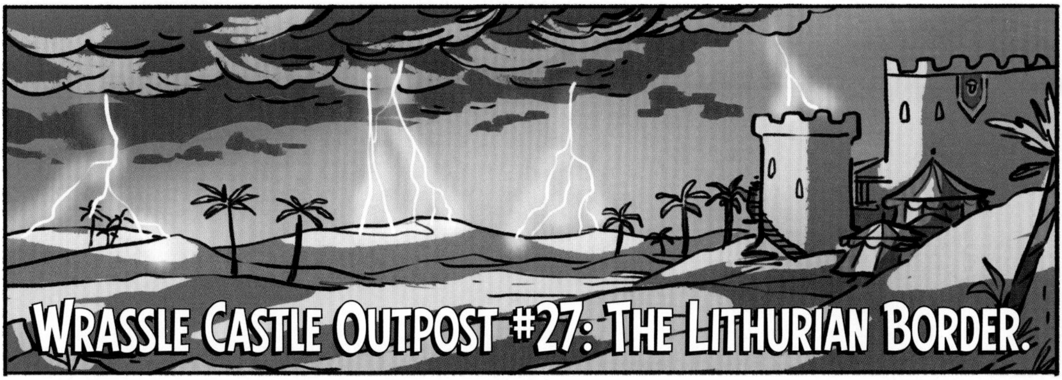
WRASSLE CASTLE OUTPOST #27: THE LITHURIAN BORDER.

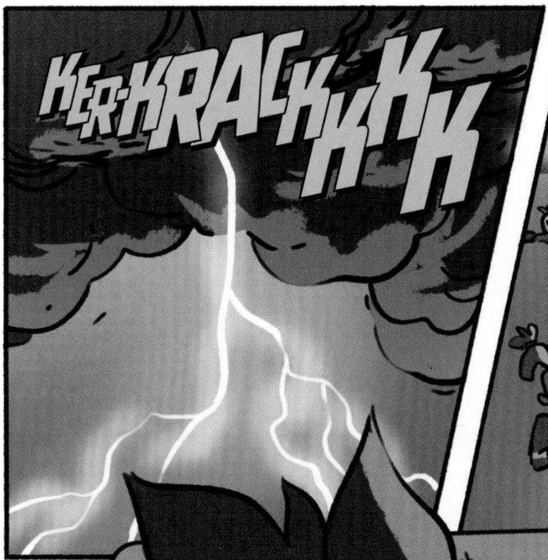
KER-KRACKKKKK

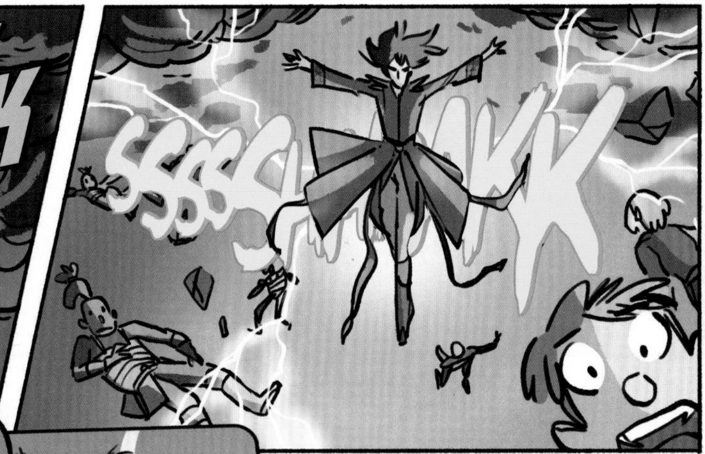

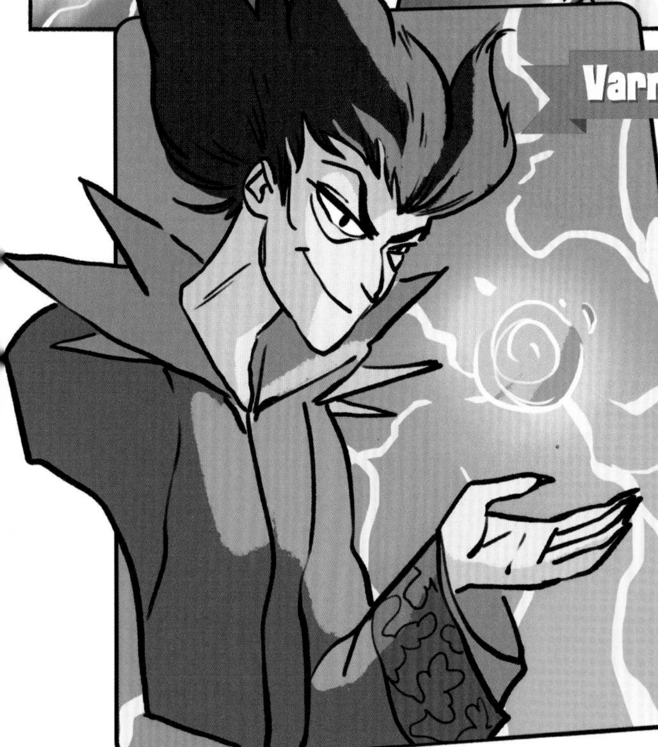

Varney "Stormslammer" Bainehollow

AGE: 72

NATIONAL RANKING: 7

OCCUPATION: Aide to Phage Leffengan.

SIGNATURE MOVE: Wild Storm (highest Power Level: 97%)

STRENGTH: 14

DEXTERITY: 13

DETERMINATION: 19

FAVORITE FOOD: Elephant meat.

HOBBIES: Historical research.

NOTES: As a child, Varney was found abandoned outside the entrance to Hellwurst Caverns, and raised by the Only End wrasslin' sect. Varney possesses a unique power to create terrible storms with the fury of his wrasslin' abilities.

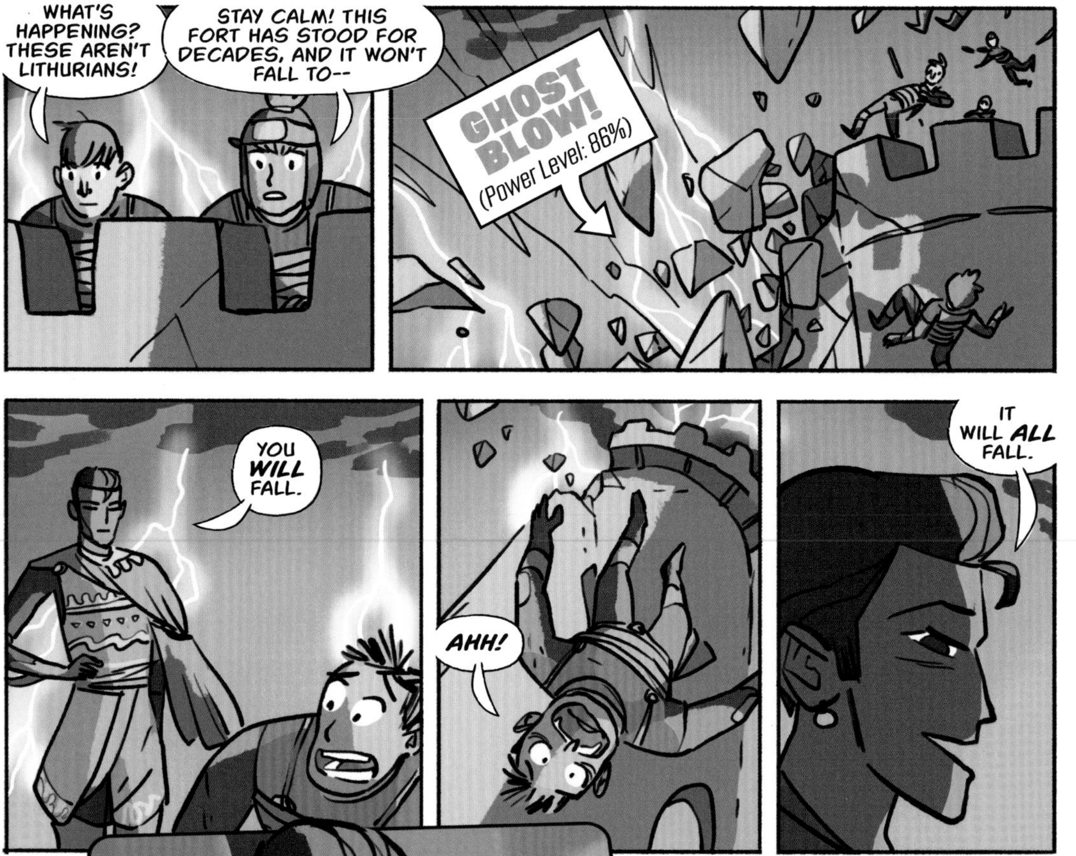
WHAT'S HAPPENING? THESE AREN'T LITHURIANS!
STAY CALM! THIS FORT HAS STOOD FOR DECADES, AND IT WON'T FALL TO--
GHOST BLOW!
(Power Level: 86%)
YOU WILL FALL.
AHH!
IT WILL ALL FALL.

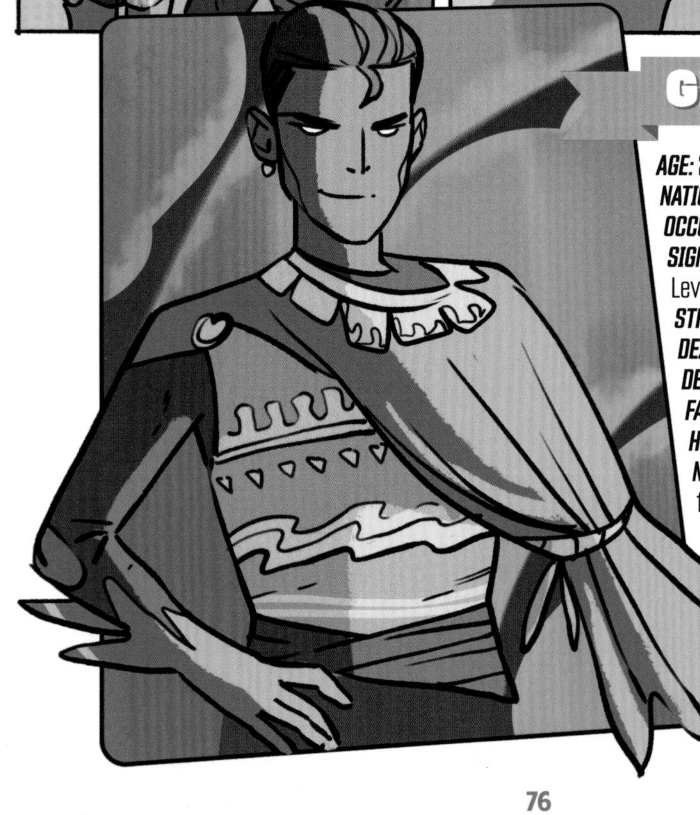

Ghostly Jeenu

AGE: 28
NATIONAL RANKING: 24
OCCUPATION: Aide to Phage Leffengan.
SIGNATURE MOVE: Ghost Blow (highest Power Level: 88%)
STRENGTH: 17
DEXTERITY: 17
DETERMINATION: 16
FAVORITE FOOD: Rice with fruit.
HOBBIES: Bar hopping. Fashion.
NOTES: Jeenu's mother was an ambassador for the textile industries, and he gained a great love for fashion in his youth. His parents were murdered by brigands during a caravan ambush, and since then Jeenu has withdrawn from the "proper" society of his upbringing and now belongs to the Street Rats, a consortium that claims ownership of sixteen of Grimslade's 117 taverns.

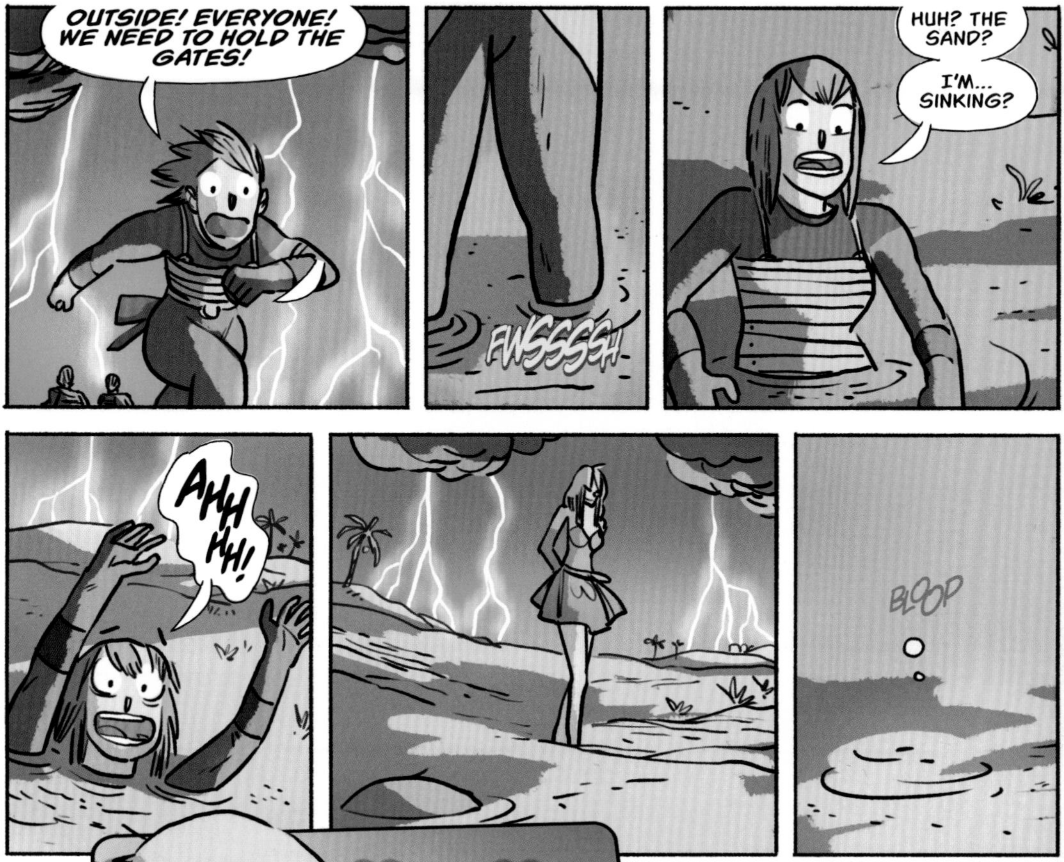
OUTSIDE! EVERYONE! WE NEED TO HOLD THE GATES!
FWSSSSH
HUH? THE SAND?
I'M... SINKING?
AHHHH!
BLOOP

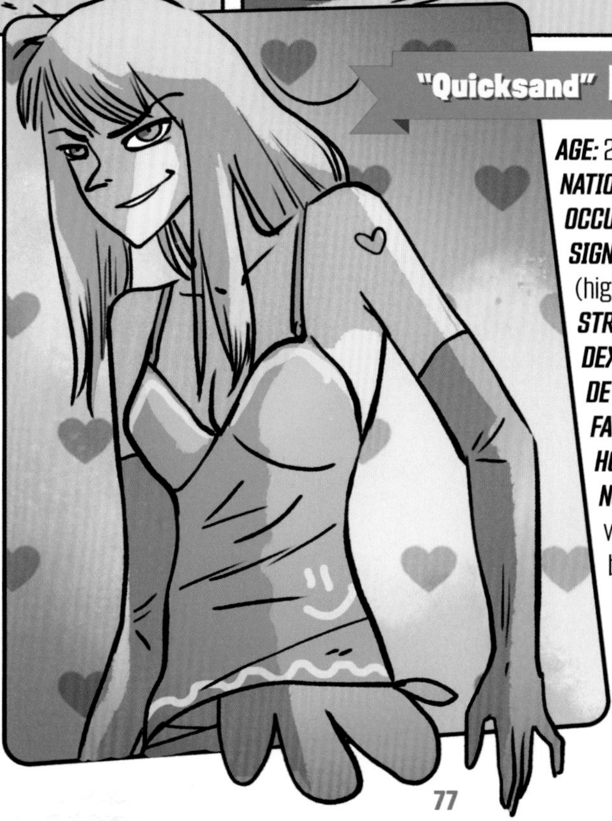

"Quicksand" Kelly Sanderson

AGE: 25
NATIONAL RANKING: 112
OCCUPATION: Diplomatic courier.
SIGNATURE MOVE: Smother Strike (highest Power Level: 91%)
STRENGTH: 12
DEXTERITY: 15
DETERMINATION: 16
FAVORITE FOOD: Kelp noodles.
HOBBIES: Swimming. Macramé.
NOTES: Quicksand Kelly's early life was spent scavenging scraps beneath the piers of Grimslade Warf. Recruited by Phage Leffengan to join his personal staff when all of Grimslade was gripped with fear by the still-unsolved "Chokehold" murders, which came to an abrupt end shortly thereafter.

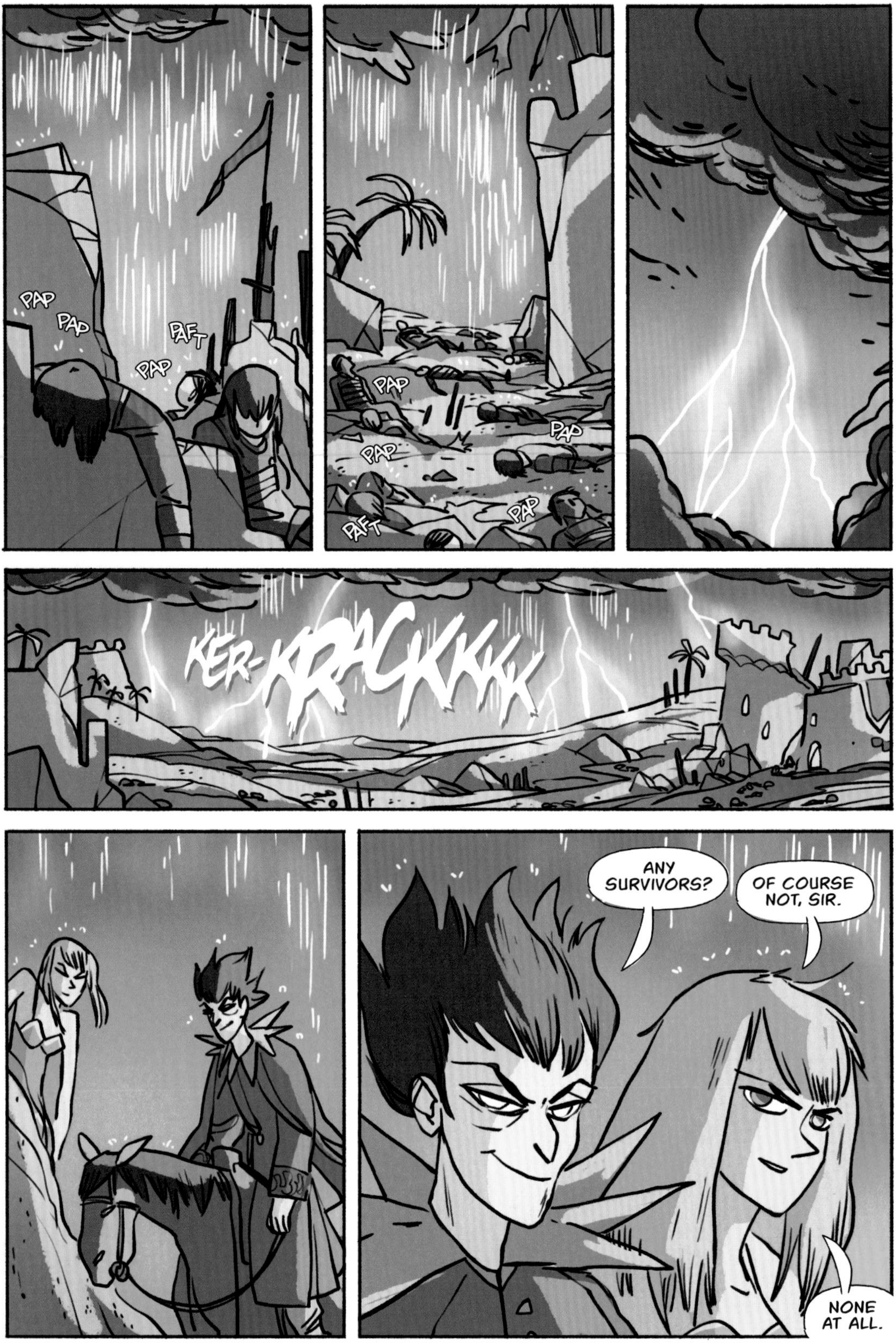
PAP
PAP
PAFT
PAP
PAP
PAP
PAP
PAFT
PAP
KER-KRACKKKK
ANY SURVIVORS?
OF COURSE NOT, SIR.
NONE AT ALL.

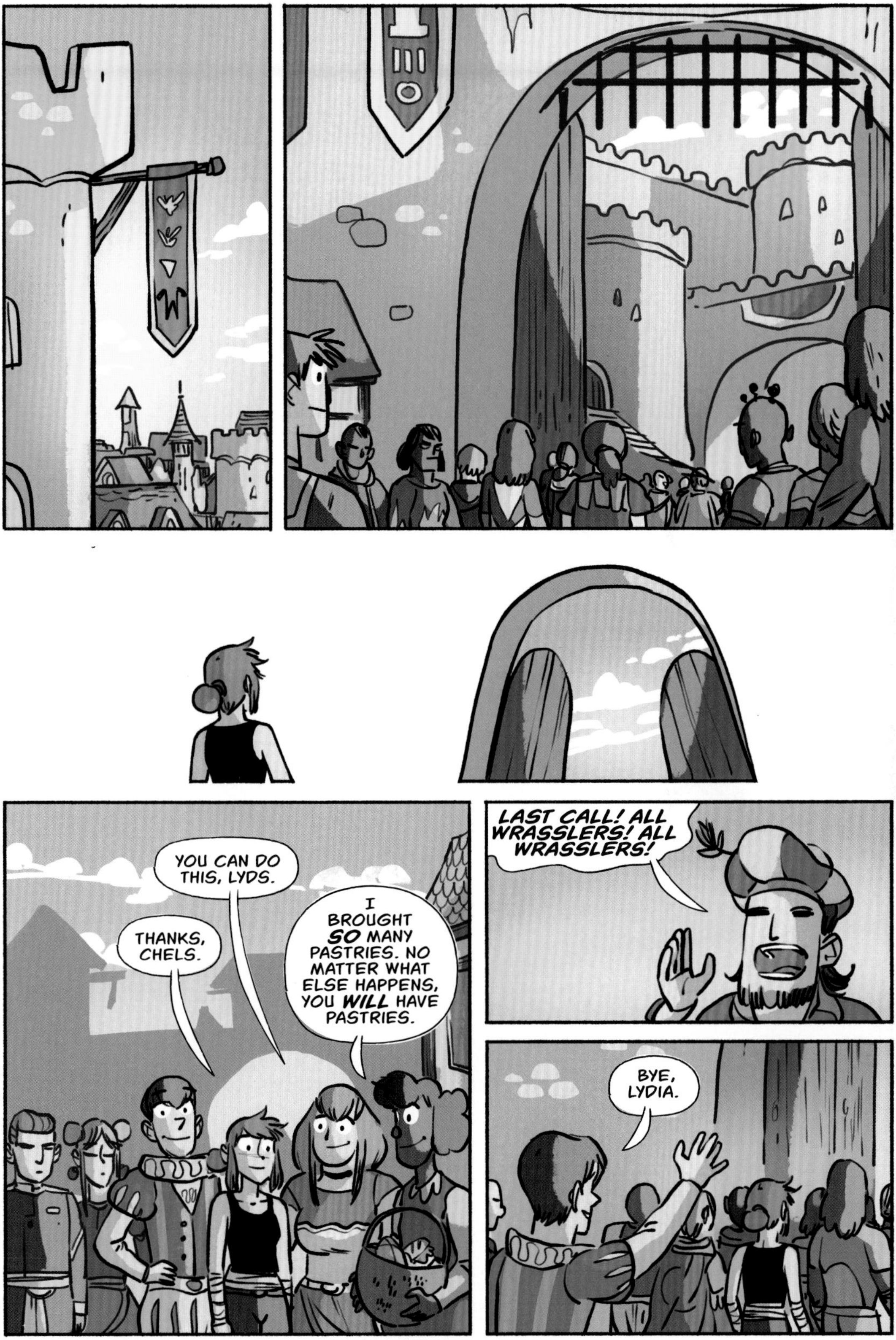
YOU CAN DO THIS, LYDS.
THANKS, CHELS.
I BROUGHT SO MANY PASTRIES. NO MATTER WHAT ELSE HAPPENS, YOU WILL HAVE PASTRIES.
LAST CALL! ALL WRASSLERS! ALL WRASSLERS!
BYE, LYDIA.

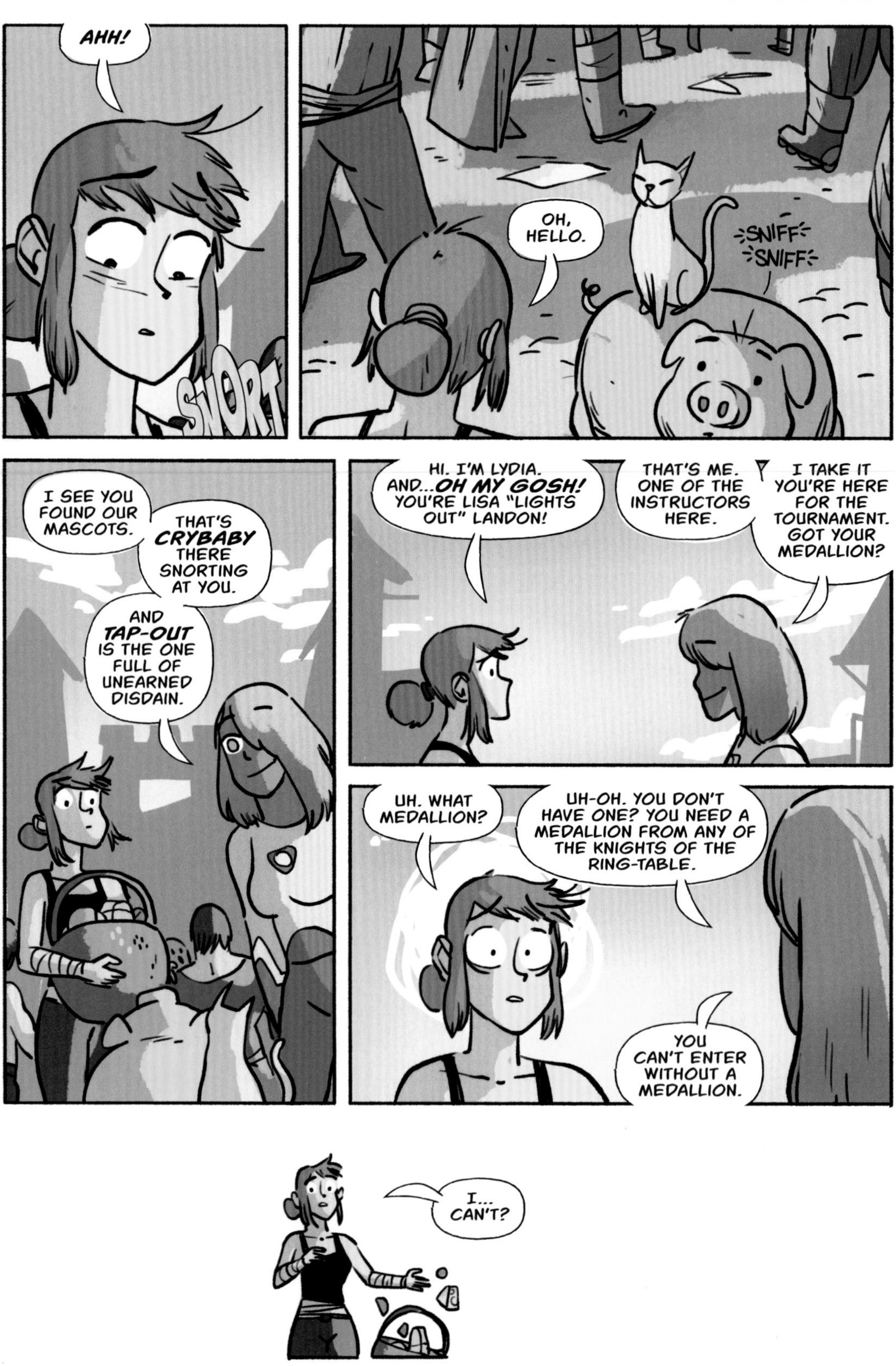
AHH!
SNORT
OH, HELLO.
SNIFF SNIFF
I SEE YOU FOUND OUR MASCOTS.
THAT'S CRYBABY THERE SNORTING AT YOU.
AND TAP-OUT IS THE ONE FULL OF UNEARNED DISDAIN.
HI. I'M LYDIA. AND...OH MY GOSH! YOU'RE LISA "LIGHTS OUT" LANDON!
THAT'S ME. ONE OF THE INSTRUCTORS HERE.
I TAKE IT YOU'RE HERE FOR THE TOURNAMENT. GOT YOUR MEDALLION?
UH. WHAT MEDALLION?
UH-OH. YOU DON'T HAVE ONE? YOU NEED A MEDALLION FROM ANY OF THE KNIGHTS OF THE RING-TABLE.
YOU CAN'T ENTER WITHOUT A MEDALLION.
I... CAN'T?

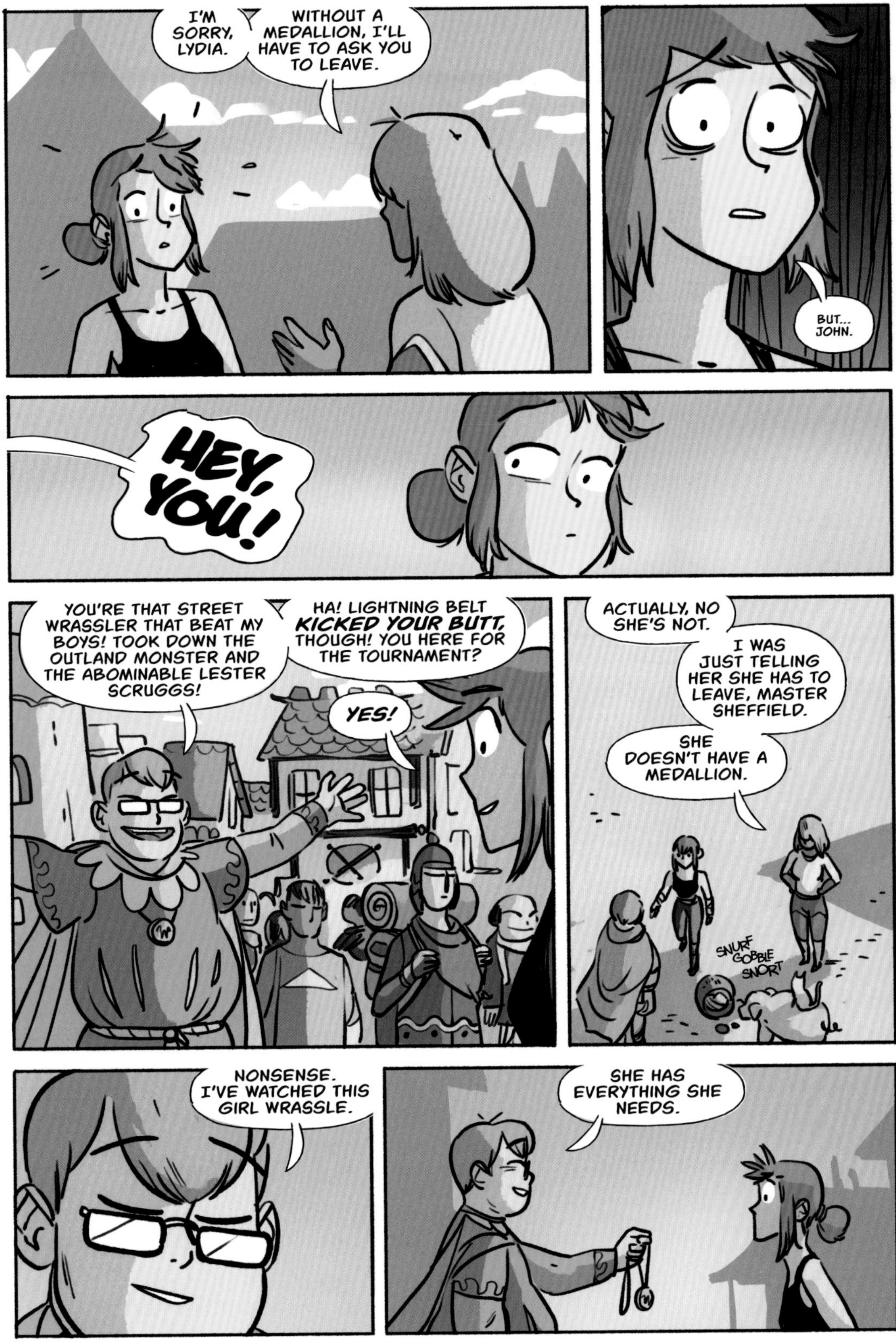
I'M SORRY, LYDIA.
WITHOUT A MEDALLION, I'LL HAVE TO ASK YOU TO LEAVE.
BUT... JOHN.
HEY, YOU!
YOU'RE THAT STREET WRASSLER THAT BEAT MY BOYS! TOOK DOWN THE OUTLAND MONSTER AND THE ABOMINABLE LESTER SCRUGGS!
HA! LIGHTNING BELT **KICKED YOUR BUTT**, THOUGH! YOU HERE FOR THE TOURNAMENT?
YES!
ACTUALLY, NO SHE'S NOT.
I WAS JUST TELLING HER SHE HAS TO LEAVE, MASTER SHEFFIELD.
SHE DOESN'T HAVE A MEDALLION.
SNURF GOBBLE SNORT
NONSENSE. I'VE WATCHED THIS GIRL WRASSLE.
SHE HAS EVERYTHING SHE NEEDS.

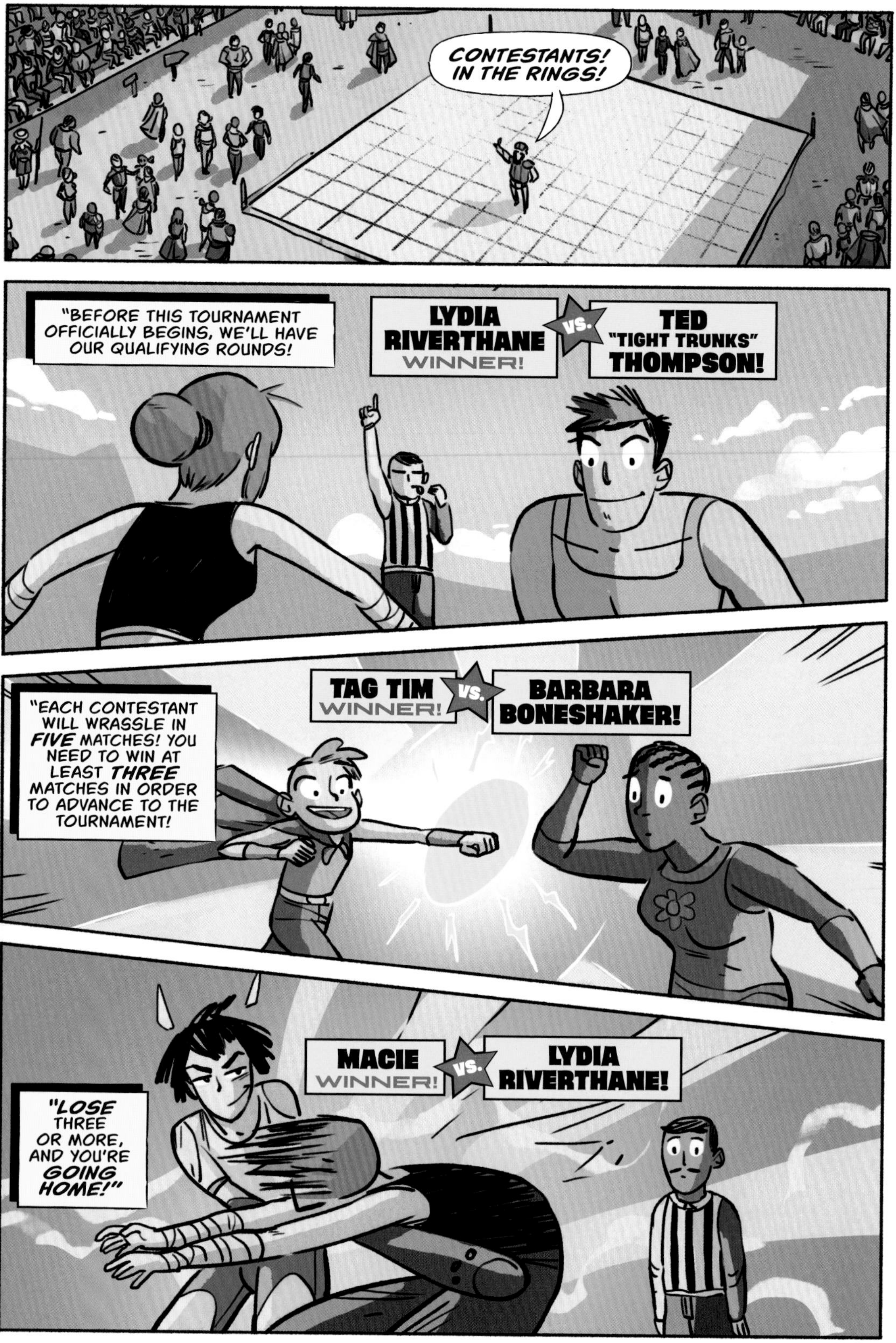
CONTESTANTS! IN THE RINGS!
"BEFORE THIS TOURNAMENT OFFICIALLY BEGINS, WE'LL HAVE OUR QUALIFYING ROUNDS!
LYDIA RIVERTHANE
WINNER!
VS.
TED "TIGHT TRUNKS" THOMPSON!
TAG TIM
WINNER!
VS.
BARBARA BONESHAKER!
"EACH CONTESTANT WILL WRASSLE IN FIVE MATCHES! YOU NEED TO WIN AT LEAST THREE MATCHES IN ORDER TO ADVANCE TO THE TOURNAMENT!
MACIE
WINNER!
VS.
LYDIA RIVERTHANE!
"LOSE THREE OR MORE, AND YOU'RE GOING HOME!"

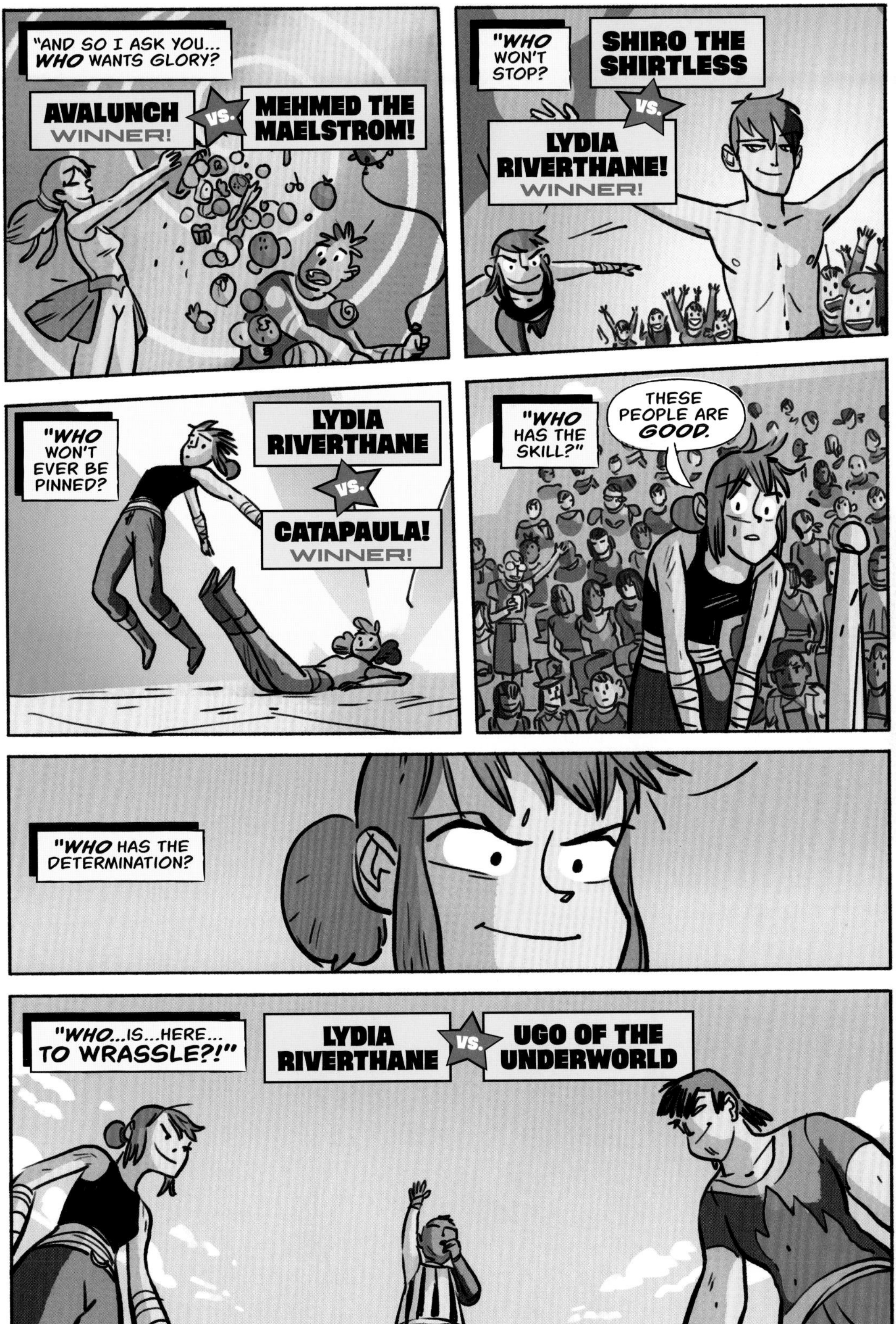
"AND SO I ASK YOU... WHO WANTS GLORY?
AVALUNCH
WINNER!
VS.
MEHMED THE MAELSTROM!
"WHO WON'T STOP?
SHIRO THE SHIRTLESS
VS.
LYDIA RIVERTHANE!
WINNER!
"WHO WON'T EVER BE PINNED?
LYDIA RIVERTHANE
VS.
CATAPAULA!
WINNER!
"WHO HAS THE SKILL?"
THESE PEOPLE ARE GOOD.
"WHO HAS THE DETERMINATION?
"WHO...IS...HERE... TO WRASSLE?!"
LYDIA RIVERTHANE
VS.
UGO OF THE UNDERWORLD

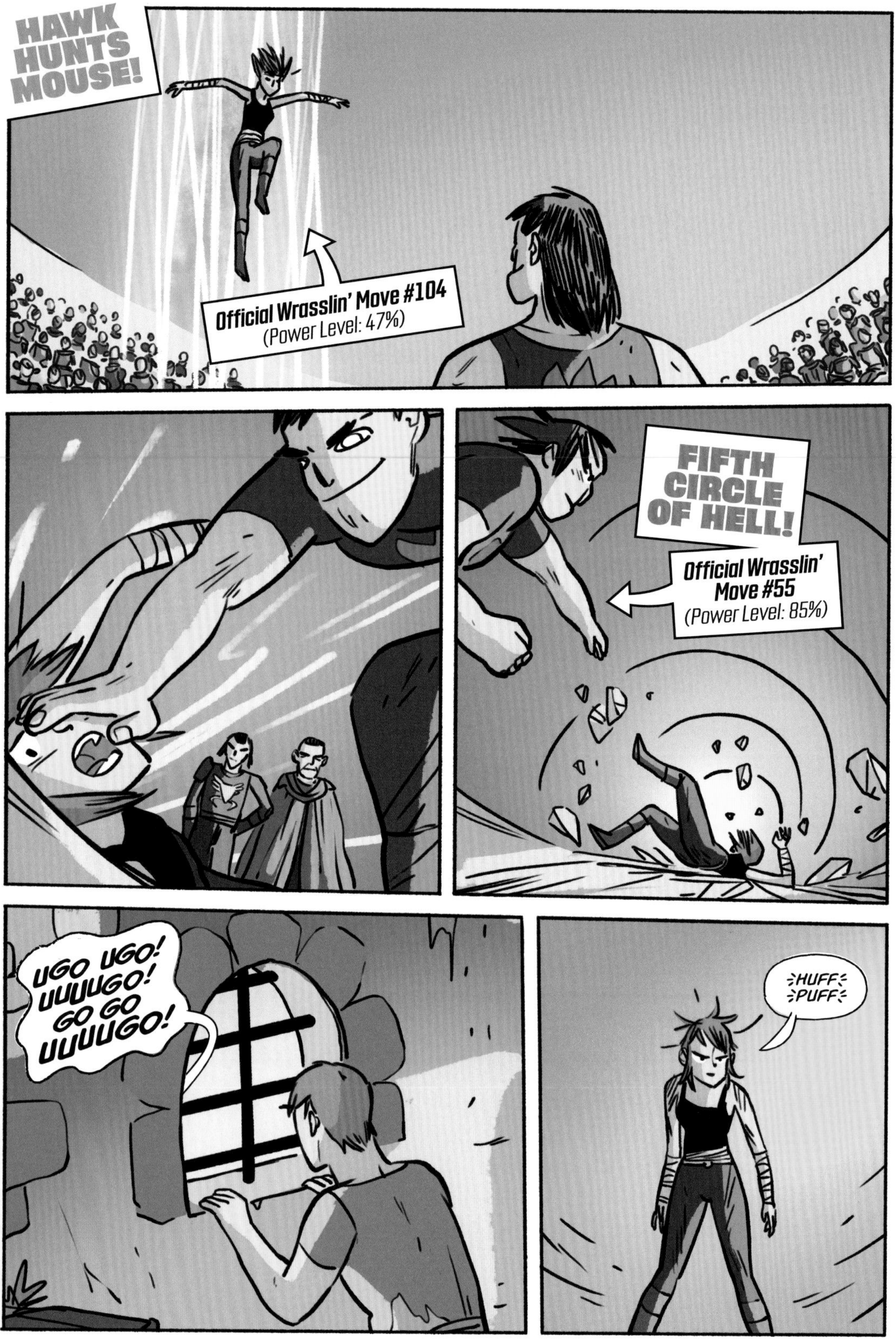
HAWK HUNTS MOUSE!
Official Wrasslin' Move #104
(Power Level: 47%)
FIFTH CIRCLE OF HELL!
Official Wrasslin' Move #55
(Power Level: 85%)
UGO UGO! UUUUGO! GO GO UUUUGO!
HUFF PUFF

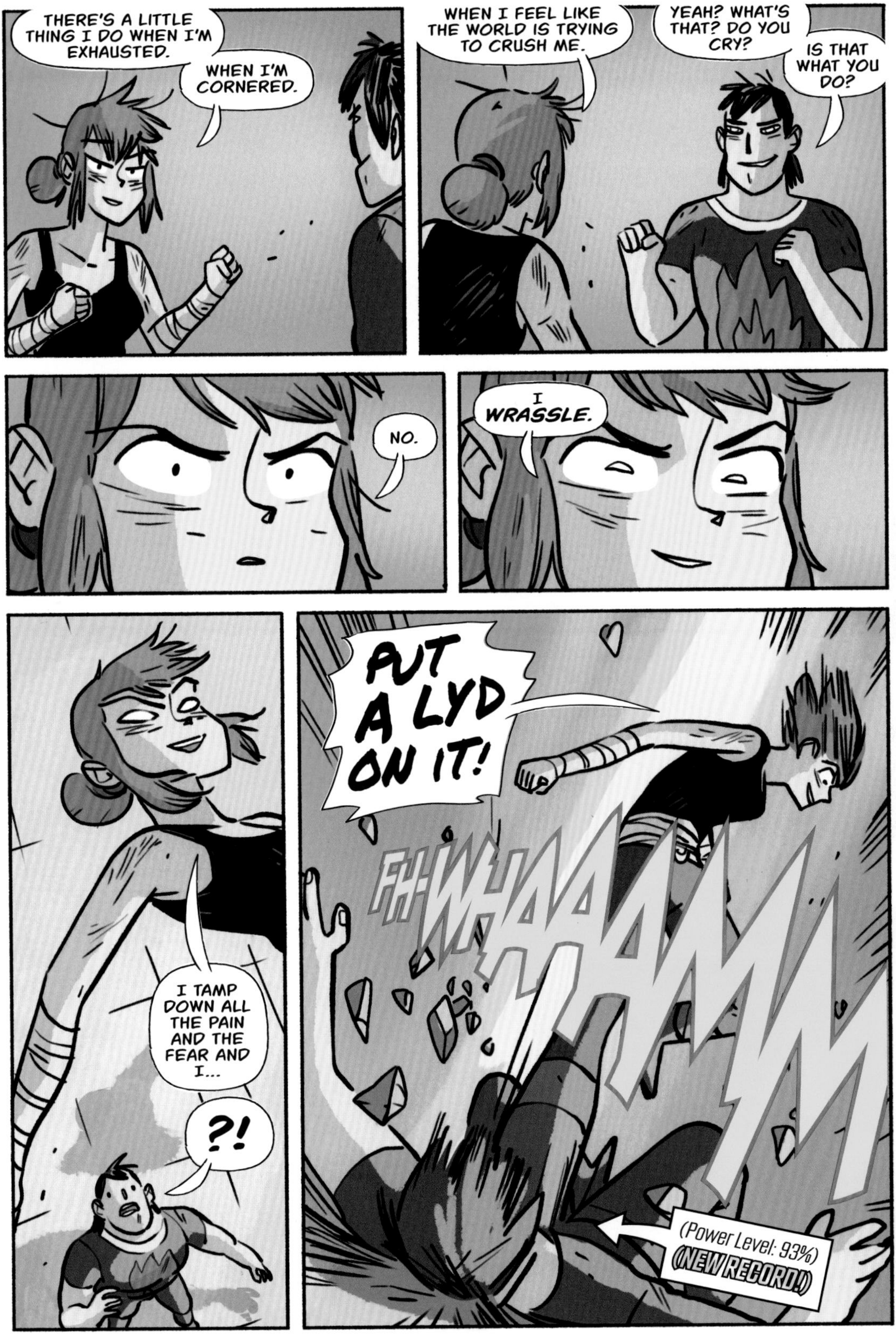
THERE'S A LITTLE THING I DO WHEN I'M EXHAUSTED.
WHEN I'M CORNERED.
WHEN I FEEL LIKE THE WORLD IS TRYING TO CRUSH ME.
YEAH? WHAT'S THAT? DO YOU CRY?
IS THAT WHAT YOU DO?
NO.
I WRASSLE.
I TAMP DOWN ALL THE PAIN AND THE FEAR AND I...
?!
PUT A LYD ON IT!
FH-WHAAAMM
(Power Level: 93%)
(NEW RECORD!)

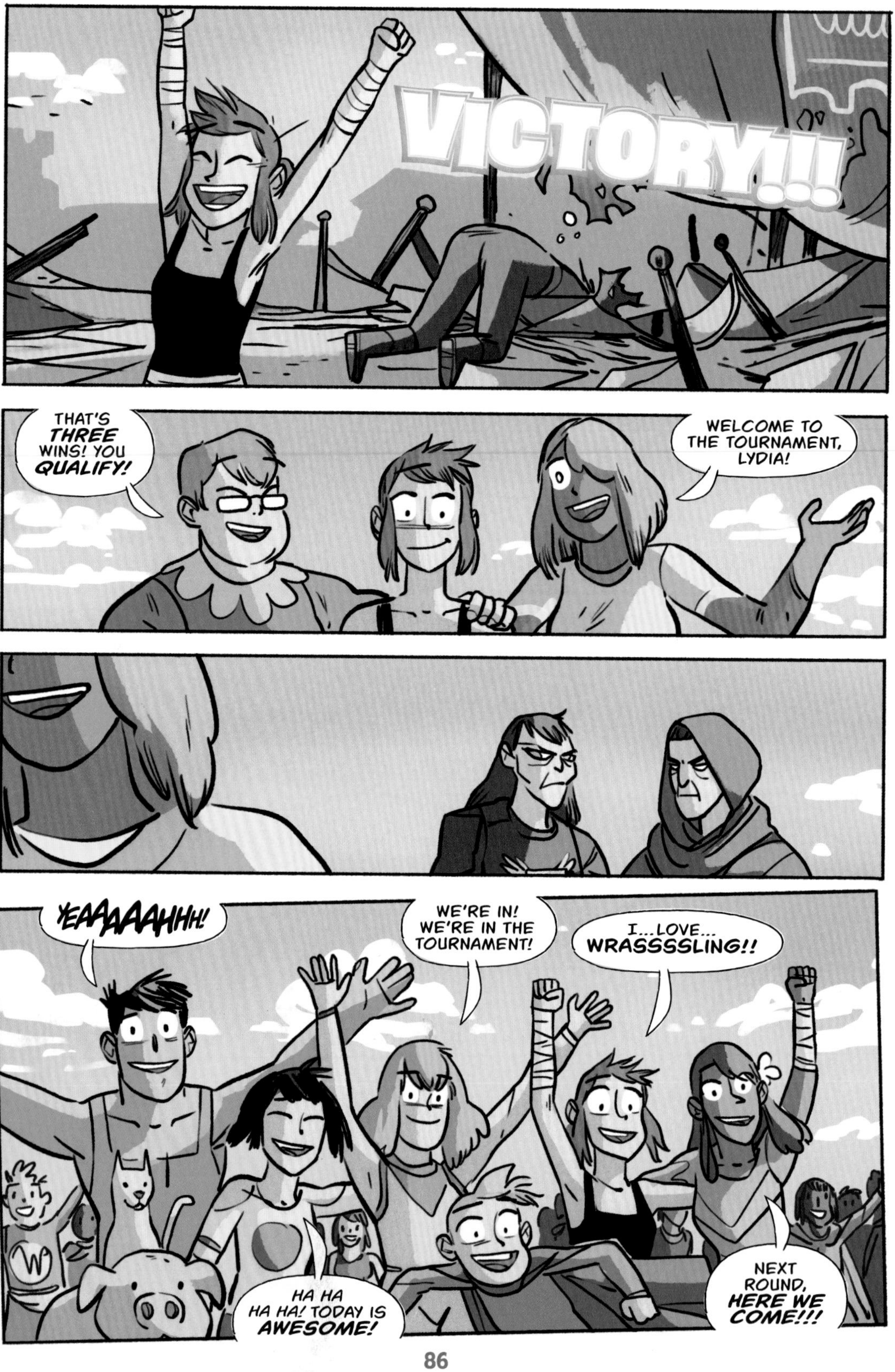
VICTORY!!!
THAT'S THREE WINS! YOU QUALIFY!
WELCOME TO THE TOURNAMENT, LYDIA!
YEAAAAAAHHH!
WE'RE IN! WE'RE IN THE TOURNAMENT!
I...LOVE... WRASSSSLING!!
HA HA HA HA! TODAY IS AWESOME!
NEXT ROUND, HERE WE COME!!!

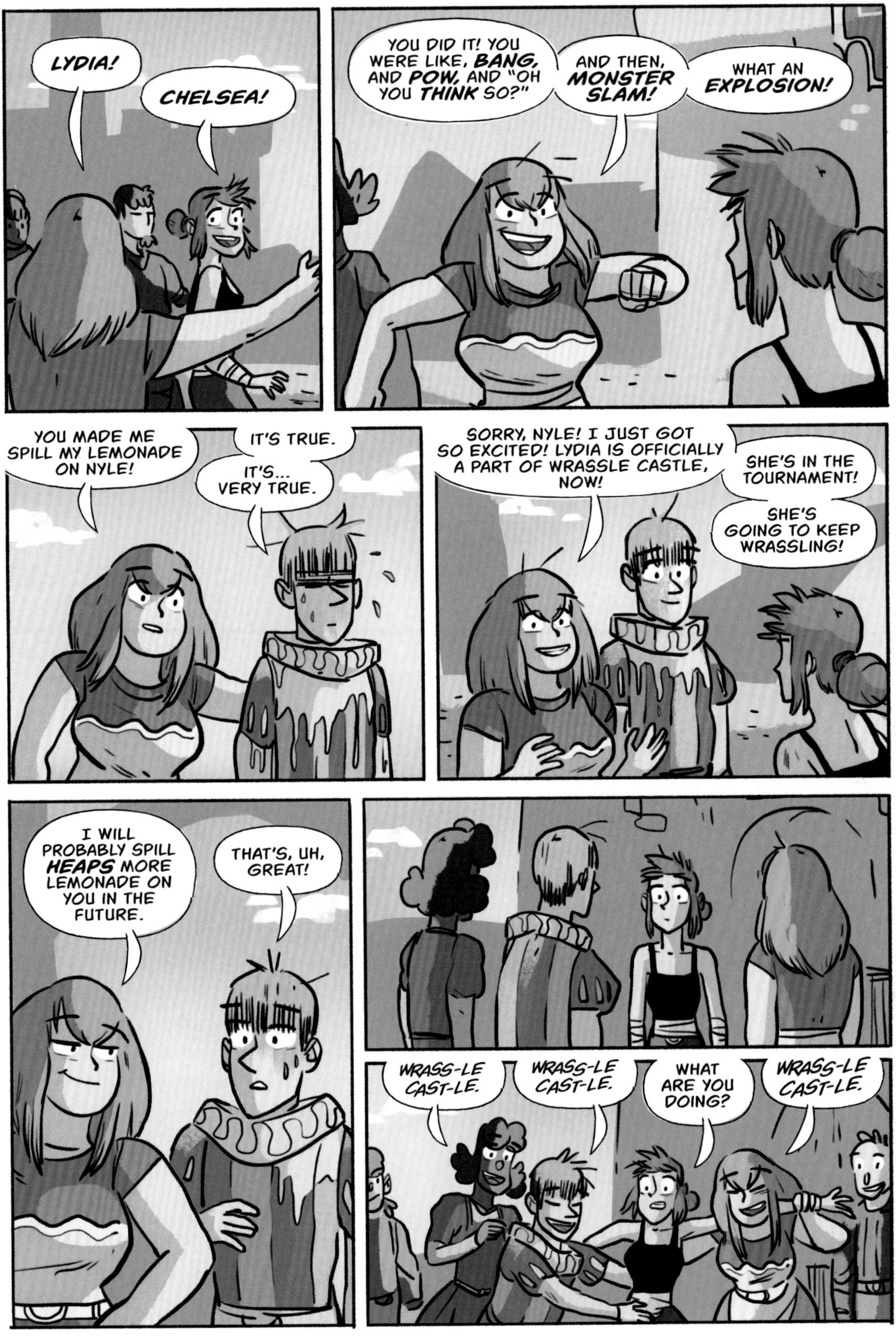
LYDIA!
CHELSEA!
YOU DID IT! YOU WERE LIKE, BANG, AND POW, AND "OH YOU THINK SO?"
AND THEN, MONSTER SLAM!
WHAT AN EXPLOSION!
YOU MADE ME SPILL MY LEMONADE ON NYLE!
IT'S TRUE.
IT'S... VERY TRUE.
SORRY, NYLE! I JUST GOT SO EXCITED! LYDIA IS OFFICIALLY A PART OF WRASSLE CASTLE, NOW!
SHE'S IN THE TOURNAMENT!
SHE'S GOING TO KEEP WRASSLING!
I WILL PROBABLY SPILL HEAPS MORE LEMONADE ON YOU IN THE FUTURE.
THAT'S, UH, GREAT!
WRASS-LE CAST-LE.
WRASS-LE CAST-LE.
WHAT ARE YOU DOING?
WRASS-LE CAST-LE.

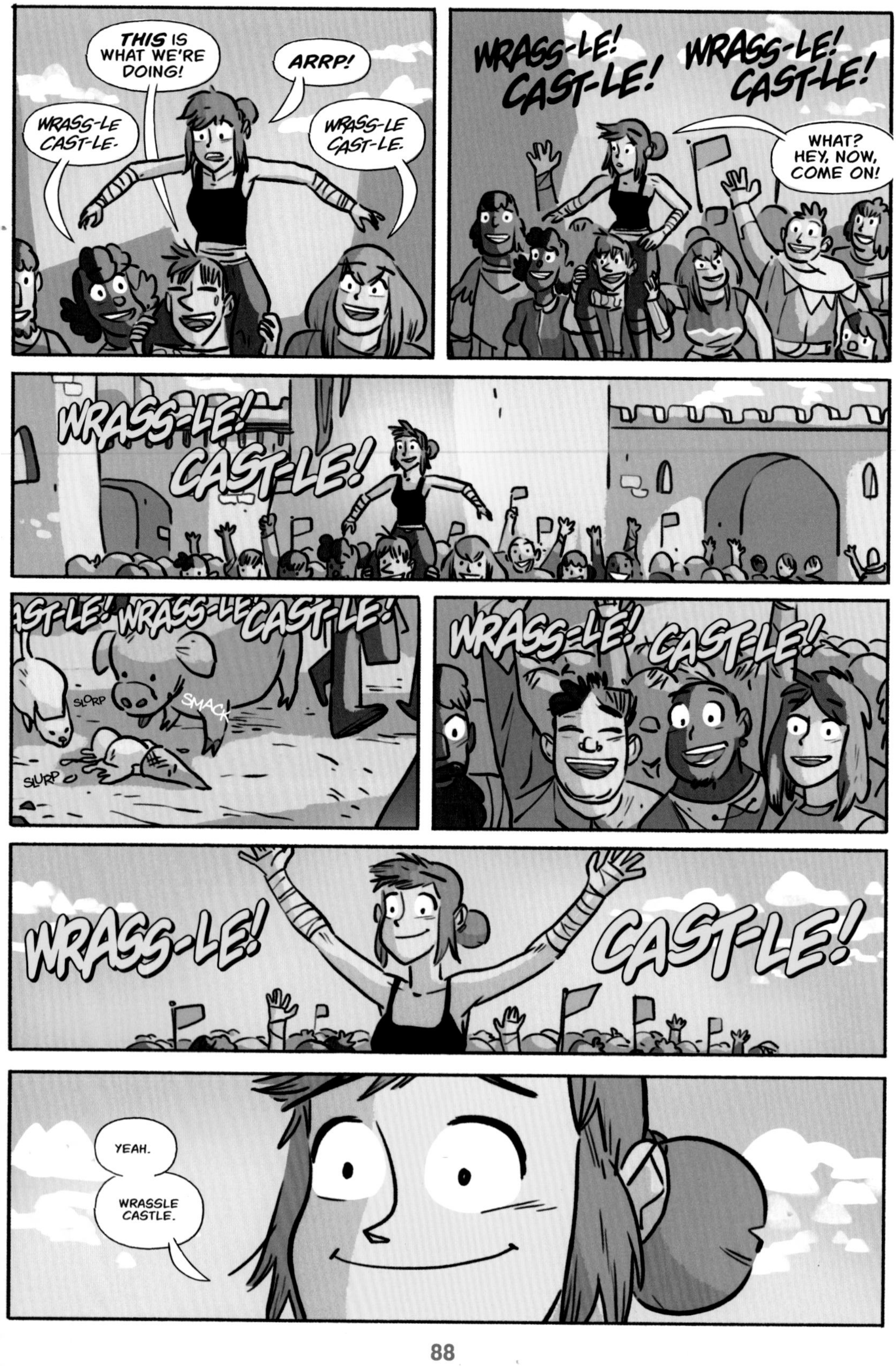
WRASS-LE CAST-LE.
THIS IS WHAT WE'RE DOING!
ARRP!
WRASS-LE CAST-LE.
WRASS-LE! CAST-LE! WRASS-LE! CAST-LE!
WHAT? HEY, NOW, COME ON!
WRASS-LE! CAST-LE!
AST-LE! WRASS-LE CAST-LE!
SLORP
SMACK
SLURP
WRASS-LE! CAST-LE!
WRASS-LE! CAST-LE!
YEAH.
WRASSLE CASTLE.

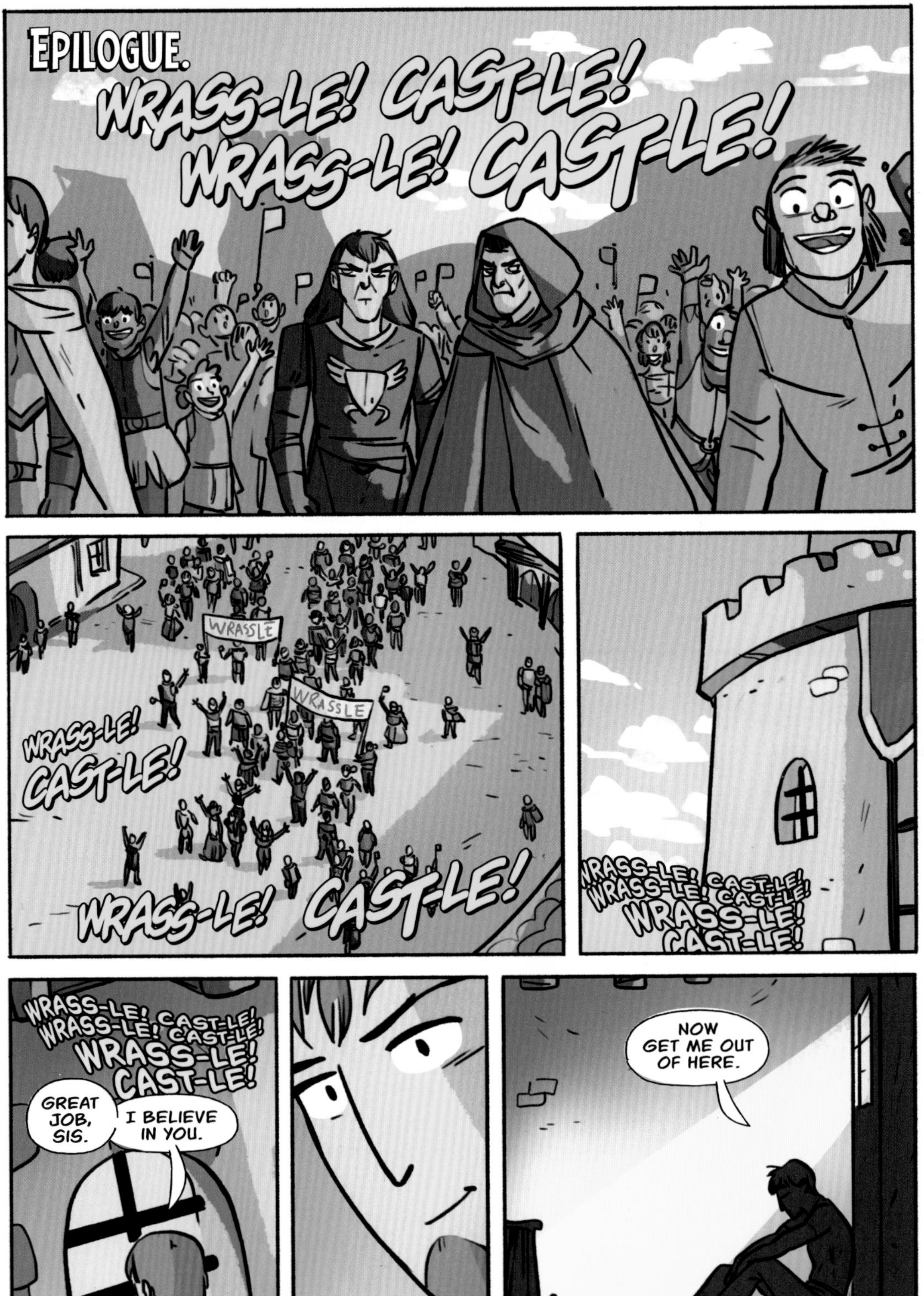
EPILOGUE.
WRASS-LE! CAST-LE!
WRASS-LE! CAST-LE!
WRASSLE
WRASSLE
WRASS-LE!
CAST-LE!
WRASS-LE! CAST-LE!
WRASS-LE! CAST-LE!
WRASS-LE! CAST-LE!
WRASS-LE!
CAST-LE!
WRASS-LE! CAST-LE!
WRASS-LE! CAST-LE!
WRASS-LE!
CAST-LE!
GREAT JOB, SIS.
I BELIEVE IN YOU.
NOW GET ME OUT OF HERE.
Continued in...Vol. 2!

AUTHOR'S CORNER

WHEN WE FIRST CAME UP WITH THE TITLE "WRASSLE CASTLE," I WAS OVERJOYED. "IT PRACTICALLY WRITES ITSELF!" I DECLARED. WHILE THAT TURNED OUT TO NOT BE ENTIRELY TRUE, CREATING THIS WORLD HAS BEEN A PURE JOY THAT I AM SO GLAD TO SHARE WITH YOU!

- COLLEEN COOVER

"WRITE WHAT YOU KNOW," THEY SAY, BUT I WROTE A STORY ABOUT WRASSLING WITH BEARS WHEN ALL I'VE EVER PERSONALLY WRASSLED ARE MY BROTHER MIKE, A FEW DOGS, AND THEN ONE SHEEP, THE LATTER OF WHICH DID NOT GO WELL, BUT I SUPPOSE WHAT THIS BOOK IS REALLY ABOUT IS FRIENDSHIP AND ADVENTURE, AND THOSE ARE TWO THINGS I'VE ALWAYS HELD AS PARAMOUNT IN LIFE AND THAT I HOPE YOU'LL ALL FIND WHEN READING WRASSLE CASTLE.

- PAUL TOBIN

WHEN I STARTED WORKING ON WRASSLE CASTLE, I THOUGHT IT WOULD BE JUST SILLY FUN AND LOTS OF PUNS (WHICH IT IS!), BUT AS I DELVED DEEPER INTO THE SCRIPT, I REALIZED THAT THIS SERIES WAS MUCH MORE THAN THAT: A CAST OF INCREDIBLE CHARACTERS, A WORLD FULL OF WONDERS AND MAGIC, A STORY ABOUT NEVER GIVING UP, WORKING HARD TOWARD YOUR GOALS, AND MAKING MEANINGFUL FRIENDSHIPS. OUR BOOK IS NOT JUST FUN AND FIGHTS, IT'S GOT HEART!

- GALAAD

COLLEEN COOVER

AGE: STILL COUNTING.
NATIONAL RANKING: ALSO STILL COUNTING.
OCCUPATION: WRITER
SIGNATURE MOVE: TRUTH BOMB
(HIGHEST POWER LEVEL: NUCLEAR)
STRENGTH: 15
DEXTERITY: -99
SOMETIMES UNCOMFORTABLE HONESTY: 20

FAVORITE FOOD: UNDISCLOSED FOR PASSWORD
SECURITY REASONS.

HOBBIES: KNITTING.

NOTES: COAXED FROM THE COMFORT OF HER
COMIC-DRAWING CAVE BY THE PROSPECT OF
CO-WRITING A FANTASY WRASSLIN' ADVENTURE,
COLLEEN HAS BEEN TRAINING HER AUTHORING
MUSCLES BY BENCH PRESSING COMPUTER
KEYBOARDS AND EATING RAW WORD DOCS FOR
BREAKFAST.

"MEAN" COLLEEN

PAUL TOBIN

AGE: SEVERAL YEARS OLD
NATIONAL RANKING: 7,898,653 (ON A GOOD DAY)
OCCUPATION: WRITER
SIGNATURE MOVE: NAPALANCHE
(HIGHEST POWER LEVEL: 98%)
STRENGTH: 20+
DEXTERITY: 20+
SELF AWARENESS: 3

FAVORITE FOOD / NEWSPAPER STRIP COMBO: PEANUTS

HOBBIES: INDOOR ROCK CLIMBING, OUTDOOR BIKE
RIDING, ALLDOOR COOKIE EATING.

NOTES: AS A FERAL CHILD IN THE IOWA WILDERNESS,
PAUL WAS RAISED BY A KINDLY PAIR OF PULP
MAGAZINES AND EVENTUALLY JOINED HUMAN SOCIETY
AFTER PASSING THE LEGALLY-REQUIRED POTTY
TRAINING TEST ON ONLY THE FOURTH TRY. HE ENJOYS
FRENZIED STORMS AND AN ASTONISHING RANGE OF
THINGS MOST PEOPLE CONSIDER STRANGE.

"TEN TOES" TOBIN

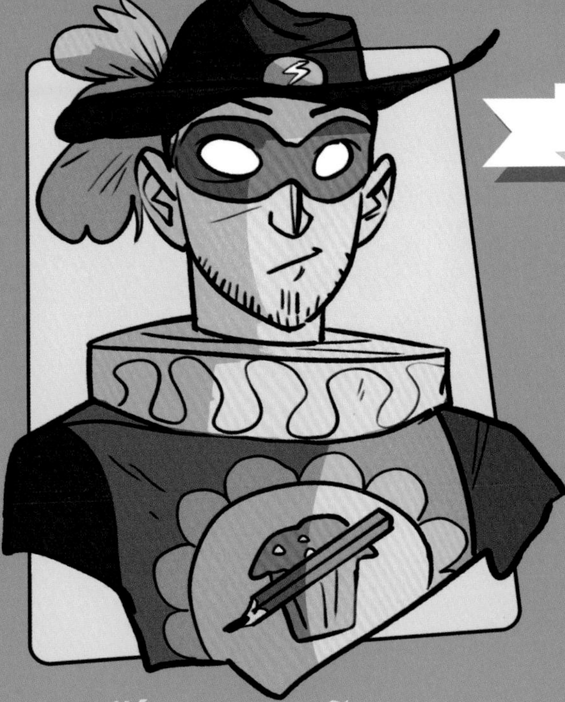

GALAADOR

AGE: UNDISCLOSED.
NATIONAL RANKING: OFF THE CHART.
OCCUPATION: DRAWS COMICS
SIGNATURE MOVE: EXPLOSIVE PENCIL OF DEATH (HIGHEST POWER LEVEL: DEADLY)
STRENGTH: AVERAGE
DEXTERITY: NATURAL 20
ABILITY TO BEFRIEND CATS: EXCEPTIONAL

FAVORITE FOOD: ANY THING THAT CONTAINS SUGAR, EGGS, BUTTER, FLOUR OR ANY ASSORTMENT OF THOSE.

HOBBIES: CRUSHING PENCILS, LIFTING DRAWING TABLETS.

NOTES: ONCE DEFEATED VEGETA IN SINGLE COMBAT. OR WAS IT IN HIS IMAGINATION?

"ÚLTIMO DISEÑADOR EXTRAORDINARIO"

JEFF POWELL

AGE: UNKNOWN
NATIONAL RANKING: 138
OCCUPATION: CALLIGRAPHER, SNAIL FARMER, PART-TIME WRASSLER
SIGNATURE MOVE: POWELL'S POWELL-FUL PILEDRIVER (HIGHEST POWER LEVEL: !!!%)
STRENGTH: JEFF POSSESSES THE NORMAL HUMAN STRENGTH OF A MAN OF HIS AGE, HEIGHT, AND BUILD WHO ENGAGES IN MODERATE REGULAR EXERCISE.
DEXTERITY: 14
DETERMINATION: VERY

FAVORITE FOOD: BACON, CURED MEATS

HOBBIES: CULTIVATING CARNIVOROUS PLANTS, CATS

NOTES: JEFF FANCIES HIMSELF A PRO AT COOKING BREAKFAST FOODS. HE'S ESPECIALLY SKILLED AT FRYING EGGS.

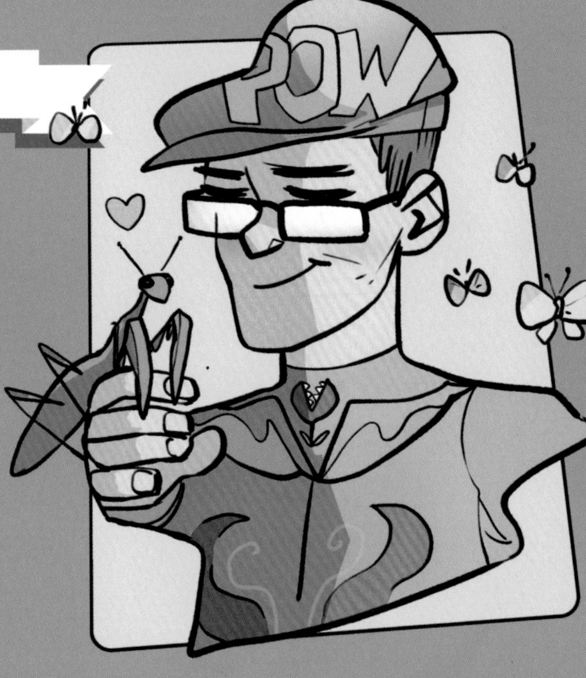
POW

"POW POW" POWELL

NEXT TIME IN

WRASSLE CASTLE

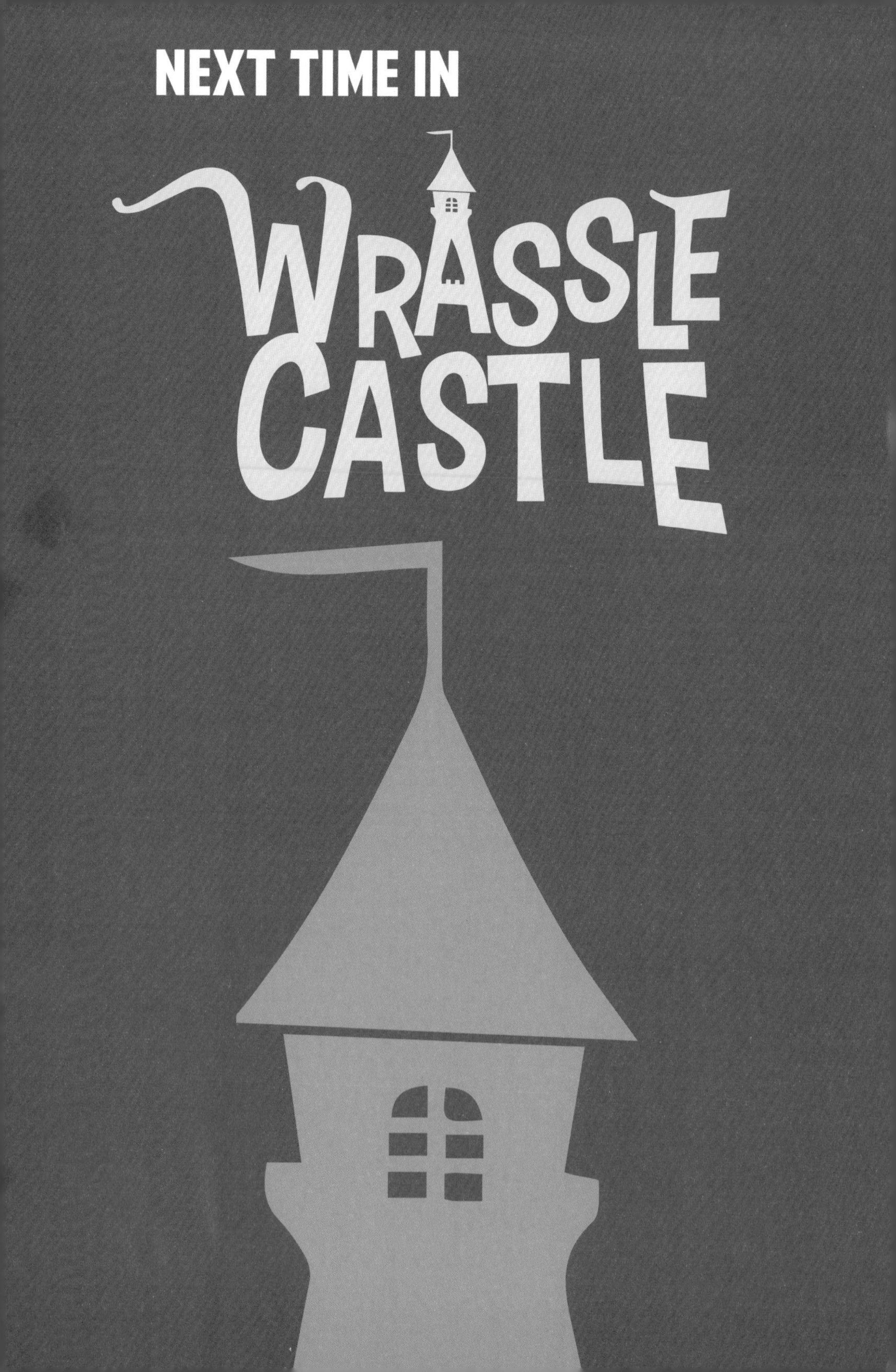

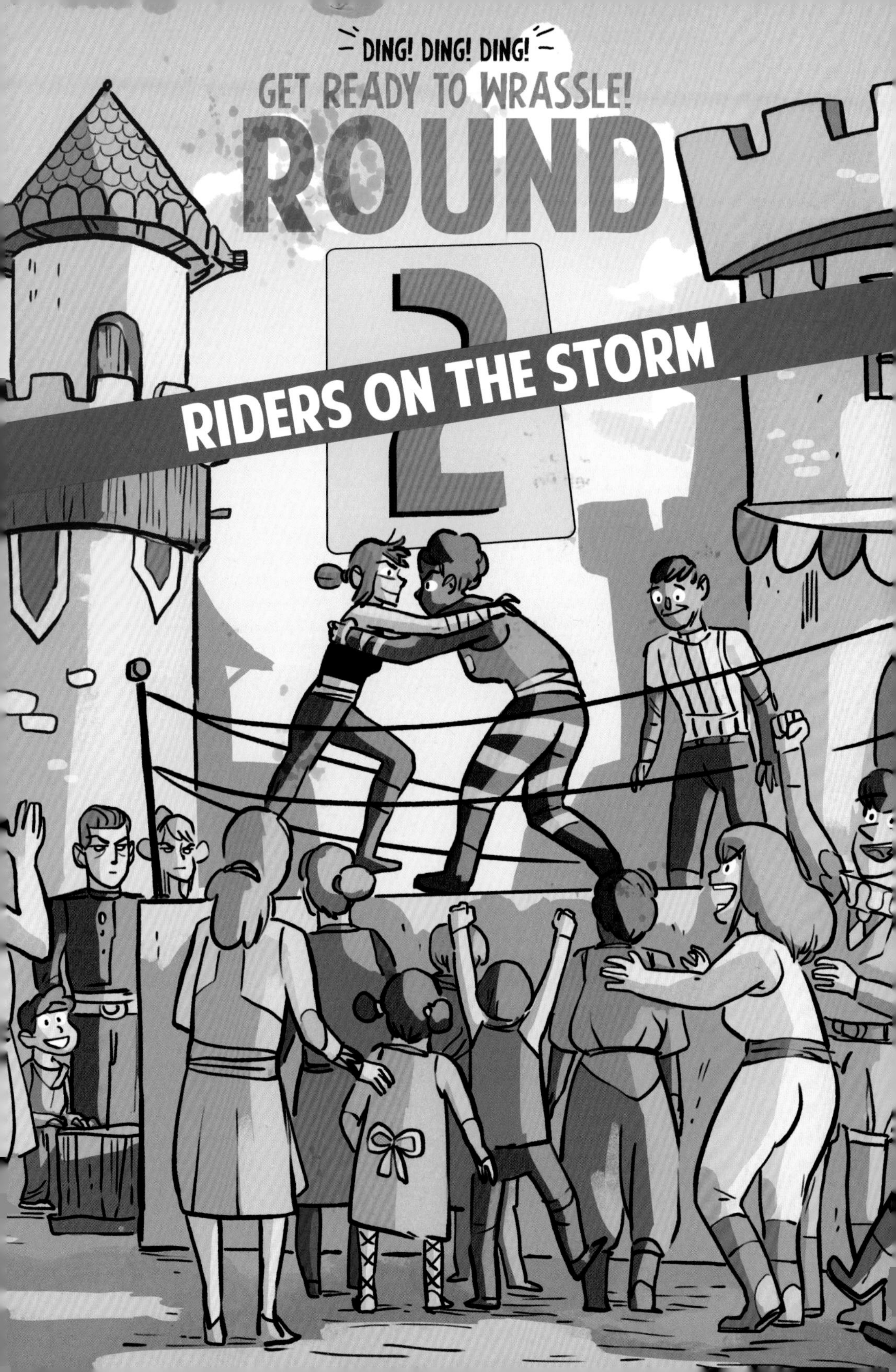
DING! DING! DING!
GET READY TO WRASSLE!
ROUND
2
RIDERS ON THE STORM

WONDERBOUND

YEAR ONE – 2021

Wonderbound publishes science fiction, fantasy, and spooky graphic novels for the young and the young at heart.

Grab a ticket to Wonder!

@readwonderbound

WRASSLE CASTLE BOOK 1: LEARNING THE ROPES
Written by Paul Tobin & Colleen Coover
Illustrated by Galaad
Letters by Jeff Powell
Price: $9.99
ISBN: 978-1-638-490-098

In Stores: 9/21/2021

VERSE BOOK 1: THE BROKEN HALF
Written & Illustrated by Sam Beck
Price: $12.99
ISBN: 978-1-638-490-104

In Stores: 9/28/2021

SEPTEMBER

THE UNFINISHED CORNER
Written by Dani Colman
Illustrated by Rachel "Tuna" Petrovicz
Colors by Whitney Cogar
Letters by Jim Campbell
Price: $12.99
ISBN: 978-1-638-490-111

In Stores: 10/19/2021

HELLO, MY NAME IS POOP
Written by Ben Katzner
Illustrated by Ian McGinty
Colors by Fred C. Stresing
Letters by AndWorld Design
Price: $9.99
ISBN: 978-1-638-490-128

In Stores: 10/26/2021

OCTOBER